WILD AND BRIGHT

A ROCK STAR ROMANCE

SKYLER MASON

To Emily, my wild and bright sister

ONE

Camden

SHE CUT HER HAIR.

It's a subtle change—short dark strands sweep from the crown of her head to her cheekbones—but it's noticeably different from the video I watched before. The time stamp on that one said it was posted two days ago. This one was from this morning, so she must have gotten her hair cut sometime yesterday, maybe even at that salon on First Street she used to go to in high school.

It's strange how a detail like that can make me feel close to her.

Stranger still that I welcome this warmth that washes over me every time I watch her stupid makeup tutorials on YouTube when I've been going out of my way these last five years to avoid seeing her in person.

This is just how it works with obsession. Nothing about it is rational. My preoccupation with Lauren Henderson should have waned the moment I left my small hometown of Coronado. By the time River of Sight got our first management deal, adjusting to tour life should have replaced her in my thoughts. Now that we've achieved the kind of success I never imagined we would, now that I have my pick of beautiful women, my childish crush on the girl next door should be a bitter-sweet memory, too silly and maudlin for even a love song.

She lifts a thin red tube out of the cardboard box and holds it close to the screen. "I've been eyeballing this mascara on Sephora for weeks," she says. "But I'm poor, y'all, so if it's not deeply discounted or $3.99 at Target, I just can't do it. Thank you, Smashbox, for taking pity on a single mother." I intake a sharp breath when she smiles. Her whole face changes—her big green eyes grow smaller and crinkle at the edges, and her wide mouth bares those white teeth with that one slightly overlapping canine on the right.

In an instant, it's like I'm sitting in a room with her rather than in a cold concert venue thousands of miles away.

I want to stay here with her.

How is it possible that one person could have this much power over my senses? Even in the depths of my obsession as a teenager, when I was so delusional that I unconsciously saved my virginity for her, I knew she was wrong for me.

If I wanted a girlfriend at all, I'd need one who's steady and predictable. Not wild, boisterous Lauren who got pregnant at eighteen years old. Not the girl who used to give lap dances at parties and let guys take shots between her tits. She'd make me so crazy that I could never write music. I'd never be truly at ease, because I couldn't trust her.

Not after what she almost did with my brother minutes after taking my virginity.

I jerk up from my phone when our stage manager, Jeff, bursts into the room.

"Hunter," he says to my brother. "Leo found you some hot twins—boy and girl. Do you want me to send them in, or do you need him to take a picture first?"

Hunter glances up from his guitar. His face is still bright red and his shirt is soaked with sweat even though it's been almost twenty minutes since our performance ended. The sight of it makes me uneasy. He always sweats more right after a relapse. It's another reminder of how close sobriety is to drunkenness—separated only by that first or last sip.

"Have him take a picture," Hunter says, looking at his hands as he strums his guitar. He's playing it mostly to give himself something to do, since his first urge after a show is to drink. I wish I found the sight of it comforting. "Tell him to make them kiss for it."

"Gross," Janie shouts from across the room, her gaze fixed on her cello as she runs a cloth over the wood.

"It's all I got," he shouts back to her. "Pussy and dick. Do you really want to take away the one thing I have?"

I resist the urge to roll my eyes. Self-pity is another staple of his sobriety, and even in jest, I can't stand it. I can't stand any reminders of how desperately he loves alcohol.

"It's still disgusting," Janie says. "And if anyone finds out that you do this creepy stuff, you'll be cancelled."

Jeff turns to me. "He's also got this leggy brunette out there begging to meet you, Cam. Makeup influencer. Ten out of ten."

It's ridiculous that the words "leggy brunette" and "influencer" make my pulse speed up. Lauren might be perfect in my eyes, but Jeff wouldn't think she's a ten out of ten, and she would never be at a concert all the way in Boston begging one of our roadies to let her come backstage.

"No, I'm good." I shoot him a stern look. "And I agree with Janie. You and Leo shouldn't still be doing this shit for him. Let him find his own groupies."

"Thanks, Mom," Hunter says, and this time I don't stop my eyes from rolling. Ever since his last relapse, he's been snippy anytime I've been too high-handed or controlling, but that's because he doesn't know what it's like to love an addict. He doesn't know the agony of being constantly at the edge of a precipice, that any phone call from an unknown number or rehearsal he's late for or text he doesn't respond to could mean the end.

If he knew that feeling, he'd be more patient with me.

"Speaking of Mom," I say, reaching across the couch and picking up an acoustic guitar, obviously placed here by a guitar maker who wants one of us to try it out. I start playing the chorus of "Old Man" by Neil Young, my fingers on autopilot. "She wants us at the house at noon now, so Brayden is rescheduling our flight to first thing tomorrow morning."

"That actually works out better for me," he says. "Lauren wants to talk to me about something, so that'll give me time to go over there before dinner."

My hand goes still mid strum, and I hate myself for it.

I ought to be accustomed to their relationship by now. She's always been much closer to him than to me. They're "besties", as Lauren often says in her videos whenever she has the audacity to use his fame to boost her views on YouTube.

Even though I know my preoccupation with her is unhealthy, when I've done everything I can to squash it, I can't overcome this itching desire to keep them as far from each other as possible. I can't stand their closeness.

I resume the melody, but there's no hiding my slipup. Hunter noticed. Hell, even Janie probably noticed all the way across the room. "What does she want to talk about?" I ask, not lifting my gaze from the guitar.

"I think she's going to ask for some kind of a job." Out of the corner of my eye, I see that he's scratching the back of his head.

"I just got that feeling from her text. Like maybe she wants to do something with our social media."

A cynical smile rises to my lips. Of course she would use her friendship with Hunter to get something out of it.

"Absolutely not," I say.

When he sighs heavily, I know he's going to argue with me. "She's really good at what she does, Cam."

"She does makeup tutorials."

He shrugs. "She has more TikTok followers than we do."

I grunt, shaking my head. "Who gives a shit about TikTok? Our fans aren't twelve years old."

"Yeah, but she's really good at YouTube, too, and she doesn't think the company we hired knows what the fuck they're doing."

"They do an adequate job, which is exactly what we pay them for. We don't need social media to gain fans. Our music should be doing that."

"I don't know. Lauren says—"

"I don't give a fuck what Lauren has to say about it."

When the room goes quiet, I want to flinch. This visit home has me more wound up than I thought. It's the first time we've been able to spend Christmas in Coronado in ages. For the last few years, we've always been right in the middle of a tour, and my parents have had to fly out to meet us.

I knew cancelling this tour would mean they'd want to see us more. Hell, since both Hunter and I will actually be living in our San Diego houses, my mom will probably try to instigate weekly family dinners and movie nights.

The prospect of it wouldn't be so exhausting if it weren't for the dark-haired girl who still lives across the street from my parents' house.

I won't be able to avoid seeing her now, not with how close she is to Hunter. She'll probably pop in to my parents' house as she pleases, like she used to in high school, letting herself in and helping herself to the food in their fridge. Her four-year-old daughter might even come with her.

The same daughter I once accused of being mine in a moment of complete insanity.

There's a good chance I'll be forced to confront our whole sordid history this Christmas, when all I want to do is get over this obsession and leave Lauren in the past where she belongs.

"I'm going to hear her out," Hunter says.

I can see on his face that he thinks I'm being unreasonable. But that's because she's always been able to bulldoze him.

"Hear her out all you want. It's not happening."

TWO

Lauren

"LAUREN," my mom calls out from the kitchen. "I need you to start making the mini quiche. Aunt Carrie texted, and they're passing through Encinitas."

My eyelids flutter. I've been in my head all morning, practically counting the minutes until Hunter's flight arrives. My frenzied brain has been so distracted it took me over twenty minutes to find the perfect angle with my tripod in order to capture the afternoon light. I don't have the time or energy to waste making Christmas Eve appetizers no one will eat.

I shouldn't let it bother me. My life will be changing after today. I'm getting myself a real, big-girl job, even if I have to sell my soul to the devil to get Hunter to agree. By Christmas next year, I won't be here to make mini quiche, because Cadence and I will be across the country touring with River of Sight. I'll finally be able to support her myself and start paying off my mountain of student-loan debt.

The fact that it will mean being close to Camden again is something I can't let myself think about it. I'll delay anxiety over that until after I have the job.

I turn around and glance at my twin brother. Just as I suspected, he's still lounging on the couch with his phone in front of his face.

"I'm working," I shout. "Have Logan do it."

"Logan is our *guest*," my mom shouts back, which immediately prompts me to look away from Logan and roll my eyes dramatically. He's visiting for the holidays with his girlfriend and his best friend, something he's done dozens of times since he left for college, but this time it's different. Now that he's a college graduate with a real engineering job in Indiana, he's been promoted to a "guest", while I'm Cinderella forced to scrub the floors and make the nasty mini quiche.

"That's right," Logan says, clearly not sensing my irritation. "That also means I get to pick the entertainment. We're turning on basketball."

I glare at him. "Absolutely not. I have exactly twenty minutes before the lighting in this room turns to shit."

"Aren't you a professional? Use that ring...thing." He gestures vaguely at my tripod.

My eyelids flutter. "Light? Is that the word you're looking for? I am using it, and it still can't beat natural light. My face needs a lot of finesse, and I know that *because* I'm a fucking professional. Artificial lighting makes my nose look twice its size."

He groans. "I'm sure it won't make your opinion on lip gloss any less credible."

Ah, there it is.

The inevitable judgment of my job. Every member of my family thinks influencing is silly. A vain job. A fake job, even, like I'm a little kid putting on a play and charging my family members for admission.

I whip around to face him. "This is my fucking career, Logan. I have a daughter to take care of. Not everyone has a job like you. Some of us have jobs you find frivolous, but they wouldn't exist if there wasn't a need for it. Some people need frivolous things in their lives."

Logan's dark brows snap together. "I was teasing you. Jesus. Chill out."

I can see that he means it, and I feel like an ass for snapping at him with such little provocation. I take a deep breath and release it slowly. My upcoming conversation with Hunter must be making me edgy.

"Go make the quiche," I say. "I'll be quick, and you can watch basketball as soon as I'm done."

He groans but still gets up from the couch. "I fucking hate that quiche."

"Put lots of cheese in it."

"I'm going to put whiskey in it," he mumbles as he walks away.

I glance at my phone. 1:06. Hunter said their flight would land at 12:30, and that they would head straight to their parents' house, which meant they'd be arriving any minute. I'll have to make this video in one take. No restarting when I stumble over my words.

Just as I'm about to set my phone to record, a small face appears in the hallway.

"Mommy, can I sit with you during your video?"

"No, honey. Not yet." I try to look at her sternly even as I want to smile. She's so like me at that age—wanting to do everything the adults do. "You still have three months before you turn five."

I don't know why I chose five as the arbitrary cut-off age

when plenty of influencers feature their children daily in their videos from the moment they're born. It's not like I have anything against it. Our lives are so saturated with social media that showing my child's face online is hardly any different than showing it at the grocery store.

It's probably my mom's voice in my head, passive aggressively ranting about the selfish, irresponsible influencer parents who "use their children" to further their careers.

"Can you put some eye shadow on me then?"

I smile. "Sure. Come here."

I reach for my metal bin and grab the two boldest colors I can find. "Do you want red or black?"

She purses her lips to the side as she plops down on the couch. "I want both. Put the black right here." She points to her lid. "And the red in the outer corner."

My lips quirk at her use of terms she's heard me say in my tutorials. "I wouldn't have even thought of that. You have good instincts."

"Yeah, I'm going to be really good at makeup when I grow up."

"You already are."

As I lightly brush red over her lid, her brows draw together. "Will I be famous when I'm five and you let me make videos with you?"

"A lot of people will see them, so I guess that makes you famous in a way, but not quite like Ryan's World famous. He has a lot more subscribers than me. A hundred thousand isn't as much as it sounds."

"Will I be famous like Uncle Hunter and Uncle Cam?"

My smile fades at her mention of Camden, and especially his honorary title of uncle. An unpleasant ache tightens my throat. Is this guilt?

If it is, there's no reason for it. Five years ago, I was certain

Cadence was Ryder's. Or almost certain. And even now, despite my growing suspicion, it's still much more likely she's his. What are the odds that a single, fevered encounter with Cam would get me pregnant when I'd had frequent unprotected sex with Ryder up until then?

It's only been these past few months that my certainty has waned. Sometimes I'll catch myself daydreaming about Cam, unsure of where the thoughts came from, and then I'll glance at those intense dark eyes of my little girl, and my whole body grows cold.

Then again, it doesn't take much to make me think about Camden.

Maybe I'm seeing things.

"No, they're a lot more famous." It's all I can say.

"Well, I'm going to be way more famous than them when I grow up, and my YouTube channel will have a hundred hundred hundred thousand subscribers, and then I'll give you some, and then you can be more famous, too."

I gasp out a laugh. "I'll be too old by then, baby. No one will want to look at my face. My nose will be as big as Grandpa's. Look at this thing." I point to the tip of my nose. "It's already a miracle that I have as many subscribers as I do."

"Mommy, I love your nose."

When I shift my gaze from my brush strokes to those sincere brown eyes, my chest aches. God, I never thought I was capable of a love like this until the first time I laid eyes on her. My love for her had broken out like blinding sunshine through my foggy delirium when I was about to collapse from exhaustion and was still slightly high from the fentanyl they gave me before the epidural.

"It's really big," she says. "Bigger than Grandpa's, and I love that it's so big."

My hand freezes mid-brushstroke, and I throw my head

back and laugh so loud it echoes across the room. "How is it possible to be so sweet and such an asshole at the same time?" I pinch her soft little cheek, and she giggles.

"Did you really call your four-year-old daughter an asshole?"

I clench my teeth as the shrill voice resonates from the hall. I smile, shooting Cadence a knowing look. "Yes," I say sweetly.

When my mom marches into the living room, I see that familiar frown. The frown of judgment.

She places both hands on her hips. "I know you think there's some kind of cultural cache from being flippant with your children—calling them assholes and..." Her pale-green eyes drift from my tripod to Cadence and then back to me, her expression growing more irate by the second. "Are you putting her in one of your videos?" Her voice is soft and menacing, which makes my stomach flutter.

What if I let her think that I am?

The thought alone makes my whole belly flip over.

God, why does no one ever talk about the malicious joy of living up to people's worst expectations? It's like a drug, it feels so good.

With effort, I keep my lips from twitching upward. "She's been asking me to do it for a long time. I think she's old enough now." I turn to Cadence, winking dramatically.

"You think four is *old enough* to decide if she wants to have her face plastered all over the internet?"

I roll my eyes. "That's such an old person thing to say."

Like clockwork, her jaw ticks, and it makes me want to laugh. How absurd for an almost sixty-year-old woman to bristle at being called old. But vain, beautiful people never adjust to their changing looks. Instead of rejoicing over their good fortune in having once been gorgeous, they consider aging an injustice—that the person within them was always meant to be beautiful, and the universe is cruel for taking away their birthright.

"There's so much social media out there," I say. "None of this will matter. People who aren't on social media are the weird ones. If you try to get hired somewhere in 2035 and you don't have a long social media history, people will automatically assume you're a serial killer."

My mom's smile doesn't reach her eyes. "I didn't realize you were a sociologist. Did you finish your degree without my knowledge?"

Rage flares at the question and the cruelty behind it. My unfinished degree is the bane of my existence, the reason I'm drowning in debt and unable to move out on my own. She's always known exactly what to say to get under my skin.

I try to keep my voice light. "Good talk, Mom. Now please get out of the living room so Cadence and I can finish our video. I don't want you in the background. If people see your wrinkles, they won't trust me when I talk about skincare."

As soon as the words are out, I want to suck them back into my mouth. Why do I have to be like her? Why can't I control this childish impulse to lash out? My mom's look of rage as she stares at me silently only makes me feel that much worse. If she's this visibly angry, it's because I hurt her.

She turns to Cadence. "Sweetie, can you go to your room for a minute? I need to talk to your mommy about something."

Much more obedient than I ever was, Cadence immediately gets up and walks in the direction of her bedroom.

When she's out of earshot, my mom turns to me. "Your dad and I can't allow this anymore. We can't reinforce your terrible parenting by paying your student loans and letting you live here rent free. From now on, you're going to have to take care of yourself."

My mouth falls open. "Are you serious right now?"

She shrugs. "It's not out of the blue. Your dad and I have been talking about it for a long time. Logan's been supporting himself since he graduated college. I think it's only fair you support yourself, too."

I grit my teeth, my nostrils flaring. "Logan doesn't have a child."

"We're doing this to protect Cadence."

"You would kick your granddaughter out onto the streets because of a fucking YouTube video? Because you're trying to *protect* her? Mom, do you, like, not know what irony is?"

She lifts a brow. "I never said anything about kicking Cadence out."

My whole body stiffens. I open my mouth, but I can't speak.

My daze is short-lived when I catch the twinges of a smug smile on her face. She's enjoying this. "You are..." I grit my teeth, but I won't be able to stop myself from saying more. I'm too far gone. "You are a miserable cunt. You're out of your mind if you think I would ever let you raise my daughter."

My mom only stares steadily at me, but I catch that faint twitch of her left eye.

I take a step in her direction, lowering my chin. "If I leave this house, Cadence is coming with me."

Her eyes widen minutely, but then she seems to recover herself. "If you try to take her with you, I'll call child protective services." Her voice is eerily quiet.

My lips part before closing again. "What for?"

She shrugs, obviously trying to look calm, but the movement is jerky. "I'll say I'm concerned about her, which is the truth. What if sexual predators see her on one of your YouTube videos?"

If I weren't so riled up, I would laugh. "Do you really think

CPS is going to take Cadence away because I put her in one of my YouTube videos?"

"I'll tell them about the bathtub thing."

That familiar aura settles over me, making my whole body hum. My gaze falls to the floor before slowly drifting back up to my mom, and I'm startled. Her face is strange somehow, as if I've never seen it before. If I hadn't grown to know this feeling so well, I would think I was dreaming.

"Mom." My voice is barely above a whisper. "Are you really reminding me of the worst moment of my life because I pointed out your wrinkles?"

She says something, but I can't hear it. I'm transported back to the moment I woke up and the water was cold. When I heard my baby crying and knew with certainty that I could never make up for my carelessness.

"I'm going on a walk," I say in an empty voice.

When Logan suddenly appears in my vision, I'm pulled into the present. I guess I walked into the kitchen. The metal ridges of my car keys cut into my hand, but I don't remember grabbing them. The look on Logan's face tells me he heard everything that happened in the living room. "She's not really going to kick you out." His voice is urgent. "She's just being a bitch."

"I know." I start walking to the front entry. "And I don't care."

"Don't do anything stupid," he calls out, and the apprehension in his voice makes me want to hit him.

Why does everyone around me think I'm a loose cannon—even the people who are supposed to love me the most?

MY WALK IS SHORT, I think, or maybe it only feels like it. By the time I make it back to my street, Hunter is sitting at the front porch table of the Hayes house, a vape pen in one hand and a phone in the other. When he smiles brightly and waves, I start in his direction, almost running to meet him. As soon as I get close, I leap into his arms, wrapping my legs around his waist.

He squeezes me tightly, burrowing his head into my shoulder. "Ah, my girl," he says against my hair. "I've missed you."

I rest my head on his shoulder. "I hate concert tours."

He stiffens before setting me down and pulling away. "We're actually not touring for a while. Not for the next six months, which means I'll probably be around here a lot."

My brow furrows. "Is this a recent thing? I thought you guys were doing the whole Europe thing again?"

"We were. Now it's cancelled. We're doing a handful of shows in the US, but that's it." His faint smile doesn't reach his eyes. "Cam's idea, of course."

"Did something happen?" My question is vague, because I never know how to approach Hunter's sobriety, and I sensed that something was off the last time I talked to him. It's a difficult topic between us. I never know what I'm going to get with him. Ever since he started recovery programs a few years ago, he wavers between total openness and vulnerability and a sort of detached cynicism I don't quite buy.

"You mean did I get wasted at an after-party and go home with an influencer, make out with him for a few minutes before I passed out and pissed myself on his couch?" He smiles lazily. "Yes, I did."

Ah, the detached cynicism.

"That sounds embarrassing."

He shrugs. "When you've done enough shit like that, it's amazing what you can let go."

"I support that. No reason to dwell on it." I reach out and set my hand on his arm. "I hope you can get this figured out. It's so shitty."

He smiles affectionately before placing his hand on mine. "It is." A notch forms between his brows. "What's going on with you? You seem kind of...down. What did you want to talk to me about?"

My gaze drops to the sidewalk. "I just got into a horrible fight with my mom, and it made me forget about everything. Shit. I had a whole speech prepared for you, and now..." I sigh heavily, lifting my hands to my head and running my nails along my scalp. "It'll all be messed up because I'm going to reek of desperation. I need a job from you because I have to get out of that fucking house."

"Ah."

Even that small sound out of the back of his throat makes me want to wince, because it has a wealth of meaning behind it. He already knew I was going to ask him for a job, and he already knows he can't give me one.

Because of Cam.

"You were going to ask if you could do social media for us, huh?"

I know my smile doesn't reach my eyes. "You sound really excited about the possibility."

His face falls. "You know I can't give it to you."

I can't keep my eyes from closing. Of course he can't. Not when Cam hates me.

"And not because I don't want to." I feel the pressure of his hand on my shoulder. "I know you'd be good at it, but it's not in my control."

My eyes pop open. "Why not? Why does he get to decide everything? Aren't there three people in your band? Why don't you or Janie ever have a say about anything?"

He sighs heavily. "It's complicated."

"I don't think it is." I can't keep the accusation out of my voice. "I think he has all the control because you both let him."

"Partly," he says right away. "But he also writes ninety percent of our songs, and we literally have no band without him."

I lower my gaze to the concrete, not wanting him to see my expression. "And he takes full advantage of both of you, even though you're family, and Janie is practically family."

"Yeah, he's a fucking dick."

My eyes snap up, and the fire in Hunter surprises me. I've hardly ever seen him angry with Camden, even when we were kids, and I've certainly never heard him call him a dick before.

"And an absolute control freak," he says. "And he's been driving me insane lately... But I can't change the decisions I've made. I can't change how much I've fucked up. I wish I could give you this job. I really do."

The compassion in his eyes makes guilt wash over me. I reach out and grab his hand. "I'm being selfish. I'm sorry. I have no clue what it's like to struggle the way you have. I know it must be so shitty."

"Don't apologize. All of my problems are of my own making, and it's not like you haven't had it hard, too." He shoots me a probing look. "You haven't even told me what your fight with your mom was about."

I smile tightly. "Oh, you know, the usual. Except this time she's threatening to stop paying my student loans *and* kick me out of the house. Oh!" I shoot him a bright humorless smile. "And call child protective services and have Cadence taken away from me. The trifecta."

"Shit," he mumbles. "Is she really serious?"

I exhale heavily, shutting my eyes. "No, but it doesn't

matter. I can't live with her anymore. I absolutely can't." I wrap my arms around myself. "I think it turns me into a bad mom."

"That's not true at all. You're an amazing mom."

I shake my head. "I do stupid things when she provokes me. Childish things. Like today, the whole fight started because I made her think I was putting Cadence in one of my videos, and I wasn't. Not that I have anything against doing it, but I only let her think it because I knew it would piss her off."

He smiles warmly. "Yeah, but that's just who you are."

"A child, you mean?"

"No, a firecracker."

When I stick a finger inside my mouth and pretend to gag myself, he chuckles. "It's a good thing."

"No, it's not. It's gross. And it's only when I'm with her, which is why I need to get out."

He winces dramatically, smiling afterward. "I don't know if it's *only* when you're with her."

I scowl at him, balling my hand into a fist. As I lift my arm to punch him in the shoulder, he reaches out and pulls me into a tight hug, pressing my face against his chest. "God, I've missed you. Come live with me if you guys need to get away from your mom. I can't give you a job, but I can give you a big bedroom."

"Don't tempt me." My voice is muffled against his shirt.

"Seriously."

The vehemence in his tone makes me push away from him. His light-brown eyes are earnest and probing.

"I'm not going to mooch off you."

"Why not? Why not mooch off me for at least the next six months before we start touring again? I'm going to be bored as hell, and my condo is big enough for the three of us. I can even cover your student loans until you get on your feet."

"Oh my God." My voice is breathless. "You're really serious."

"Yeah."

I step back, shaking my head. "Absolutely not. I'm not taking your money just because you're rich now. I refuse to be one of those people."

"Lauren, it wouldn't be like that. Come on. You know it wouldn't be like that. I love you and Cadence—"

I lift my hand to silence him. "I need you to stop talking, because the more I think about your gorgeous condo and being able to look out at the ocean all day, the more I want to say yes, and it isn't right. I'm sick of being dependent on people. I need to do this on my own."

He frowns. "Why?"

"Because it's time for me to be a real adult. It's part of being a good mom. The only way I'll take money from you is if I work for you."

He shrugs. "What if you blew me on occasion?"

When my mouth drops open, he laughs. "Jesus, it was a joke! I'm not really going to charge you rent in blow jobs."

"What if I did everything except that?"

His brows draw together. "What do you mean?"

"What if I was your wife for the next six months? What if I take care of you in exchange for free room and board and my monthly student loan bill? I'll give you everything a wife would give you, except blow jobs or sex. I'll be like an old-fashioned fifties housewife. I'll clean your condo, do your laundry, make your meals, and when you need sex, I'll politely look the other way. Like a good fifties housewife would." I smile. "We could even have twin beds."

"I really don't need you to do that, though. I have a house-cleaning service. And a laundry service."

"Cancel them. Let me do it instead."

He frowns, lifting his hand and scratching the back of his head. "I don't know how I feel about putting you to work like that. I'd rather you just live with me, no strings attached."

I take a step in his direction. "I'll give you head massages. Every night." I lower my voice to a melodic hum. "Imagine laying on my lap while we watch trashy reality TV. I'll even get acrylic nails like I had in high school. And instead of whining that I'm tired, I'll keep going until you drift off to sleep."

He lifts his head, narrowing his eyes. "Now you're manipulating me."

"Yep. I think this is an ideal situation for both of us, and I'm going to fight dirty if I have to. It keeps me from being a freeloader."

His frown deepens. "I fucking love your head massages."

I smile widely at the fervor in his tone. "I know you do."

He shakes his head, his eyes growing unfocused, as if he's mulling the whole thing over.

"Say yes," I whisper.

He smiles faintly.

"Do it." My tone is harder this time.

His smile grows.

"You know you want to do it. Just say yes."

His smile vanishes, and he shoots me with a probing look. "It's not going to be pleasant for you. You know Cam won't like it—especially if we say you're my *wife*—and he'll take it out on you."

Heat prickles at the back of my neck, my stomach sinking. Cam has resented my relationship with Hunter for as long as I can remember. When we were teenagers, I thought it was all for Hunter's sake. Cam is an extremely protective older brother, and he made it clear that he didn't approve of how young I started partying.

But on that beautiful, miserable night five years ago, I

learned it was much more complicated than that. I'll never forget the wild look in his eyes when he held my hips and sank deep inside me, or the words he whispered in my ear.

"I've wanted this for as long as I can remember."

I swallow to ease the tightness in my throat. "You're talking about it like it's a sure thing. Does this mean we have a deal?"

When his smile fades, apprehension prickles at my skin. I realize for the first time that I really, really want this.

"I'll come over after dinner. I'll have an answer for you then."

THREE

Camden

HER FULL LIPS part into a wide, toothy grin as she lifts a thin black case. "*This,*" she says, "is what I've been waiting months for. I'm not kidding when I tell you this is not your mom's contour palette." She points to her nose. "I'll make this big ol' honker half its size right before your eyes. It's literally magic."

I snort, smiling to myself. She's so ridiculous. How can she say shit like that with a straight face?

"Watching her videos again, I see."

I jump back in the lawn chair and practically slam my phone on the metal table. When I glance at Hunter, a faint smile is twinging at his lips as he sucks at the black vape pen. After lowering it from his mouth, he exhales a small white cloud. "You don't have to hide it. It's not like I haven't caught you doing it plenty of times. Don't think I forget everything when I'm drunk."

Heat creeps along my neck as I look away. "What did she have to talk to you about?"

He exhales heavily, and this time, a large cloud rises into my line of sight.

I hate that he vapes—a habit he picked up in rehab number two. It's certainly a mild vice compared to alcohol and pills, and yet every time I see him do it, I get this irrational, skin-crawling anxiety that makes me wish I could shrink him into a little boy again, back to when we used to hide our dad's cigars because we were afraid they'd give him cancer.

Long before all the rehabs and sponsors and Al-Anon meetings.

"It's a long story," he says. "And mom says dinner is ten minutes out."

"Give me the short version." My tone is curt.

"It was what I thought. She wants to do our social media. I told her it's not my place to give her that job."

A cynical smile rises to my lips. "I'll bet she didn't like that. I'll bet she tried to bulldoze you into it."

"No." His voice is quiet, almost hesitant. "She didn't have to, because I'm pretty sure I'm going to give her another job."

Uneasiness settles over me. "What kind of job? Don't tell me you're going to make her your PA and pay her twice what she's worth?"

"No." Again, there's that far-off tone, and it sounds alarm bells in my mind. I never know what to expect when it comes to these two. Ever since we were kids, it's been bossy Lauren leading him around like a puppy on a leash.

I hated her for it then.

I hated him for all the attention he got from her.

And I hated myself the most for my disloyalty.

"I think I'm going to be her sugar daddy for a while."

My eyes snap to his face. "What?"

It's only when he jerks back that I realize I nearly shouted at him. "You can't be serious," I say, lowering my voice with effort.

His brows draw together in a puzzled frown. He probably didn't expect I'd react this way. He thought I'd be angry and domineering.

Not frantic.

"I mean..." His frown deepens. "I guess...not really a sugar daddy, but she'll be my wife. Paid wife. Like, she'll take care of me and stuff, and I'll give her some money and let her and Cadence live with me."

It's the "take care of me and stuff" that makes my pulse race. What does it mean?

"It's a good situation since we'll be in San Diego for the next six months. I was going to just let them live with me no strings attached, but Lauren doesn't want to be a freeloader. She said she'll be my fifties housewife." He smiles slowly, and it makes me want to hit him. "She'll make my meals, do my laundry, give me massages—"

"And I assume sex is included?" I wish my voice weren't so tight, but I couldn't tone it down if I tried.

The wide-eyed frown forming on his face makes me wonder if I jumped to conclusions, and the tension in my shoulders eases a little. But then he smiles lazily.

Oh God. This is as bad as I feared.

"I mean that's what wives do, right?" he says, and I feel like the concrete has opened up underneath me.

In a flash, I see them together, just as I found them at the college party five years ago when I opened that laundry room door. His jeans hang loosely at his hips, and her long willowy fingers are wrapped around his limp dick. In the moment, I could barely comprehend what I was seeing. I was still in a sluggish daze from what I had just done with her. She'd crawled over from the passenger seat, straddled my lap, and given me what felt to my horny virgin brain like my heart's desire. And even though I stopped her and Hunter from whatever they were about to do, the juxtaposition of both those things was too much.

She gave me what I always wanted. Then she gave me what I always feared. All in the span of twenty minutes.

As usual, the memory of it all makes my pulse beat like a hammer against my throat, and a prickling heat breaks out over my skin. I hate thinking about it.

It's almost unbearable.

Especially when I think about my part in it. I'd practically dared her to fuck Hunter. I was crushed and humiliated when I found out she wasn't a virgin, too. The full weight of my one-sided obsession finally hit me, and I wanted to shrink inside myself.

Instead, I slut-shamed her.

"You can't do it," I say, surprised at how even my voice sounds.

The smile fades. "Is that a command?"

I grit my teeth at the ice in his voice. "She isn't good for you, especially not so soon after a relapse. She's a party girl. What would your sponsor say to you right now?"

"You don't know anything about her if you think she's still a party girl. And Dave has much better boundaries than you. He wouldn't say a damn thing."

I clench my teeth, trying without success to get my rapid breathing under control.

A reckless thought occurs to me, and everything around me grows still. My breathing steadies, and the roaring in my ears fades. I can even hear the gentle murmur of a car engine a few houses down.

"How much are you paying her?"

When his brows draw together, I realize how little he's thought this through. It fills me with triumph.

"I'm going to cover her student loans every month."

"So what, like...a thousand a month? That doesn't seem like much given your income. She'd have a right to expect a lot more from you."

And I could give her *much* more.

His frown deepens. "It's a lot more than a thousand. Her student loans are, like, well over two-hundred K total."

"You're not doing it."

"Okay, Mom."

The ice in his tone doesn't bother me this time, because I know exactly what I'm going to do.

This has been brewing for five years. No. Much longer than that. My obsession with her began when I was too young to understand what it meant. When she could be twenty feet away, and she'd move or talk or laugh, and my gaze would find her in an instant, as if it had a will of its own. When I wanted to chase her and kiss her and touch her skin. When I wanted to watch her tongue while she licked her ice cream cone and inhale her scent when I hugged her.

The only time I've ever felt like I hated Hunter was when she gave him the things she never gave me—the warm smiles and full-body hugs and pet names like "darling".

But I won't have to feel that way anymore.

I'm going to conquer this once and for all.

FOUR

Lauren

LOGAN STRETCHES his long arms over the edge of the hot tub before settling one hand on Leilani's shoulder. When his hand drifts to her boob, he gives it a squeeze.

Armaan grimaces. "Logan, no one wants a peep show. Save it for the bedroom."

Logan smiles lazily. "It was a reflex."

"It's not his fault," Leilani says. "We both have a public-sex kink." As usual, Leilani's delivery is so stoic, it's impossible to tell if she's joking.

Armaan grimaces before turning to me. "I don't know how you stand it. I think they've been worse since they got back together."

I smile. "I'm used to it."

"I thought you said Hunter was coming over," Logan says. "Or should I say your new boss?"

Armaan smiles. "Or should we say your future husband? I guess that would make him your fiancé."

Just as I open my mouth to answer, I hear footsteps along the walkway of the front yard, and my stomach flips. "That's him. You guys, I'm about ready to seal my fate." I shoot Logan a probing look. "I want you to make it sound like I've gotten way better at cooking."

Logan's brow furrows "He'll never believe it."

"Probably not, but do your best. Talk up my crockpot Mac 'n' Cheese." Water slushes down my skin as I leap out of the tub. I'm so eager, I nearly slip on the concrete as I walk to the back gate. "Hunt!" I shout. "We're in the spa!"

Something about the sound of his footsteps sends a prickle of foreboding down my spine.

"Hunter's not coming."

Heat washes through my veins at the mellifluous sound of Cam's deep voice. He has such a beautiful speaking voice. People with beautiful singing voices usually do, but there's something about his... It's so deep and smooth.

I grit my teeth, inwardly refusing to let him intimidate me. After straightening my spine, I glance down at my chest. When I notice I have side-boob on my right, I adjust the triangular cloth on my left to match it. I smile before pushing open the gate and marching outside, but as soon as our eyes meet, it fades.

After so many years of seeing him mostly on social media, I'd forgotten how beautiful he is in person. His dark eyes and square jaw would make him look so forbidding if it weren't for that plump bottom lip of his pouting mouth. I remember exactly what it felt like as he pressed those soft lips against my jaw and whispered words I'd never thought I'd hear him say.

"You're the most beautiful thing I've ever seen."

I know he wants me—or at least, wanted me at one time—so

why does his presence always make me feel this way? Why do I want to cross my arms over my chest and hide the fact that my boobs don't quite sit where they used to now that I've had a baby? Why do I feel like I could never be enough for him?

At the sound of Logan's laughter, Cam glances in the direction of the hot tub. "Can we go somewhere private?"

"No." My tone is hard.

I refuse to let my vain insecurities make me weak. He doesn't get to choose our battleground.

His grim expression doesn't change, but I sense that he's straining his eyes to keep them from rolling. "Hunter told me everything."

I swallow, trying to squash the flutter of nervousness threatening to make my voice quaver. "Of course he did. He has nothing to hide."

"That's not why he told me." He narrows his eyes. "He wanted me to talk him out of it. He knows you're a bad influence on him. He knows he'll be tempted to go out and party with you if you're living in his house."

I almost want to laugh at his assumption that I haven't changed, as if I still do all the things I did as a teenager now that I have a four-year-old daughter. As usual, he judges me without evidence.

This is why I shouldn't feel guilty, even if I have begun to question the assumption I made five years ago. I could never co-parent with a person who trusts me this little. It wouldn't be good for Cadence, because who knows what he would do? He might even try to take her away from me, just like my control-freak mother.

The thought makes my throat tight. I swallow to ease it away. "That sounds like your opinion of me. Not Hunter's."

Though his look is still forbidding, he doesn't deny it. How could he? I know Hunter didn't say any of that. Hunter doesn't have the slightest worry that I'd jeopardize his sobriety. Unlike Cam, he actually knows me.

"And either way," I say, "you don't have any control over Hunter's choices."

"I know that. I'm here to offer you an alternative."

Startled, I jerk back. "What do you mean?"

"I want to make you a similar offer. Except my house is a lot bigger than Hunter's condo, which will be better for Cadence. And you won't have to clean it or make my meals. And I'm willing to pay you much more."

I take a deep breath to calm my racing heart, trying to ignore the flutter in my stomach.

"What would I do for you?"

He hesitates for a moment, his dark eyes roaming my face. Whatever he's about to propose, it seems like even he's not completely sold on it. He seems to come to some kind of decision, because his eyes harden, and his posture straightens. "Hunter wanted you to be his housewife. Well, I want you to be my party wife. I want you to come with me to events and parties and make sure I'm able to talk as little as possible. To as few people as possible. I know you love parties, and I absolutely hate them. I'd be happy if I could never attend one again, but that's not a possibility in our industry. And since we won't be touring again until June of next year, I won't be able to use our rigorous concert schedule as an excuse to skip them."

I stare at him blankly, my head swimming.

"What are you thinking?" His dark gaze roams my face.

I take a deep breath, trying to give myself another moment to collect my thoughts. "It's insane that you would ask me to do that. Most of the time we're around each other, you barely even make eye contact with me. Why would you want me to be your party wife? It seems like you could find a million women to do that for you. Women who would do it for free. Women who are more charismatic and *much* prettier. Wouldn't it make more sense to choose one of your fans?" I frown at him. "I don't even like your music that much. I mean, don't get me wrong, I think it's very pretty if you like dad music like *Mumford & Sons*, but it's not my cup of tea, and I wouldn't hesitate to tell anyone at a party. Just like I'm not hesitating to tell *you* right now."

I nearly drop my jaw when he chuckles. The sight and sound is so unfamiliar—that deep rumble of a voice growing lighter, those shoulders shaking and normally stern eyes crinkling at the edges.

"Dad music." His voice is tight with laughter. "Brutal, Lauren."

My lips quirk. "It's not an insult. My dad loves your music, so it's literally true."

His smile softens. "You still say exactly what's on your mind, huh? That hasn't changed a bit."

The affectionate look in his eyes makes me a little dizzy. I have to look away, needing to keep a clear head. "You said you would pay me more. How much more?"

His voice grows firm. "I'll pay you ten grand a month."

This time, I can't keep my jaw from dropping. "You can afford that?"

"Of course." He says it like it's nothing. "It'll be for six months, so sixty K total. That should be enough to get you on your feet."

I huff out an almost hysterical giggle. "Yeah, that should be enough."

He narrows his eyes, staring at me for a moment with what looks like contemplation. "It's really not that much money. It might seem like it now, but you'll want to spend it carefully."

Somehow, I'm able to keep my eyes from rolling. It's a sign of how much his life has changed that he doesn't think sixty K is a lot of money. He can't even remember what it was like to be an average person.

"Don't worry about how I spend my money."

"I'm sorry." His voice is much softer. "I was just speaking from experience. I thought I struck gold when I made my first sixty K, and it was gone pretty fast."

When he was still living in New York, he means. When River of Sight was just starting to take off. But that was different. He knew he'd be getting another sixty K soon. He was probably blowing most of it on his Brooklyn apartment. He didn't have a daughter to take care of.

It wasn't a life changer for him.

"Well, you weren't drowning in student-loan debt, so it was different for you."

He sighs. "You're right. I don't know what that's like. It must be stressful, especially for a single mom."

Warmth spreads over me, and I hate myself for it. That was hardly a complement to my parenting. And yet, as always, I find myself devouring Cam's crumbs of validation.

It's gross.

Steeling myself against it, I narrow my eyes at him. "You still haven't explained why you want me of all people to do this for you. Why can't you just find someone to do it for free?"

His eyes grow hesitant. "Hunter said sex would be part of it. He said it was sort of a—I don't know—a sugar-daddy situation. Would that be the case with me, too?"

My eyes nearly pop out of my skull. "Hunter told you that?"

My question seems to set something off in Cam. "You thought he wouldn't, huh? You thought he'd keep the secret from me." He huffs, shaking his head. "But I would have known if you were living with him, even if he hadn't told me. It's always been this way with you two. This was bound to happen eventually."

The accusation in his tone would raise my hackles if I weren't so bewildered. Why on earth would Hunter have told him that? It doesn't even make sense, especially if he wanted Cam to go along with our plan without raising an issue. Then again, Hunter did seem pretty fed up with Cam's behavior lately. Maybe he's finally reached his limit.

Maybe he wants to fuck with him.

A smile rises to my lips. "We really only agreed on blow jobs."

Cam's look of horror makes me want to giggle, but I can't show my cards yet. With effort, I keep my lips from twitching.

Seeming to compose himself, his expression grows stern. "I would want more than that, and I don't think that's unreasonable for ten grand a month. It's nearly five times what Hunter was willing to pay, and I'm only asking you to go to an occasional party with me. If you're really okay with this, I want everything."

The electric heat that shoots into my groin would make me hunch if I weren't making such an effort to compose myself.

Holy shit.

He really means this. He really wants me to be his sugar baby. Doesn't he know that I'd have sex with him for free?

Jesus Christ, I'd pay *him* to have sex with me.

When his gaze narrows on my face, I realize he's waiting for an answer. And now is my cue to tell him the truth. A mature person, a *real* adult—the person I'm striving to be—would tell him right now.

But damn it, this is too tempting.

"Why would you do this? Why would you pay me for sex when you could get almost anyone you want for free?" My eyes are drawn to the notch in his chorded neck as it rises and falls.

"It seems like a pretty good setup for me. I don't like people. I don't like having to pretend I'm interested in women just to get sex. It's all..." He shakes his head. "Exhausting. I'd rather have someone who knows what to expect from me. Someone who won't get their feelings hurt when I ask them to leave my bed after we've had sex. Someone who won't expect me to ask them about their day."

I nod slowly, still dazed. Sensing his intent stare on my face, I look up.

"What are you thinking about?" There's a hint of something in his voice that I can't quite decipher. Is it nervousness?

Heat pools in my belly. I shoot him a sultry smile. "Maybe I can use your offer as leverage against Hunter's. Maybe if I tell him you're willing to pay me ten K a month, he'll do it, too."

"Use my offer as leverage against Hunter's," he scoffs. "Hunter didn't even make you an offer. You wrangled one out of him."

"Yeah, because he would have done it for free."

He smiles faintly. "But you wouldn't let him. For some reason, it matters to you not to take charity. But you know it would be charity coming from him, even with on-demand—" he hesitates for a moment, as if struggling to find the next word, "—blow jobs. Hunter doesn't need that. He's not like me. He loves people. Hell, he even loves groupies. He has sex all the time when we tour, with men and women. He doesn't need you, and you know it."

Though he may be completely wrong about my plan with Hunter, he's still right about that. Hunter *doesn't* need me. And for the first time, I wonder if our plan was really fair. Hunter doesn't need a housekeeper. He wasn't even comfortable with my whole proposition. The only reason he considered it is because he loves me and didn't want to leave me hanging when the situation with my mom is so dire.

Still, I refuse to cower to Cam. "Are you implying that you need me?"

His expression doesn't change, but when his lips close, I know I've stumped him. He lifts a hand and scratches the back of his head, an uncharacteristic gesture for Cam.

"I don't like people. It's a better situation for me." His repetition confirms my suspicion that I've rattled him. "And the fact that you and I don't particularly like each other makes it even better, because I won't have to worry about hurting you."

Heat prickles at the back of my neck as my stomach sinks. I know Cam doesn't like me. I know his attraction to me is purely physical. So why do I feel like he squashed a hope? Like something was building when he first asked me to be his mistress, and with a few words, he destroyed it.

"I need an answer now." Cam's command startles me out of my head.

My brow knits. "An answer to your offer?"

"Yes." He crosses his arms over his chest. "What's the situation like with your mom? Hunter says you need to move out right away."

"I mean... I don't think she was serious about kicking me out, but still, I'd like to move out soon if I can."

"Good. We have a concert in Seattle Sunday night. If we're going to do this, I want you to already be moved into my house by then. I don't want to have to think about any of this when we perform. I've already been too in my head since Hunter's relapse."

Sunday night? Is he crazy?

"Well, I'm going to need to think about it."

"What is there to think about? You need the money. It's only six months, and you'll have sixty grand. You'd be an idiot to turn me down."

"It's a big step. I'll need time to figure out what it will mean for me."

"You should be thinking less about yourself and more about your daughter," he says under his breath.

A chill runs down my spine. In an instant, we're sitting across from each other in that San Diego Denny's, and he's accusing me of being pregnant with his child and not telling him about it. And I'm filled with that same stomach-hollowing uncertainty.

Am I a terrible mother? Is all of his judgment—his belief that I'm a reckless, careless human being—founded in truth?

No. I can't let myself fall back into the insecurities of my youth just because I'm around him again. I'll never survive the next six months if I do.

I straighten my spine, lowering my chin as I stare up into his inky-dark eyes. "Don't you ever talk about my relationship with my daughter. It's none of your business."

A look flashes on his face, so quickly there and gone that I can't quite interpret it. But somehow, I know in my gut that I'd hurt him.

Does he still think about that conversation? Does it haunt him like it haunts me?

"I'm sorry." His voice is soft.

"It's *because* of my daughter that I need to think about it. It's a huge deal uprooting her life like this."

"You're right. I shouldn't have said that." He exhales heavily. "I know it's none of my business. Somehow I can never seem to help myself when it comes to you."

His vulnerability touches me somewhere deep inside. "You have to be nice to her. If I'm going to do this, I mean."

His eyes harden. "How could you even think that I wouldn't be?"

"I don't know you at all anymore. You've made sure of that."

The hardness in his eyes fades, and as we stare at each other, the entirety of the last five years stretches between us. All of those wasted hours when we were in the same room and hardly looked at each other. Is he thinking about how it could have been different? Is he, like me, living again in that heavenly moment in his car when I straddled his lap and wondering what might have happened if we'd both behaved differently afterward?

"Come over tomorrow," I say. "I'll have your answer."

My words seem to catch him by surprise. He blinks once. "What time?"

"We usually open presents first thing and then have breakfast around eleven."

He frowns. "I don't want your entire extended family around when we're planning on moving you into my house."

I lift a brow. "You sound pretty confident you're going to get a yes."

He looks like he wants to roll his eyes. "Just give me a time."

"Come over here around one."

He nods once and takes a step back as if to leave, but then he hesitates. His eyes grow hooded as they drift down my barely covered body.

"Can I kiss you?" he asks, his voice breathy.

Another jolt of heat shoots into my belly. I almost forgot he thinks he's going to be paying me for sex. God, he's going to kill Hunter when he finds out. I would laugh if I weren't so overwhelmed by that hungry look in his eyes. With an effort at nonchalance, I shrug one shoulder. "Sure, I don't see why not. We could think of it as a Costco free sample. You'll be spending a lot of money on me if I say yes. You should get to try a bite first so you can find out if you really want to buy the whole eighty-four pack of frozen tamales. Although I guess you've already had a whole tamale…"

I trail off when his eyes fill with laughter. Oh God, if I'm going to do this, I'll have to shield myself from that affectionate gaze.

I'm in danger if I don't.

When he takes a step in my direction, a pleasant shiver runs down my spine. He stares down at my mouth, and he's so close now that I can feel his breath on my forehead. My lips part slightly as I tilt my chin upward. He lowers his head, and my eyelids grow heavy in anticipation. But then he steps back, snapping me out of my daze.

"No, I think I'll wait. I'll kiss you tomorrow after you say yes."

And with that, he turns around and walks in the direction of the Hayes house.

Camden

MY DICK STRAINS in my jeans as I walk away from her.

God, if I didn't know any better, I'd think she wore that bikini just to tempt me. And why didn't I take what I wanted? Why did I let my frustration with her get the better of me?

It's not like she isn't going to say yes ultimately. What she did back there was a power move. Lauren loves thwarting my expectations. She should realize now that I expect her to thwart my expectations.

Except I wasn't this time.

I thought she was going to say yes, and now I won't be able to rest until I have this whole thing locked down.

I need this. A six-month exorcism of Lauren Henderson.

Ignoring her for the last five years has been a mistake. Deprivation has had a reverse effect. The deep recesses of our consciousness are a fertile soil, and repressed desires sprout and take root when we aren't looking. Five years ago, this whole thing was a childish crush. And today I asked her to move in with me.

God, what have I done?

I take a deep, steadying breath. I can do this.

Six months.

It will all be over in six months. I'll spend every moment getting everything I've ever wanted from her.

The elation that flows through my veins makes me almost dizzy. I speed up my pace. As soon as I walk inside the house, I head in the direction of the guest bathroom.

"Oh my God," Hunter says, stopping me in my tracks. "You went over there, huh? You went over there and asked her to be your mistress." He shakes his head, looking dazed. "I can't believe you actually did it."

I told him I was going to after dinner, but I could see in his eyes he didn't think there was a chance in hell I'd go through with it, because he's never fully understood my obsession with Lauren.

His eyes grow suddenly focused, narrowing on my face. "What did she say?"

There's something in the question... Something I don't like.

As if he can't even imagine a universe in which she'd say yes.

I grit my teeth. "She said she'd think about it."

His eyes widen slightly before growing dazed again. "You're not doing this to keep her away from me, are you?" The words sound faraway, as if he's lost in thought.

I glare at him. "I'm not insane enough to invite a single mother and her daughter to live in my house to keep her away from my brother who's a grown-ass man. But I'm not going to lie that it's an added advantage. She's not good for you. Especially after a relapse."

Hunter grunts, shaking his head. "Unbelievable."

"She's not." My volume raises a notch. "She's a party girl. She always has been."

"You don't know a goddamn thing about her. You don't know her at all."

His words send an icy shiver down my spine, making my jaw clench. I've always hated his implied ownership of her. *He knows her best. He's her confidant.*

I turn away and walk down the hallway, hoping he doesn't sense the direction of my thoughts. I've never wanted him to know. Never wanted him to see how this petty jealousy warped my thinking and made me, in moments, hate the person I love most in the world.

It's disgusting.

"You need to stop doing this," he calls out. "Say the serenity prayer."

"Fuck off," I shout back, wishing it were as simple as that. I wish this were just another instance of me being an overprotective brother.

As soon as I walk through the door of the bathroom, my body recalls my purpose. My partially softened dick grows fully erect even before those wide green eyes and pretty pink mouth come into my mind. After I pull down my pants, I grab my cock. I imagine her lying on my bed, her dark hair spreading like spilled paint across my white comforter. Her heavy, round tits falling to each side of her chest.

I don't even have time to get through my usual rotation of Lauren fantasies—that time I caught her sunbathing naked in our backyard or the blissful moment in my car or one of the more porny scenarios my imagination created on its own. After three strokes, I'm hunching over, fighting a groan as my come spurts into the toilet.

That was fast.

Oh Jesus Christ, I'm in trouble. Fantasizing about her has become almost a ritual. Even when I try to think of someone else, thoughts of her always intrude during moments of abandon.

I've told myself that's how it works with our earliest sexual fantasies. They're too formative to go away.

I've told myself it doesn't mean anything significant.

I stare into the toilet in a daze. Did I make an epic mistake committing to this?

She hasn't even moved in yet. I haven't even started to purge myself of her, and already I feel this certainty in my gut that six months could never be enough.

FIVE

Lauren

"ARE YOU OKAY?" Armaan asks.

With effort, I form a smile on my lips as I turn to him. I've been going out of my mind all day waiting for Cam to show up. I hate him for it, because I was too distracted to fully enjoy watching Cadence open her presents. And I took two jobs last month from makeup companies I would never represent under normal circumstances just to save money for her gifts.

It's now almost two o'clock. I thought for sure he'd be banging on the door the moment the clock struck one, in typical high-handed, control-freak Camden Hayes style.

Maybe he changed his mind. It would make sense if he did.

It was a crazy proposition.

"Yeah, I'm fine."

Armaan nods, but he looks like he doesn't believe me. "I wanted to talk to you about something."

By the sound of his voice, I can tell it's important, and I'm thankful for the distraction. "What's going on?"

"So you know how I'm working on making an online store for my edibles?"

"Logan was talking about it the other day, and I'm super excited for you. Your brownies are ungodly delicious, and they give you such a good, relaxing high."

A wide grin spreads over his face, and it makes my heart clench. Armaan has never shown this kind of enthusiasm over a career before. Like me, he struggled to focus in college, and his poor grades made him the outcast of his accomplished family. That's why we bonded immediately. I understand his situation in a way Logan never could.

"I've got a lot more recipes now than only brownies. This past summer, Leilani basically put me through a whole culinary school, and not to brag, but I'm a hella good baker. Even she thinks so."

I smile. "And she wouldn't sugarcoat it."

"No, she wouldn't. Anyway, I'm nowhere near ready to launch. It's weed, you know, so it's not as simple as making a website and selling my shit. It will probably be six months or even a year before it's ready—with all the manufacturing and legal shit I have to work through. But I've got one investor locked in, and I'm working on another."

"Damn!" I reach my hand out and slap his thigh. "Look at you. You have an investor? That's insane."

"I know right?" His smile is rueful. "I'm like a real adult now."

I keep my grin fixed, even as my throat grows tight.

I hate myself. Why can't I be happy for him? Why do the successes of my peers always make me feel like I'm in a bad dream, trying to run toward something and yet unable to move my feet?

"And I want you to do social media for me."

My eyes widen.

"I want to get started on all of that early. You know—to build momentum before we launch. I wouldn't be able to pay you much of anything at first, but—"

He halts when the doorbell chimes, and my stomach flips over.

"Is that him?" he asks.

"I'm not sure." It takes all my willpower to keep myself from running to the front entry.

"It's Camden!" my mom shouts from the kitchen, obviously looking at the doorbell camera.

My overwhelming relief must be visible on my face, because Armaan chuckles. "I don't believe you that you think this whole thing is crazy. I think you want to be his mistress."

I wave a hand in his direction. "I'm only fucking with him."

He narrows his eyes, his lips quirking at the edges. "Sure you are."

When I slap his thigh much harder this time, he chuckles. I turn my head in the direction of the hallway, straining my ears to hear my mom's conversation with Cam. I can't make out the words, but I catch that her voice is slightly higher than usual. If I weren't so riled up, I would laugh. Her entire demeanor changes when she's around handsome men. I can almost see her brows arching and her lips pouting as she makes small talk with Cam, as if he would have any interest in the fifty-nine-year-old mother of his childhood friends. It must be a reflex after so many years of being accustomed to the adoration of men.

I ought to feel sorry for her, but instead, this familiar anger settles over me. This strange, euphoric anger that makes my skin uncomfortably hot even as my stomach flips.

She would die if she knew why he's here.

She'd never think someone like Cam would have any interest in someone who looks like me.

I stand up and march to the front door, trying hard to wipe the childish smile from my face. Without glancing in my mom's direction, I meet Cam's dark gaze. "Should we go to my room and talk?"

Cam's brows draw together, a question in his eyes. "No." His gaze drifts to my mom and then back to me. "Let's go outside."

"Good idea. That will give us privacy." I'm barely able to keep my lips from twitching.

As I open the door, I strain my focus to my peripheral vision, and I can see that my mom's expression is a mixture of confusion and annoyance.

"Why are you smiling?" Cam asks as we walk to the front lawn.

"Because my mom would lose her shit if she knew why you're here."

"You have such a weird relationship with her. I've never met anyone who talks about their mom the way you do. It's like you're both mean girls."

"*She's* the mean girl. I only act in self-defense."

His lips quirk. "You can be pretty mean sometimes, too."

I wave a hand. "It's just insecurity. Look at my nose." I gesture at my face. "Anyone with a nose like this would be mean sometimes. I'm angry at God for being so unfair."

He's quiet for a beat, and when my gaze roams his face, I find something that takes me completely off guard. His smile looks almost...

Tender.

"You still have that thing about your nose, huh?"

"Of course." I lower my gaze to the grass, trying to hide how his uncharacteristic expression is making me lightheaded.

"Have you seen my mom's old modeling pictures? Do you remember what she looked like even ten years ago? She was a fucking bombshell. Why didn't I get that shit? Why did Logan get her face? He's a man." I shake my head. "He doesn't even need it."

"You're just as beautiful as your mom used to be."

My lips part. "Are you out of your mind?"

He stares back at me steadily. "I prefer the way you look, actually."

I scowl. "Now I'm less flattered by the fact that you're attracted to me and want me to be your mistress. You obviously have horrendous taste, and as a beauty influencer, that means something to me. I'm not sure I even trust you as an artist anymore."

That affectionate smile grows, and his eyes even crinkle a little around the edges. Who is this person?

His face grows serious. "You haven't given me your answer."

And that's when I hear it. The urgency in his tone.

When I give him a glance over, my suspicion is confirmed. Though his face gives nothing away, his thumb is drumming a quick beat on his thigh, which is unusual for Cam. He's usually so still all the time.

He wants this. He really wants this.

The thought makes me hot everywhere.

"My answer is yes."

His mouth doesn't move, but his eyelids grow—ever so slightly—heavier. My cheeks grow warm under his gaze.

"Good," he says quickly, as if snapping out of his daze. He reaches into his pocket and pulls out his car keys. "Come on." He gestures with his head toward the black car parked on the other side of the street. "I have a meeting set up with my lawyer."

With that, he turns around and marches away.

After a beat, I start following frantically behind. "Wait! We have to talk about something first."

Now is the time to tell him about Hunter's lie.

Oh God, I just hope it doesn't make him change his mind about the whole thing.

He shakes his head sharply. "We're not talking about anything else without a lawyer present."

My brow furrows. "What do we need a lawyer for?"

"I have one more thing I have to talk to you about, and he'll need to be there for it."

I have to nearly run to keep up with him. "Why?"

"I'll have him explain it to you."

"You can't even give me a hint?"

"No."

WE DRIVE in silence for several minutes, my head swimming.

"Here," Cam eventually says as he reaches one hand into his pocket and pulls out a folded piece of lined paper. "It's a list of your responsibilities. I wrote it out last night."

My lips part as I grab the list from his hand, my stomach fluttering. "My responsibilities..." I unfold the paper and scan Cam's neat, even handwriting up and down and back again, still too dazed to process the words in front of me. "You mean like...sexual stuff?"

When he gasps out a laugh, my eyes snap in his direction. He tightens his lips, as if to repress a smile. "Just take a look."

My cheeks warm when I realize how wrong I was. The first few lines are a list of River of Sight events and parties. "So you want me to block off these dates?"

"Yep. These are what we have on the calendar so far. More

will be scheduled in the upcoming months, but not nearly as many as usual since we're taking it easy. In fact, I specifically asked my agent to book as few as she can. For Hunter's sake, of course. I want him at as few parties as possible."

I press my lips together to fight the retort rising to my mouth. *Isn't it Hunter's responsibility to protect his sobriety?* But Cam has never liked it when I come to Hunter's defense.

"I can't avoid socializing entirely," he says. "Your job will be to stay by my side and talk to people so I won't have to, which should be easy for you. And that right there—" he takes his eyes off the road and points to a column of names, "—is a list of people I never want to talk to under any circumstances, so you're going to need to be extra talkative when they're around."

My brows draw together as I scan the names. "You don't want to talk to Brayden—*your PA*—under any circumstances?" I glance up at Cam. "How do you communicate with him now?"

"I mean, I don't want to talk to him at any kind of social event. He's so fucking awkward with me when he's trying to make conversation. I think because he's nervous, but it puts me on edge. And he's fantastic at his job, so I could never fire him in good conscience."

I shift my gaze back to the list, my bewilderment growing by the moment. Good Lord, Camden *really* doesn't like people. "Are you a sociopath?" I find myself mumbling.

"Possibly," he says right away.

When my gaze snaps to his face, I see that fond smile again.

I won't let it distract me. I go back to the list to look over the other fifteen items. It's mostly basic stuff I would have expected, like staying out of his home studio while he works, but there are some odd things on it, too. Things I don't quite understand. I point to item seven. "Does this mean I need to be home *every* evening after six?"

"You can have time off, of course, but that's usually when I'm done for the day, unless I'm really onto something with my writing and I work through the night. But in general, that's when I'd be...in need of your services."

I try to ignore the jolt of heat that shoots into my belly. Now is my cue. I can't let this go on any longer.

"Cam, you don't need to pay me for sex. You can pay me to be your party wife, and I can even clean your house and make your meals if you think ten grand a month is too much for only that job, but as far as the rest of your needs..." I shoot him a sultry smile. "I'd gladly take care of them for free. In fact 'gladly' is too small a word. I'd *enthusiastically* take care of them for free."

He doesn't respond directly, but he shifts in his seat, and I want to giggle in triumph.

Looks like he needs to make room for something growing in his jeans.

"I want to pay you," he eventually says.

"But you don't have to—"

"But I want to. This is an exchange of services. You're helping me, and I'm helping you. It's not a real relationship. I want that to be clear."

The coldness in his voice sends a chill down my spine. I try to keep my expression blank, not wanting him to sense how his words gut me.

So this is how it is, huh? Nothing has changed.

He hates me just as much as he did five years ago.

"If you were going to do it for Hunter, you can do it for me."

The hard words cut into my reverie, making my head jerk back. He sounds almost...petulant. Like a child insisting on having the same size ice cream scoop as his sibling.

He's jealous.

The thought makes me smile. "Fine. You obviously have way too much money if you want to throw it away on something you could get for free. I'll gladly take it from you and put it to better use."

"How long does it take you to read a list?" The sharpness in his tone tells me he didn't like what I said.

I lift the paper from my lap, about to say something sassy when I glance over an item that shocks me. I have to read it twice to make sure I understand it correctly. "You want me to share my phone location with you?"

His jaw clenches, but he doesn't answer. I only belatedly recognize that we've now parked, and he's opening his door. "Why does it look abandoned?" I ask as I glance around the parking lot.

"Because it's Christmas. They aren't open."

Minutes later, we're standing in a large, sparsely furnished office, and Cam's lawyer, Chris, gestures for us to sit on a burnt-orange mid-century modern couch across from his desk.

"I love this," I tell him as I run my hand along the tight fabric.

"My wife picked it out. It's not comfortable at all." He smiles at Cam. "So my clients don't linger too long."

"You said it was fine. I could have waited until tomorrow."

Chris's smile stays fixed on Cam. "Could you have, though?"

A notch forms between my brows. "What is this about? What's so important that we had to meet on Christmas day?"

Chris gestures at Cam to cue him to speak, but Cam remains silent. I get the distinct impression that he's trying to intimidate me. Ironically, it does the opposite. My belly flares with heat. I love it when he's domineering.

It makes me want to taunt him.

"Please tell me we're here to discuss some kind of sex

contract," I say. "Cam, I could totally see you having a kinky dungeon with whips and handcuffs and sex swings and stuff, and I'm down for all of it."

When his brows shoot together, my smile widens.

"Whatever you want," I say. "You can spank me, flog me, clamp my nipples—"

"Jesus Christ, Lauren." Cam's dark voice sends a jolt of heat to my groin. "Keep your word vomit in check for once, please. Of course this isn't about a sex contract. That's not even legal. None of this is legal, in fact. We can't even make an official employment contract. Not if sex will be involved. Why do you think I handwrote your responsibilities? And you need to stop saying you're my mistress. I don't know who you've told already, but from this point on, you're my live-in girlfriend."

What? "That's what everyone will think? Like news sources and stuff?"

He shakes his head sharply. "News sources don't give a shit about my personal life, and that's because I've worked hard to keep it private." His jaw ticks. "I'll expect you to do the same."

"Damn." My brow furrows. "That's a shame, because my subscribers would absolutely love it, especially since I'm so aggressively average looking. It makes them root for me more than your typical beauty influencer. They'd love it if I landed someone like you. I mean none of them probably listen to your twangy banjo rock music, but you're exceptionally hot and a *real* celebrity, instead of another YouTuber..."

I trail off when Cam's hard look softens, and his eyes alight with laughter. "What?"

"My twangy banjo rock music." Cam utters the words slowly as he glances in Chris's direction. "She doesn't pull her punches, does she?"

"No, she doesn't." I hear a smile in Chris's voice, but my eyes are fixed on Cam's face.

That smile. I've seen it so many times in the last twenty-four hours, I ought to be immune to it by now. Instead, it pulls up long-forgotten memories.

Cam and I had so few moments of harmony growing up. Depending on the circumstances, his attitude toward me wavered between annoyance and disdain. But every once in a while, I'd glance in his direction and catch a look in his eyes that would tie my stomach into knots.

A hungry look.

Though my cheeks warm, I fight to keep my expression blank. I can't let him see how much that look affects me.

This is only sex for him. Not a real relationship.

"So you don't want me saying anything to anyone about our situation?"

"You can tell your friends and family we're in a relationship. You just can't say anything publicly. So nothing on your YouTube channel—"

"Cam," Chris interrupts, lifting a piece of paper in front of him. "This seems like a good time to have her sign the NDA."

Cam nods, and Chris sets the document in front of me. He starts explaining what it means—item by item—but I barely hear him.

My thoughts are racing. I can't believe Cam would make me do this. I can't believe he trusts me this little. He's treating me like a groupie.

"Are you really making me sign an NDA?" I keep my voice low.

His eyes grow slightly hesitant, though his voice remains as hard as ever. "It's standard in our industry. Most people do it when they start a new...relationship."

He's barely able to utter the word "relationship," because it's obviously so repulsive to him, which only fans my fire. My jaw clenches. "You've known me almost my entire life. Since I was fucking five years old. I was in your backyard when I got my period for the first time. And you're really making me sign an NDA?"

He doesn't respond. His expression is almost blank, and I could cry.

"I know all kinds of things about you already. Things about your whole family." I shake my head. "Hunter would never make me do this, even with all the stupid shit I've seen him do when he's drunk—" Wrath flashes in Cam's eyes, and my lips close.

"I'm not Hunter." The words are delivered softly, but they send a chill down my spine.

Somehow, I'm able to hold his stare. "Obviously not. Hunter trusts me."

Cam leans forward, and I get the distinct impression that he would grab me if he could. Oddly, the thought warms me. Turns me on, even. And I'm thankful for the feeling. Without it, I'd be tempted to storm out of here, if only for the thrill of thwarting him, and I can't do that.

I need this.

I need this for me and Cadence.

"Hunter lets you walk all over him." His tone is ice. "And I won't."

I scoff, waving a hand and leaning back in my chair. "No way. If this was really 'standard in your industry', I would have seen Hunter do it with other people. I bet you made that up because you're a psychotic control freak."

Cam doesn't even flinch. He already knows he's a control freak, and he doesn't care.

"Alright, whatever. I'll sign." I grab the pen and paper from Chris's hands. "It's not like I'm planning on blabbing anything anyway. If you knew me half as well as Hunter—"

"I know you every bit as well as Hunter."

Cam's booming voice startles me, making the "H" in my signature a little more jagged than usual. There's that same petulance I heard earlier in the car. I keep my head down as I scribble out the date in order to hide the small smile rising to my lips.

Good Lord. Does he realize how jealous he sounds?

I school my face to look blank before turning in Cam's direction. "Is that all?"

His dark brows draw together. He looks like he forgot what we were talking about, which makes me wonder if he's regretting his lapse in self-control.

His eyes grow hard again. "No, that's not all. Not even close. The NDA was mostly a formality. I brought you here because I want to propose a change to what we agreed on yesterday. Chris says paying you monthly looks suspicious. Like I said before, since sex will be a part of our arrangement, you can't officially be called my employee. So we'll have to be creative in how I pay you the ten K every month. I thought of something that will work better for you in the long run."

I frown. "What are you proposing?"

"I'll pay off your student loans."

I stare at him dumbly for several seconds, his words not computing. But the moment they do, my whole body starts to hum—a low rumble that tickles my belly and makes my skin prickle. I do my best to ignore it. He can't possibly mean what he said.

There's no way.

"What do you mean by that?"

"I mean exactly what I said. I'll pay off your student loans."

My breath catches. "All of them?"

His brows draw together. "Do you have more than two-hundred something? That's what Hunter told me."

I lean forward. "Two-hundred and thirty-six. You're telling

me you'll pay all of my student loans for being your mistress and party wife for six months?"

"Yes," Cam answers right away.

"Live-in girlfriend," Chris says, or at least I think he does. My ears are roaring, and my arms and legs seem like they belong to someone else. Am I even in my body right now, or am I floating above it?

The pressure of a hand on my arm pulls me back down.

"Are you okay?" Cam's voice is gentle.

"I understand what people mean when they say they died of shock. I think I literally just died right now."

A warm smile tugs at his lips. "You didn't, but you looked like you were about to have a panic attack."

I'm about to speak when the pressure of his hand on my arm turns into something like a caress, sending a tickling heat into my belly. I glance down to see his fingers moving back and forth across my skin. Who is this person? Who is this person treating me with so much affection?

"Those student loans must weigh pretty heavily on you." Again his gentleness startles me, and this time not in a good way. How could he be so kind when a moment ago he'd unabashedly told me I'm not trustworthy?

"Over two-hundred fucking grand? Yeah, they weigh pretty heavily. It's over two K a month, and that's the *lowest* amount I can pay. It basically only covers the interest, so I barely make a dent in the total. Up until now, I had no clue how I would ever live on my own." My brows draw together. "How could you possibly pay it off like it's nothing? Do you really make that much money?"

"Yeah, I do."

"How? Hunter doesn't have that kind of money. I mean, he's loaded, but he couldn't drop two-hundred K like it's nothing."

"I write all of our music. And while you might not like my *twangy banjo rock,*" he smiles faintly, "we've had quite a few artists cover our songs. Plus, I've published songs we don't perform. Most of my income is from royalties."

I nod slowly, not fully understanding the concept of royalties, but not wanting to reveal my ignorance by asking about it. All that matters is that I'm not dead, and he really is able to pay off my student loans.

My whole life could change.

Cadence and I could finally have a real life in a small condo somewhere. We could decorate her bedroom by painting our own pictures on the walls, like those boho influencer moms I've always envied. And I could enroll her in preschool and work regular hours. I could hustle and make a real income for us.

I could be a real mom instead of this stunted child-mom who can't raise her daughter without the help of her domineering mother and weak-willed pushover father.

"But if you want me to pay it all off, you have to agree to two things." Cam's hard voice pulls me out of my fantasy. When I glance at his face, he has his usual stern look. "I'll still pay you the sixty K, no matter what. We already agreed on that. I can't pay it monthly, because that would look suspicious, but during the time you live with me, I'll cover all of your expenses. Cadence's, too. Anything you need, just ask for it."

Heat creeps into my neck. "What two things do I have to agree to get the full loan paid?"

His jaw works. "The first one is straightforward. You have to be faithful to me."

My body grows stiff, heat flaring over my skin. So this is the full depth of his mistrust? He's willing to pay me almost four times as much money for something that I would have considered a given.

Will that night always haunt us?

"I wasn't planning on being with anyone else." My voice is so small, it brings me back to childhood when my mom would talk about me to my Aunt Lisa right in front of me.

"I worry about her," she'd say while she did something affectionate, like stroke my hair. "She's defiant."

"She's strong-willed like her Aunty," Lisa would say. "She'll be the president someday. Or she'll be a female Steve Jobs."

"Or she'll..." And then my mom would mouth something to Lisa, something I couldn't understand even as I saw the words on her lips, but I knew it was bad.

It scared me.

"Yeah, well, the problem with your plans," Cam says, "is that they can get derailed on a whim. I want you to take this seriously. I won't deal with your bullshit. I've put up with enough already, but I'm willing to put the past behind us."

Rage flares, making me feel bigger and more powerful. "Obviously, you're not. Obviously, you're not willing to put any of it behind you if you don't trust my word that I'll be faithful to you."

He scowls. "Would you trust your word if you were me?" He looks away, shaking his head. "It's insane that I'm even doing this."

"Why does some impulsive thing I did when I was eighteen have to define me in your eyes? And you never even..."

I can't finish, because he won't like what I have to say.

You never even told me why you were so upset.

I wasn't his girlfriend. I owed him nothing. Even if I had gone through with having sex with Hunter—and I never would have—it wouldn't have technically been wrong of me. The only rational reason Cam would get so upset—upset enough to avoid me for five years straight—is that the moment in his car must have meant much more than he admitted.

"Either take it or leave it," he says. "If you're too insulted by my condition, we can go back to the sixty grand I originally offered."

"I'll take it." My voice is small again.

Triumph flashes in his eyes. "Good girl."

My bravado returns at his smugness. I shoot him a lazy smile. "Oh, do you like it when I'm weak and submissive? Should I start calling you, 'Sir?' Or what about, 'Master?'"

His dark brows snap together. "Can you not with Chris here? You're making him uncomfortable."

"I'm fine." Chris's voice is strained, as if he's holding back laughter.

"What's the other condition?"

Cam glances at Chris and then back at me. "You won't be allowed to enter into a similar situation with Hunter. Ever. And if you ever try it, I'll sue you for all the money I gave you."

My jaw drops, my eyes darting frantically to Chris. "Can he do that?"

Just as Chris opens his mouth, Cam interrupts. "Why are you asking him questions? He's my lawyer, not yours. And if you're asking what legal grounds I'd have to take the money back, the answer is none. But I'll still do it. And good luck dealing with the legal fees on your influencer salary."

I scowl at him. "You're a fucking terrible person."

He only shrugs, but I can see from the set of his jaw that his teeth are clenched.

My stomach sinks when a thought occurs to me. "What if you suspected I was cheating on you, but I wasn't?" My eyes dart to Chris. "Could he not pay me, even with zero evidence?"

Chris starts to speak, but I can't hear what he says because Cam's deep voice booms over his. "None of this is legal, Lauren. Do you not understand that? This is all under the table. Neither of us has any contracted obligation to the other.

You can stop working for me at any moment, and I can arbitrarily decide not to pay you at the end of this."

When his gaze roams my face, his expression softens. "But I think you know me better than that."

I lift a brow. "I know you're such a control freak, you would sue a single mom to get your way."

His mouth tightens, and his shrug is jerky. "Well, it's up to you. You can always walk away and get substantially less from Hunter."

That's not an option any longer, and he knows it. Cam's offer is a game changer. When I glance up, he's staring at me with an intensity I've never seen before. He really wants this.

And that gives me power.

When the notch at his throat rises and falls unsteadily, that inkling of power becomes something visceral, settling in my core and making my stomach flutter. He doesn't know who I am anymore, and I'm going to show him.

I'm no longer the impulsive, sensitive teenager who betrayed him over hurt feelings. I'm a hard-working single mother who is damn good at my job, and he's going to see it. At the end of these six months, he'll be begging me to work for River of Sight.

He'll finally give me the respect he's always withheld.

In an attempt to extend his misery, I stare at him for a long moment before finally giving him my answer. "Alright, I'll do it."

SIX

Camden

IT'S DONE.

Finally.

I knew she would agree. For all her impulsivity, she's a smart girl, and it's an incredible offer, unlike anything she could get elsewhere. There's no way she'd go to Hunter now. He could never afford to pay off her student loans, not with the way he's mishandled his money these last few years.

I didn't think I was nervous. So why am I almost dizzy, so much so that it takes effort to keep my eyes on the road? Why did my arms and legs turn to jelly the moment she agreed to my terms? I could barely stand up from my seat and walk with her to the car.

She's been quiet for most of the drive, probably angry that I backed her into a corner, but what choice did I have? It's madness that I'm even considering this arrangement given our history, but if I want to get over this obsession, I have no other choice.

When I pull up along the sidewalk next to her house, I turn to her. "I don't know what your plans are for tomorrow, but I already booked the moving truck."

Her brows shoot up her forehead. "You what?"

"Yeah, I booked it last night. I wasn't sure how hard it would be to book something last minute the day after Christmas."

"Cam..." A notch forms between her brows. "My whole extended family is visiting. Am I supposed to tell my Uncle Jack and Aunt Carrie that I'm becoming your sugar baby, and moving me and Cadence into your house?

Are we really having this discussion after that meeting? "I thought you understood that we're keeping quiet about that. Just tell them we've been dating long distance and we've been planning to move in together for a while but didn't tell anyone. That's what I'm planning to tell my parents."

"And you really think they'll be okay with that?"

"Yeah." I frown. "Why wouldn't they be?"

"Because we've never gotten along."

I shake my head. "They don't question my decisions. They know I wouldn't tolerate it."

She stares at me wide-eyed, as if she's stunned. Her own relationship with her parents—and in particular, her mom—is quite different. In many ways, she's still a child.

"Anyway," I say. "I think you should tell your parents the same thing. It just makes it simpler."

She shakes her head. "My mom would never believe it."

"Make her believe it."

"No way. Haven't you noticed she has a crush on you? If I had been dating you for months, I'd never keep it a secret from her. I'd make her eat it for breakfast, lunch, and dinner, and she knows it."

An involuntary smile tugs at the edges of my lips.

I love how she does this.

I love how she's so open about her faults. How she acknowledges them without shame.

"Alright, fine," she says, turning away from me. The motion makes the long, beaded earrings around her strong jawline flutter and tinkle.

I've always loved the way she dresses. Huge, sparkling earrings, bright-neon dresses, and clacking high heels that lift her already tall form to nearly six feet. She's so undeniably herself.

I find myself drinking in the sight of her. God, I've missed that face—everything from those beautiful green eyes and that plump pink mouth to that bump on the bridge of her nose and that small scar on her cheek that she got from a loose metal bolt on my old backyard swing set. How in the hell have I been able to stay away from her all these years?

"What time are the movers coming tomorrow?"

Her question makes my head jerk up. "Eleven o'clock. Packers, too. You can oversee the move if you need to, but I want you at my house right afterward. That way you can be all settled in by the time I get home from rehearsal."

"No, sorry. I won't be able to get there until later. Probably after you get home. My whole family is going to SeaWorld tomorrow."

"SeaWorld?" I can't keep the disgust out of my voice. How the fuck could she even consider going to that hellhole after the agreement we made a half hour ago? I can hardly breathe from anticipation. I'm ready to pull her onto my lap and fuck her right now, right in front of her parents' house. "Can't you get out of it?"

She scowls. "Do you think I'm going to SeaWorld for my benefit?"

"So get out of it."

She stares at me steadily, as if there's something I'm missing. When she says her next words—with that cool, detached voice—I want to flinch in shame.

"Did you forget that I have a daughter?"

I exhale heavily, wishing I could hide my face from her view. I did forget. Probably willfully, too. Ever since I found out that little girl wasn't mine, I've been going out of my way to forget her.

"Do you think I can dump her off on my parents any time I feel like it?" she asks, snapping me out of my head. "If you do, then our arrangement isn't going to work. I can get babysitters for her sometimes, but I don't love doing it. I already only get to spend half of my week with her."

"I'm sorry. I forget you're a real mom."

When my gaze returns to her, I catch the flare in her nostrils and the rigidity of her posture.

"Shit, Lauren. That's not what I meant at all. I know you're a real mom, but I haven't been around you much since you had Cadence, and it's a little weird for me. You were such a wild kid yourself, it's weird to think of you as a responsible parent." When she opens her mouth, I raise a hand in defense. "Not because I don't think you're capable of it, but because I still imagine the Lauren I grew up with." A smile rises to my lips. "The one I caught tanning naked in my backyard."

As soon as I say the words, a vivid memory of that day rushes through my senses. I can even smell the sweet scent of the freshly cut grass in our backyard. I see the dusty-yellow sundress that she laid over the back of the lawn chair. Her perky, round tits that dipped slightly to each side of her chest.

And that gorgeous V between her legs that I couldn't quite see, though not for lack of effort.

She did it to taunt me, as she always did back then. She flaunted her naked body in front of me and my other teenage friends because she wanted to fluster and arouse me and get me back for being a high-handed prick to her all the time.

But that's because she didn't understand the mind of a teenage boy. She couldn't have known that for probably thousands of subsequent nights, I would call that memory to mind when I couldn't sleep, put my hand on my cock, and let my imagination run wild.

Or maybe she did. Maybe it was what she'd wanted.

When I catch her questioning frown, I straighten my posture. "That's fine if you have to go to SeaWorld with your family, but I want you to come over as soon as you're done."

"You got it, boss." Her full lips spread into a lazy smile. "Or do you prefer sir?"

My stomach turns to knots. It takes every ounce of my self-control to keep from reaching out, grabbing her, and pulling her onto my lap like I did on that night so many years ago.

How the hell am I going to get through the next twenty-four hours?

SEVEN

Lauren

"I WANT the red eye shadow next," Cadence says.

I can't help but smile as I run a featherlight brush of baby-blue across her lid. Red and blue. She's such a ham, just like I was at her age.

"These colors make your big brown eyes pop," I say as I grab another eye-shadow brush from the pile. I run it lightly over the deep-crimson square on the palette before lifting it to Cadence's eyelid. "Honey, I have to tell you about something." I smile brightly. "Something exciting."

Her eyes widen. "What?"

"We're going to be moving to a new house soon. Very soon. In fact, the next time you come back from your daddy's, it will be to our new house instead of here."

She frowns. "Where is our new house?"

"It's not too far away. But it isn't exactly *our* house. It's your Uncle Cam's. He's letting us stay there for the next six months."

"Is six months a year?"

"No, baby, six months is just six months. It's a half a year.""

I'm startled when my door opens. My mom stands with one hand on her hip and a big glass of wine in the other—a constant since my aunts arrived. "Cady, honey, Leilani and Aunt Lisa are working on a puzzle. They need your help with it." She smiles sweetly. "They aren't as good at puzzles as you are."

As my mom knew she would, Cadence leaps off my bed and darts toward the door.

"I didn't even finish your makeup," I call after her, but it's futile. Her bouncing footsteps are already pounding on the kitchen tile. I frown at my mom. "I was talking to her about something important."

"What's so important?" She narrows her eyes. "Where did you and Cam take off to?"

Something about the question draws my attention to her face. Her eyes are hard and her jaw is set.

She's jealous.

And that's why I don't feel guilty for my childish triumph. On the contrary, that look of death on her face makes my stomach flutter. Just wait till she knows the full extent of it.

She'll want to kill me.

"We went to his lawyer's office."

Her irritated expression shifts to bewilderment, and it makes my stomach flip.

"Why would you go to his lawyer's office?"

I stare at her steadily, wanting to savor this moment. "Because I'm moving in with him."

Her mouth falls open. "Is this a joke? Why on earth would he ask you to move in with him?"

"Why do you think?"

My mom's eyes are saucers now. "I really don't know."

"He's been into me for years. He's finally owning up to it. He wants me to move in with him so we can finally have the kind of relationship he's always wanted."

Her face grows almost completely expressionless. She looks like she's in a sort of trance. "This isn't funny," she eventually says, her voice barely above a whisper.

"I'm not joking."

"You're telling me all this time he's wanted a relationship with you?"

I clench my teeth, and my skin grows hot. "Yep."

Her eyes narrow. "And you're doing it? Out of the blue? You're moving in with him because he wants you to." Her voice lowers into a menacing rumble. "You have a daughter."

"Thank you for pointing that out, Mom. You're absolutely right. I have a daughter I need to support. And thanks to you— and dad, according to you, though he doesn't seem at all aware of the fact that you threatened to kick me out yesterday—my financial situation has changed dramatically."

"I can talk to your dad about that. Maybe we don't need to... We can probably afford—"

"It's too late to take it back. There's no way I'm changing my mind about this. It's done. And Cam's going to pay off all my student loans."

Her mouth drops open. "What?"

My stomach jolts. "Yep. He wants me that much."

Her eyes grow dazed. "I can't believe it."

She really can't—I can see it all over her face—and it makes my mountain of triumph fade into dust. I ought to have expected it. I knew she thought he's out of my league. So why does thwarting her expectations leave me strangely hollow?

"Will you go find Cadence and tell her to come back in here?" I ask. "I need to finish telling her we're moving tomorrow."

Her eyes snap to my face. "Tomorrow?"

"Yep." I try for a smug smile, but I find my lips are quivering slightly. "Cam is impatient to start our new relationship."

"Honey, what are you thinking moving out so suddenly like this? Cadence has lived here for nearly her whole life."

"And with Ryder." I wave a dismissive hand. "And he's lived in a bunch of different apartments since she was born. And with a bunch of different roommates and girlfriends. She's used to the change."

"Yes, but you're her stability."

"That's right!"

When she jerks her head back, I realize that I nearly shouted at her. I take a deep breath before speaking again. "*I'm* her stability, and you kicked me out yesterday."

She exhales, lowering her gaze to the floor. "Honey, I was angry." Her voice is small, because she hates apologizing. Even when she's cornered.

"And it's a good thing you were, because it led to this opportunity. It's a game changer for me and Cadence."

She licks her lips, shaking her head. "I don't know if it's the opportunity you think it is."

I snort. "You're only saying that because you can't relate. If you'd ever had someone like Cam offer you something like this, you would have jumped at the opportunity."

That finally gets her. She narrows her eyes, and her jaw hardens. "You don't know what you're talking about. I have a lot more experience with men like Camden than I ever told you about—"

"Mom!" We both jerk at the sound of Logan's voice. His thudding footsteps sound down the hallway.

"Uncle Jack needs you," he says.

My mom turns toward the hallway. "What for?"

"I don't know. It's important though." With that, Logan

sweeps into my bedroom and closes the door practically in her face.

Now that we're alone, I roll my eyes. "Traitor."

"Are you kidding me? I saved your ass, and you know it. I couldn't even see your face, and yet I knew you were about to snap. You were Eddie Brock turning into Venom."

"Anything I said would have been deserved."

His expression grows piteous. "Why do you still do this shit?"

"Don't say that like you're so much more evolved than me. You have mommy issues, too."

"Yeah, but I deal with mine by ignoring them." His lips twinge. "Like a healthy fucking adult."

"That's because you don't have to live under her dictatorship."

"It's only a dictatorship because you've let her have it. She can't control you. You can do whatever the fuck you want."

I raise both hands in the air. "Mom and Dad have been paying my student loans. Do you know how much they are? Two grand a month! Two fucking grand. And she threatened to stop paying them."

"Yeah, but you know she was never going to do that." His expression softens. "This isn't about that, and you know it. This is about the same thing it's always about with the two of you—her hurting your feelings, and you not wanting her to know how sensitive you really are."

I avert my gaze, unable to respond.

He sighs heavily. "You need to accept that you're never going to have a good relationship with her and let it go. She's old. She's not going to change, but it's really not that hard to appease her."

I grit my teeth. "Maybe I don't want to appease her."

"You'd be a lot happier if you did."

"*You're* happier when you appease her. Because you're a pushover."

"So what if I am?" He shrugs. "As long as I don't have to deal with her bullshit, I really don't care about anything."

"Her shit would drive you crazy if you had to live with her. You would turn into Venom, too." I narrow my eyes. "You know just now she was seconds away from bragging about some eighties celebrity who almost asked her to move in with him. And you also know 'almost asked her to move in with him' is code for said hi to her one time."

His determined expression shifts into a scowl. "God, it's bullshit when she does that, because there's literally no way of verifying it. I bet you she's making at least ninety percent of it up."

"And it's such a dumb thing to brag about, too, because no one under the age of sixty has ever heard of these so-called celebrities. Seriously, who the fuck is Harry Hamlin? And she talks about him like he's Chris Hemsworth."

Logan cringes. "That's my least favorite of her stories. It's so fucking long for how little happens in it."

"Yes! Finally, we agree on something."

His expression grows stern again. "Only on that, and honestly, I think you're on the road to becoming just like her if you don't figure this out. Think about that." He shoots me a probing look. "Think about being in your late fifties and still bragging about the folk-rock star you hooked up with in your early twenties."

My whole body grows cold. I want to say something sassy back, but I find my throat is too tight to speak.

"Shit," Logan mumbles. "I didn't mean that the way it came out."

I swallow. "Yes, you did."

"No, I really didn't. I've been..." He winces. "I'm kind of

worried about you with this whole thing with Cam. I wish you had stuck to the fifties-wife thing with Hunter."

"This is a better opportunity for me." Anger has made my voice regain much of its volume.

"I don't know. This whole thing is all so weird. I worry Cam is up to something."

"What are you talking about?"

"Don't get me wrong." He raises both hands in the air. "It's not that I don't think you're beautiful, or that he's not into you, because it's obvious he's always had kind of a twisted crush on you. But he's like a legitimate celebrity now. Why would he ask you of all people to do this? He's probably hooked up with movie stars."

I scowl at him incredulously. "Are you out of your mind? He's a *folk*-rock musician. Who listens to folk rock? I know literally no one. He's not the fucking Weeknd."

He looks like he wants to roll his eyes. "I want you to be careful."

"Are you worried he's going to murder me?"

"No." His tone isn't nearly as confident as it ought to be. "But I do worry he has some kind of ulterior motive with this whole thing."

I frown. "Like what?"

He stares at me for long moment before answering. "Cadence."

I stiffen, but only for a moment before I'm able to shrug it off. I shake my head. "He has no interest in her. These last two days, he's forgotten she even exists twice. I don't even think he remembers that day at Denny's."

"I don't know. The older she gets...the more she looks like him. And if he lives with her, he'll probably notice."

"That's a matter of opinion." My tone is firm. "She has Ryder's chin. And anyway, Cam wouldn't notice even if she did look like him, because he doesn't want to. Who on earth would want a baby mama when they have the kind of money he does?"

"I don't know. It all seems really weird." His gaze is fixed on the carpet, his brows drawn together.

I wave a hand in his direction. "Even if he was her real father, and the chances of that are slim, he'd have to prove he wants her before I'd give him any rights. And he literally has nothing without my say. I've researched the hell out of this. It doesn't matter how much money he has, he couldn't force a DNA test by claiming we had sex once. But anyway, it doesn't matter. He doesn't want her, and he doesn't trust me at all. If I ever said I suspected he was her father, he'd probably accuse me of trying to take more of his money."

And I don't even want to think about what it would mean for Cadence. His thinly veiled disdain for me was hard enough to bear these last five years.

If he rejected my little girl, my heart would break in two.

EIGHT

Camden

IT SMELLS LIKE HER.

How strange. It's only her clothes in boxes, makeup in giant tin cases, and one pillow she insisted is "more comfortable than the clouds in heaven" when I told her that her new bed already has plenty of them. And yet the whole room smells like Lauren Henderson.

I'm brought back to those moments in high school when I'd open the front door and let her into our house. She'd brush past me with hardly a look, intent on seeing Hunter. Even in the midst of my disdain for her rudeness, her scent would wash over me, and I'd be filled with longing.

Attraction is visceral, and it's unfortunate. I've always wanted her, even when I couldn't stand her.

And in a few hours, I'll have her.

That scent of hers will be all over my bed. All over me.

God, my heart is racing like I'm on something. I'm so frantic to get her home.

She texted me two hours ago to say that her family was about to leave SeaWorld, but knowing Lauren's sense of time, it will probably be another two hours from now.

I was so eager to get this night started, I stupidly ended our rehearsal early. Since then, I've been wandering around the house trying to pass the time. I tried watching TV, but I couldn't concentrate. I tried tidying up the kitchen, but my housecleaning service took care of everything, so there was hardly anything to do.

So here I am in her bedroom. I've been standing here as if I can piece together the last five years of her life by staring at the piles and boxes of her clothing and makeup.

The doorbell chimes, and my stomach jolts. I keep my steps measured as I walk downstairs, not wanting to show how eager I am, and yet I'm still almost dizzy by the time I make it to the foyer. When I yank open the door, a tingling sensation runs over my skin.

She stands with her hands on her hips and a frown on her face, wearing what looks like athletic wear and a messy knot of hair on the top her head, like coming to this house is the most normal thing in the world. Like she's only been out for a bit, and now she's home.

She looks tired.

She looks beautiful.

"How was SeaWorld?" I'm surprised at how nonchalant I sound, as if I haven't spent the last three hours roaming the house like a lonely lapdog whose life revolves around her.

"Ugh," she groans, pushing past me as she makes her way inside, and that scent washes over me, just like I remember.

"Packed, of course. God, don't you hate SeaWorld?"

My eyes still closed, I smile to myself. I school my face into a blank expression before turning around. "Yes."

"I'm sorry I'm late." Her tired green eyes meet mine. "Fucking Logan and Armaan had to go on every single roller-coaster, because they're apparently both still twelve years old, and then Cadence started crying because the sea otter exhibit was closed, so I had to buy her a forty-dollar stuffed otter in the gift shop. Oh!" She raises both hands in the air, and I want to laugh. She's so vivacious when she talks—her bright-green eyes expressive, her gestures wild. "And then she left it in the car when I dropped her off at her dad's, so obviously she loves it and fully appreciates my financial sacrifice."

When I smile warmly, she looks surprised, and I don't like it. She's given me that look almost every time I've smiled at her these past few days. Have I really been that much of an asshole these last few years that even a smile is shocking? "You won't have to worry about forty dollar purchases anymore."

A slow smile spreads across her face. "I still can't believe you're paying off all of my student loans. And I get to live in this gorgeous house!" She spreads her arms wide and turns in a circle as she glances around. "I love all the glass. You can see the ocean everywhere. It reminds me of... What's that famous architect's name? Something Lloyd Wright..."

"Frank Lloyd Wright."

Her head snaps in my direction. "Did he design this house?"

My smile stays fixed. I stare at her, trying to read her expression. "Are you joking?"

"No, why would I be joking?"

I gasp out a laugh. "This is a nice house, but not *that* nice. And it's new. It was built probably fifty years after Frank Lloyd Wright died."

"I'm sorry I'm not an expert in architecture."

"Neither am I, but I know enough to know that the most famous architect of the twentieth century didn't design some random house in La Jolla."

When she sucks in her lips, my stomach sinks. That's the look she used to give me when we were teenagers. It means I'm being a dick. Goddamn my terrible interpersonal skills.

I clear my throat. "Are you hungry?"

Thankfully, her cynical smile fades. "No, I had shit food all day at SeaWorld. What I do want is a stiff drink. Can you make me a dirty martini, but don't even bother with the olive juice? Just give me what I want, darling. Straight vodka and maybe one olive." She frowns. "What's wrong?"

And that's when I realize I'm staring at her with my lips parted.

Darling.

She's never called me that before. She used to say it all the time to Hunter. But never me.

"Nothing." I turn around and walk toward the living room. "The bar is over here. I'm not very skilled at making cocktails, but I guess if you only want vodka and an olive, it shouldn't be too difficult."

She follows close behind, and her willowy shadow stretches out ahead of me. The sight of it makes the hairs on my forearms stand up.

I still can't believe that she's here.

I pull out a glass of whiskey from the bar cabinet. "Doesn't look like I have martini glasses. I really only drink whiskey."

She rests the side of her hip against the counter. "I'm flattered you're even making me a cocktail. You're not someone who makes drinks for people. I'm not sure I've ever seen you do it before."

"I'm a lot of fun, is what you mean." I pour the cold vodka into her glass and hand it to her. After pouring a whiskey for myself, I raise my glass in the air. "Should we say cheers to our new...relationship?"

She narrows her eyes, pursing her lips as she stares down at her drink, as if giving the question earnest thought. "Why don't we say cheers to Pepperdine for shackling me with debt and making me desperate enough to do this?"

I smile, raising my glass higher. "To Pepperdine."

She shoots me a cheeky smile as she clanks her glass with mine.

"Do you think you'll ever go back to school?" I ask.

"God, no. I love what I do now. I only really went because I got to use the loans on this insane apartment in Malibu. Cadence even had her own room"

I gulp back a laugh, trying not to choke on the whiskey I just sipped. "I wondered how you were able to run up that much debt in a year and half."

"Student loans are designed for morons like me. People with no impulse control, who can't do math and think their psychology degree—that they don't even have yet, by the way— could reasonably pay back hundreds of thousands of dollars in ten years. It's literally not possible. It should be illegal."

"You're not a moron. I bet you would have figured out how to pay it off. In two days, you conned two relatively wealthy people into taking you into their homes and giving you money."

"Is that what I did? A con? If so, I'm good, because I didn't have to work that hard, especially with you. You offered it up out of nowhere."

I smile warmly. "I was already sold. Based on that Costco free sample you gave me years ago."

She places a palm over her mouth as she snorts, her shoulders shaking, and I can't help but laugh along with her. How does she always do this to me?

I haven't laughed this much in months. Not since I

suspected Hunter was taking benzos and trying to hide it, and definitely not since that miserable night two weeks ago when his one-night stand had to call an ambulance because Hunter passed out and was unresponsive on his couch.

"Remember when a trip to Costco felt like a Caribbean cruise?" she asks when her laughter subsides, and thankfully, it draws me out of my head. "When we'd beg our moms to take us?"

I grimace. "You and Hunter maybe. I never felt that way. I fucking hate Costco, and any store like it. So many people..." I shake my head. "I'm so glad I have a PA now to arrange all of that shit for me."

She smiles, narrowing her eyes. "I didn't think you hated people that much. I knew you were a dick, but this is crazy. You really hate talking to women so much that you'd rather pay someone for sex? Someone who would give you sex for free?"

My gaze falls to my drink. "I don't hate all people. I have five I like."

"*Only* five?" Her tone is incredulous. "Does that number change? What happens when you get married? Will you have six people then?"

My smile turns rueful. "I like to keep it at five. It keeps me from overcommitting. If I ever get married, someone will have to be demoted."

Her loud cackle is followed by a snort, and it warms me everywhere. It's so achingly familiar even after so many years away from her.

"You're such an asshole." Her voice is strangled with laughter.

I shake my head. "It's all about temperament. People fall into two categories. They either like all kinds of people—you're that kind of person—or they like a select few. I'm a misanthrope, so I like a *very* select few. I can't help it. It's just how I'm built."

"You're wrong about me. I don't like all kinds of people."

"Really? You were always so loud at parties. And it seemed you had a new best friend every week in high school. Maybe you've changed."

"Oh, I still love being around people because I'm vain and I love attention, but I don't like very many people." She narrows her eyes. "Who are your five?"

I lift one finger. "Hunter, obviously."

"Of course. You're such a good big brother."

My brow furrows. "You think so?"

"Absolutely. You're so protective of him. Like I know you would literally commit murder to keep him safe. It used to give me mad older-brother fantasies when I was a kid."

I nearly jerk back at that. "What do you mean?"

She smiles a bit ruefully, averting her eyes from mine, as she lifts her drink to her lips. "Logan is a wonderful brother, so don't get me wrong. And he's technically my older brother by eleven minutes. He is protective in his own way, but he's so easygoing. I used to fantasize about having an older brother like you who was just a little bit of a dictator, you know?"

"No, I don't know. I never had any brotherly feelings for you, even when we were young."

"It was when I was really young. It was definitely a sexual fantasy, though I didn't know it at the time." She smiles slowly as she runs her gaze down my body and up again. "I definitely don't have any sisterly feelings for you now."

Heat washes over me. I swallow as I lean in closer and stare down into her heavy-lidded eyes. "What do you feel for me now?"

Abruptly, she pulls back. She grabs her drink from the bar

counter and takes a small sip. "I'll tell you later. Who are your other four?"

"Tease." I roll my eyes. "I don't think I'm going to tell you. You'll have to guess."

She smiles to herself. "Well, obviously your mom and dad—"

"Nope."

Her gaze darts to my face. "You're saying you don't like your mom and dad?"

"I love them, obviously, but I don't love hanging out with them. In fact, hanging out with them is a chore—something I do only because it needs to be done."

"Like doing laundry."

"Exactly. But I can be around my five people all the time, and it doesn't bother me. I can talk when I need to, but I can also be silent. They're people I can share a space with. I didn't like living with my parents, which is why I moved out as soon as I turned eighteen."

"You're sharing a space with me..." She raises questioning brows.

My pulse starts to race, and I avert my gaze. This conversation is dangerous, and I need to change the subject fast. "Yeah, well...I won't be hanging out with you all the time. This is a big house, and I spend most of my time in my studio. You probably won't even see much of me when we aren't..."

"Going to parties. Or fucking."

The harsh word on her lips makes my already half-hard dick grow fully erect. I look at her face—that beautiful face with her big green eyes, thick dark brows, and wide expressive mouth. "Goddamn, you're so fucking gorgeous."

Her brow knits. "Do you really think so? Even with my big ol' honker?" When she lifts her fingers and touches that bump on the bridge of her nose, my body grows lighter than it has in years. Like I might float away if I'm not careful.

How is it always this way when I'm with her? How do I always feel so light and easy when we have these rare quiet moments with just the two of us, when at other times she drives me to absolute insanity?

"Even with your big ol' honker," I say.

She gasps when I grab her by the waist and press her against the counter. My body flush with hers, I lower my head and press a hard kiss against her neck. "Sorry," I whisper against her skin. "I've been waiting hours for you to get home, and I don't think I can wait a second longer."

NINE

Lauren

I CAN'T BELIEVE I'm here, standing on this polished wood floor and surrounded by walls of glass. I feel almost dazed, unable to believe that I live here now. Cam, on the other hand, didn't glance at the ocean when he brought me inside his bedroom, even as the sun set behind the water, turning the whole coastline purple.

His gaze hasn't left my face.

He now hovers over me, his breathing unsteady after all those kisses. He's nearly undressed with only boxers covering that fully erect cock that peeks out slightly at the waistband.

My God, he's even more beautiful than when we were teenagers.

He was always lean with broad shoulders and a narrow waist—a gift of nature—but all of this muscle is new. It's yet another sign of how drastically our lives have drifted apart these last few years. He looks like this because he's rich. He can afford an in-house gym and expensive food, and he has the type of job that allows him to do what he likes, when he likes it.

I refuse to let it intimidate me, even though my belly is softer now with an array of stretch marks. Even though my boobs hang much lower than they used to, and my nipples are bigger from breast feeding.

I lift my chin and meet his eyes, making an effort to stare at him boldly. I grab the bottom of my shirt and lift it up slowly. As if on cue, his eyelids grow heavier. Just as I pull the shirt over my shoulders, I catch the scent of my armpits.

Shit.

So much for boldness.

After tossing my shirt on the floor, I frown. "I've been sweating all day at SeaWorld. I stink. Do you mind if I take a shower first?"

He scowls. "Yes, I mind! My dick minds. I don't care if you're sweaty."

"I care though." I smile ruefully. "I need to feel sexy in order to enjoy myself. I don't feel sexy right now. And I know what a hygiene freak you are, which only makes me more self-conscious."

"I'm only a hygiene freak with myself. With you it's different. I like the way you smell. And I can't wait another second." His eyes grow intent on my face. "I think I might die if you make me wait."

His words make my belly catch fire. I give myself a moment to take in the intensity of his gaze as he stares at my half-clothed body. Goodness, it feels good for him to want me this much.

"Trust me when I tell you won't like the way I smell right now." I lift my hands and point to each armpit.

He shuts his eyes and groans. "I really don't mind. I like the smell of your pussy. It's pheromones. Your sweat won't bother me. It's science...probably."

I can't keep my mouth from falling open. "You've only ever been around my pussy once."

He stares at me for a long moment. "I have a good memory. A *really* good memory when it comes to you." He winces, looking almost pained. "Can we please have sex now? I'll plug my nose if it will make you feel better. I'll do fucking anything." His eyes are pleading.

"Oh we can have sex now, and don't bother plugging your nose. That might be the hottest thing I've ever heard in my life, what you just told me. Like, literally the hottest. I feel like a fucking sex goddess right now. I want to rub my pussy all over your face."

He exhales heavily as he approaches me. "Please do."

And with that, he lifts me by the waist and tosses me onto the bed.

I sit up, thrusting my chest forward and reaching behind my back. "Self-consciousness gone," I say as I unhook my bra strap. As soon as my bra falls, I hiss. I lift my hands to my tits and cup them to ease the pain. "It always hurts after being in the same bra all day."

When I look up at Cam, his eyes are fixed on my tits. "Rub them."

I lift a brow. "You like this."

"Yes." His voice is tight.

A slow smile spreads across my face as I massage my tits in circles. It doesn't feel good, but I won't tell him that. Not when he stares at me so reverently—his eyelids heavy, his lips parted.

"Oh God." His eyes spark. "Take your pants off now." His gaze shifts to my hips. "Now!"

"Wow, you're bossy." My voice is breathless.

"I've been thinking about this for two days straight. I'm ready to fucking explode."

I'm only able to pull my yoga pants to my hips when he reaches for my waist and yanks them down along with my underwear. I gasp when he lowers his head and presses soft kisses down my belly. When his mouth settles at the cleft between my legs, I release a whimper.

"I've wanted to lick your pussy since I was a teenager," he says after pulling away.

Warmth rushes over me. This is what I've always wanted to hear from him. Do I have a praise kink, or is it specific to Camden Hayes? Have I always craved his validation because he withheld it from me?

He places two fingers between my pussy lips and spreads them apart. "It's so pretty, I could write a song about it."

Even as heat rushes over my body, laughter rises to my chest. I slap my hand over my mouth and gulp it back.

"You don't understand." I hear a smile in his voice. "You'd have to like pussy to understand."

I lift my head to give him a skeptical look. "How do you know I don't like pussy?"

He doesn't seem to hear my question, his eyes glued to the area between my legs. His head drops down, and he sucks my clit with his entire mouth. The pleasure is so overwhelming, my hips start to flail of their own volition. "Holy shit! What are you doing to me?"

My response seems to spark something in him. He grips my hips tightly, his tongue moving frantically.

"Oh my God!" I shout. "You're really good at this!"

"Mmm," he hums, and I can feel the vibration against my clit.

"I never would have guessed it." My voice sounds faraway. "I always thought you'd be bad at oral."

I gasp when he yanks his head away. "What do you mean by that?"

Reality settles over me, and I want to hit myself for my lack of filter.

"Nothing." I wave a hand. "Keep going. Please."

He shakes his head sharply. "Not until you tell me what you meant."

"You're a hot guy," I shout, ready to explode with frustration. "Hot guys are usually bad at oral. It's not an insult. It's just how the world works."

I can't see his face fully, but I sense he's not satisfied with that response.

"Hot guys have nothing to compensate for," I say.

"No." His tone is hard. "You said you always thought *I'd* be bad at oral. You were talking specifically about me."

"Ugh," I groan, unable to believe he's torturing me like this. "Fine! *You specifically* like everything your way. You have no desire to please anyone but yourself."

There's a black frown on his face. Great. I'll probably never get his mouth on my clit again.

"You think I'm selfish." His tone is incredulous, and I don't understand it. Of course I think he's selfish.

He *is* selfish.

"Yes! But I was wrong about your oral skills, okay? You're excellent at oral. Now, can you please get back to it?"

He either doesn't sense my sexual frustration, or he doesn't care. His jaw is set as he stares down at the bed. "I'm going to make you come ten times tonight. And I won't let you sleep until I do."

The vehemence in his tone would make me laugh under different circumstances. I'd never guess that stern, unselfconscious Cam is like every other guy, wanting to prove his sexual prowess.

"Okay," I say sweetly. "Can you start by putting your mouth back on my goddamn clit? Because I was on the verge of having my first of ten when you stopped to have this delightful chat."

And just like that, he snaps out of his dark mood. He lowers his head between my legs, and the next two minutes are electricity and fireworks. Before I know it, I'm screaming. When his face enters my clouded vision, I see that smug half smile typical of men who know they've given you a good orgasm. It tugs at me, because it's so unexpected. He seems so much more human. Almost boyish.

He kisses me feverishly, rubbing his tongue hard against mine as if to remind me of his skill by making me taste myself. When he pulls away, he stares down at me, his expression almost tender. But then his expression grows hard again. He stands up and walks toward the bedside table. After opening the drawer, he pulls out a small square package. He puts on the condom and crawls back onto the bed, settling his body over mine and gripping my hips tightly. I gasp when his cock probes at the base of my pussy. "I'm going to fuck you now, because I'll explode if I don't come soon." His jaw clenches. "But after that, you're mine. Save your energy. Nine more orgasms, do you hear me?"

I can't help but smile. "Cam, darling. There's no need."

His whole body grows still.

My brows draw together. "What?"

"Nothing."

"Do you not like it when I call you darling? Is it too girl-friendy?"

His gaze shifts to my collarbone. "No, I like it." The words are rapid and hushed.

God, he's so much more tender and vulnerable than I ever expected.

When his cock pushes forward, and all thoughts of tenderness vanish. I gasp as he stretches and fills me. I'm so slippery after my orgasm that he's able to sheath himself in one thrust. He releases a groan that I feel in my bones.

"Lauren." His voice is breathless.

"I know."

"I haven't been able to stop thinking about this."

"Me, neither."

"I wish..."

He doesn't finish his thought, and it makes me irrationally angry with him, because I can't stand the hope that springs into my chest, making my whole body warm. I can't start wishing for more from him when I know it will only lead to disappointment.

His next hard thrust pulls me out of my head, and I'm thankful for it. I'm still too sluggish from my orgasm to feel the full effect of his big cock pounding into me again and again, but, oh God, watching him is almost as good. His eyes are glazed, his dark brows drawn together as if in pain. As if the pleasure is too much. He grits his teeth. "Jesus Christ, I'm not going to last long."

"That's okay. I like you like this." I shoot him a sleepy smile. "At my mercy, I mean."

His eyes harden. "Enjoy it. It won't be like this next time."

"In that case..." I reach my hand under the comforter and run my fingers along his hard stomach. I reach his hips and trail my fingers inward. When I find what I'm looking for, I cup his balls, squeezing softly.

"No," he shouts, his eyes frantic. "You're going to make me come."

And I'm going to enjoy it.

I bite my lip. "I know."

When I massage the velvety skin, he grimaces, his body

growing stiff. He's struggling for control, trying to last as long as he can, which makes me want to be bad.

I raise my mouth to his ear. "Why don't you finish in my mouth, baby?" I whisper. "I want to taste your come."

He jerks away from me, his eyes wide. When I giggle, he glares at me. "Goddamn you!"

My smile widens. "Or you can come all over my face, and I'll lick my lips."

His thrusts become faster and harder, his grip on my hips tightening like a vice. "Goddamn your filthy mouth!"

My giggle fades when he releases my hips and abruptly pulls out of me. I gasp when he pins my arms down on the bed with his knees. After ripping off the condom and tossing it on the floor, he grabs his cock and strokes it up and down. "You want my come? Here you go."

"Oh my God." My words are breathless.

It takes only a few strokes before warm liquid spurts all over my tits. My eyes snap to his face, and I see that he's staring down at my chest. After the last few drops shoot out, he rubs an index finger along the slippery mess, the look in his eyes almost reverent. "I've always wanted to do that."

I swallow. "You've never come on someone's tits before?"

"Oh, I have." When he lifts his gaze to meet mine, a faint smile twinges his lips. "Just not yours."

A tingle runs down my spine. My God. He needs to stop talking this way or I'm going to be in serious trouble.

"Alright," he says, reaching his hand back and patting me on the hip. "Let's get you cleaned up so I can start working on orgasm number two."

As he gets up and walks to the bathroom, I smile to myself, the memory of his earlier determination flooding back.

"Cam," I call out, "it's going to take me at least another twenty minutes before I come again. I'm literally numb after an orgasm. You really should give up your goal. You're going to wear yourself out."

"No." His tone is firm as he emerges from the bathroom with a towel in his hand. "You will have ten orgasms by the end of the night. That's a promise."

I take the towel from his hands and rub the wet spot along my chest. When he reaches into the bedside table and pulls out a small pink device, I roll my eyes. "Seriously, give it up. I don't like vibrators. My clit's too sensitive."

He smiles to himself as he looks down at the bullet. "You told me that years ago, and like any other remotely sexual thing you've ever said to me—" when his eyes meet mine, they crinkle at the corners, "—I never forgot it. You'll like this vibrator. It's designed for sensitive clits." His smile fades, those dark eyes growing hard. "Alright, get on your hands and knees."

My stomach flips over. "Yes, Sir."

After I get into position, my stomach jolts in anticipation, and I realize my post-orgasm numbness might have faded early. When I glance back at him, he's still standing a few feet away. "What are you waiting for?"

"Just enjoying the view. I'm fully hard again already. I don't know how you always do this to me."

As expected, his praise makes my whole body heat.

I could get used to this.

I inhale sharply when grabs me by the hips and starts pushing his cock into my pussy. His voice grows strained as he speaks. "Okay, we're going to try this. The lady at the sex shop said it's a vibrator for people who don't like vibrators."

I roll my eyes as he brings his arm around my hips and sets the little pink bullet against my clit. "They always say that. I've tried plenty, and I've never—Jesus Christ!"

The low rumble makes my whole body grow taut with electricity. I fall forward, my face smashing into the mattress. I'm so lost in the sensation I barely feel the pressure of Cam's arms as he lifts me up and pulls my back against his chest.

"Do you think maybe they were right this time?" he whispers in my ear.

I'm too lost in my sexual haze to call him out on his smugness. "Yes," I nearly whimper. "Yes." My words sound like a plea.

Cam chuckles, and I can feel the vibration of it radiate through my body. When he starts to move in me, I whimper again, and moisture gathers behind my eyes.

"God, Lauren." His voice is hoarse. "You feel incredible."

His thrusting sends waves of electric heat from my core to the tips of my fingers and toes, and before I know it, I'm screaming and sobbing and begging for something I can't name.

Then the whole world grows quiet.

The next thing I know, I'm lying on my back, my body limp and languid. I finally open my eyes at the brush of his fingers against the damp hair on my forehead. Cam is staring intently at my face. He takes one finger and brushes it down my cheek. "You were crying."

"Yeah." It's all I can muster.

A small smile tugs at his lips. "You don't seem like someone who cries when you come. You didn't when I went down on you earlier, or..."

That night.

He can't say it. But he doesn't need to, because it's always between us.

"I don't usually." I shake my head slowly, surprised at how much effort it takes for such a small movement. "I don't think I've ever loved anything more than I love that vibrator."

He chuckles for a moment before his warm lips press against my cheek. "Don't I get at least a little credit? I mean, it was my idea to get it for you."

I frown when a thought occurs to me. "Did you actually go to a sex shop to buy this vibrator specifically for me? Between yesterday and now?"

"Brayden did, actually." He winces. "I figured you wouldn't mind if he knows about our situation since you're not shy about things like this."

"So you sent him to a sex shop to buy me a bunch of toys?"

"I think he arranged a shopper. And they bought you all kinds of things. Not just the vibrator."

"Like what?"

"Uh..." He scratches the back of his head. "Lotions and conditioners and all that beauty shit. I made Brayden look at your YouTube channel to find out what to get, so I hope you don't lie in your videos. I also had him get Cadence some things. Art supplies, Marvel toys... Stuff like that."

I can only stare at him, my incredulousness probably all over my face. He averts his gaze. For some reason I can't explain, my throat grows tight, and moisture gathers behind my eyes. I swallow before speaking. "How did you know to get Cadence Marvel toys?"

His eyes are fixed on the bed. "I asked Hunter what she likes."

I can't say anything more. My voice would quiver if I did.

"Don't fall asleep."

The sharpness of his voice makes me realize my eyes have drifted shut.

"I'm not nearly done with you yet." The low rumble of his voice makes my limp body come alive again. "And I don't want you sleeping in here."

His words make me go cold. My shock must be obvious, because he winces.

"I'm not trying to be a dick, but I don't like sharing a bed.

And I don't want..." He closes his mouth, his lips tightening. "I want the boundaries of our relationship to be clear."

I'm barely able to keep myself from flinching. I suppose I should be thankful for the reminder.

When he lowers his lips to mine, I don't even find it difficult to kiss him back.

All of the rising hope has now been squashed.

TEN

Camden

I WALK into the kitchen and glance around the sparse white counters, trying to figure out what I'm looking for.

Am I thirsty? Do I want coffee?

I roll my eyes. I've been doing this constantly for the past two days. I'll be driving or playing an instrument or writing lyrics on a notebook, and I find myself seized by images of her. Images so vivid that everything around me fades away.

Her big green eyes heavy-lidded and glazed. Her soft, warm lips wrapped around my cock. The sweet sound of her whimpers.

I can't get any goddamn work done.

My eyes are drawn to a flashing light on the counter. When I turn to the source, my stomach flips.

Her phone.

I glance back at the hallway before reaching for it, and my

eyes widen when I swipe the screen and instantly see a page of apps. She doesn't even have a passcode.

Oh God, I'm going to do it.

My conscience barely even prickles as I pull up the app and press "share location". By the time I'm done, I feel nothing but relief. A quiet voice tells me I'll regret it, but I push it away. It's only for six months. And I already told her I was going to do it.

After deciding that I don't feel thirsty, I grab a mug from the cupboard. I reach for the coffee carafe and pour the now lukewarm liquid into the mug. This whole thing had better work. Six months better be enough to expunge her from my system. If not, I'm in trouble.

She makes me do crazy things.

"Uncle Cam!"

I jump, spilling coffee on my white undershirt.

"I made slime!"

When I turn around, I see Cadence standing at the entrance of the kitchen, a pile of purple sludge in her hands.

Good God, how could I have forgotten?

How could I have forgotten that my obsession is so out of control that I invited a single mother with a child to live in my house? I'm not good with children, and this particular child has always been a bit of a sore spot for me. I make an effort to give her a warm smile, not wanting her to sense how I feel. None of it is her fault.

"You made it? How do you make slime?"

"Mommy bought a kit!" She rushes to the kitchen table, where an array of plastic cups, spoons, and bottles are spread over the surface. "Grammy hates slime, and she never lets me make it, but we live in your house now, so Mommy says I can make slime all the time. Do you want to play with it?"

I open my mouth, about to tell her I can't. I've been so

distracted all day thinking about her mother that I've hardly gotten any writing done, but something about her question gives me pause. There's something so sweet about her earnestness, as if she can't imagine why a twenty-five-year-old man wouldn't want to play with slime.

"I'd love to," I find myself saying. I walk over to the kitchen table and pull out the chair next to hers.

"What color do you want?"

I glance at the two piles of slime sitting on my table. God, it looks disgusting, like brightly colored snot. And I can see that she's handled it quite a bit from the specks of dust and fuzz clinging to it. I have to keep myself from cringing. I forgot how messy kids can be, but I'm going to have to get used to it. She lives here now.

"I'll take pink."

She smiles brightly. "That's my favorite one. I made it for Mommy because she loves glitter."

"Are you sure you don't want it then? I can take the purple."

She stares at me for a moment, a concentrated frown forming on her brow. "You can play with it first, and then I'll get a turn."

The authority in her tone fills me with warmth, reminding me so much of Lauren when she was a little girl. "That's a great idea. You're way better at sharing than I was at your age."

"Mommy says you're sharing your house with us. She said it's not our house, but you're letting us live here for six months. She told me I have to say thank you for my new toys, but I forgot."

"You don't have to thank me. I want you to feel at home here."

Sensing someone's gaze, I glance up to see Lauren at the kitchen entry, and the sight of her makes an involuntary smile tug at my lips. She's standing there with a laundry basket at her hip and big headphones around her ears.

I love it.

I love having her in this house. I love that she prances around in that baggy sweatshirt and yoga pants and sings shitty pop songs loud enough for me to hear all the way in my sound-proofed studio.

But all warmth vanishes when I notice that she's staring at me with her lips slightly parted, her eyes wide. She looks utterly shocked.

Like she can't even imagine that I'd be nice to her daughter.

"We're playing with slime," I say, the words feeling foreign on my tongue.

"I thought you were writing."

"I was, but then I came out here to get coffee, and Cadence invited me to play with her." Though stilted, the words sound affable enough, but it doesn't change that look on her face.

She glances at Cadence. "Sweetie, why don't you bring the slime into your room? Uncle Cam is really busy. We have to try not to distract him during the day."

"It's fine," I say immediately.

Cadence glances at me and then back at Lauren, looking like she wants to protest, but she eventually grabs her slime and walks out of the room.

"Why'd you do that?" I ask when she's out of earshot. "She probably thinks I'm an asshole now. Making her stay in her room."

Lauren waves a hand. "She's fine. Kids don't read that far into things. And you were the one who said you wanted to be left alone during the day."

I want to deny it, but what could I say? She's right. I didn't want to be distracted during the day, but I mostly made that dictate because of her.

Because I knew I could lose myself if I didn't set boundaries with her.

"I'll go work at our downtown studio. That way she won't feel like she has to stay cooped up in her room all day."

She smiles. "She loves her new room. It's twice the size of her room at my parents'. And it was so sweet of you to buy all those toys."

I wave a hand, averting my eyes from hers, not wanting her to see how her shock at my kindness makes me hate myself. Why did I have to be such a dick all these years?

"It's not a big deal." I stand up from my chair and walk to the counter where I set my keys yesterday. "I'll probably be home around dinner time. Do you want me to pick up food on my way back?"

"It depends on if I go out or not. I was planning on meeting a friend for happy hour, but my mom still hasn't texted me back to tell me if she can babysit." She lifts a brow. "She's been an absolute delight these past few days."

She keeps talking—something about how her mom resents her for taking away her granddaughter, but I'm only half listening.

Happy hour.

A friend.

"When will you be home?"

When her eyes widen, I realize my curt question interrupted her mid-sentence.

"I'm not sure." She tucks a strand of hair behind her ear. "I don't even know if I'll be able to go out with him. It all depends on my mom."

Him. My teeth clench as I imagine who it could be.

I want to tell her no—to forbid her from going—but I can't do that. And though I don't doubt for a second that after one drink too many she could end up blowing her "friend" in a public bathroom, it's not reasonable for me to dictate her life based on hypotheticals. Our agreement was that she'd be faithful to me, not stay away from men entirely. I take a deep breath, trying to keep myself from lashing out. "I don't want you coming in and out of the house at odd hours. It's too distracting for me. I need you to give me a time."

Based on the black scowl forming on her face, my guess is that wasn't the right thing to say, either. She places indignant hands on her hips. "And I just told you I'm not even sure if I'm going."

"Well, once you find out, let me know."

Her nostrils flare. "I'm not going to report to you like you're my fucking parole officer."

I flinch, recalling similar things Hunter has said to me over the years. I know I'm not being fair, but goddamn it, she's given me a lot of reason to fear her impulsivity.

I search my brain for a way to save myself, something that won't make me sound like a jealous control freak. "You've never lived with anyone who has a creative job. I need a regular schedule so that I can focus. If I'm wondering where you are and when you're going to get home, I won't be able to write."

She shakes her head. "You're so full of shit. This has nothing to do with your creativity. This is about you wanting everything your way and thinking you have the right to tell everyone around you what to do."

"Not everyone." My tone is ice. "Just the people I employ."

At her stunned look, I wince. Good God, I sound like a fucking maniac.

This woman makes me crazy.

"So that's how it is, huh? Paying my student loans means you get to order me around all the time?"

"No. Fuck. I really didn't mean that." I lift both hands to

my head and run my fingers through my hair. "I need to get out of here before I say anything more."

She lifts one brow. "As soon as I hear from my mom, I'll report back to you, Master."

Master.

The word goes straight to my dick.

I shouldn't be turned on right now. Not when she said it with so much disdain. But God, how I would love it if she called me that under different circumstances. Like tonight. When she makes her way into my bedroom like she has for the last two.

"I'll probably stop at the Thai place across the street from our studio," I say to change the subject. "Can you tell me if you're going to be home and what you want?" When her expression doesn't soften, I lower my voice. "I'm asking you. Not ordering you to do it."

She looks like she wants to say something snarky but thinks better of it. "I'll text you."

I nod.

"Just get the fuck out of here. I'm about to strangle you." She smiles faintly. "And if you're dead, you won't be able to pay off my student loans. You'll be useless to me."

I force a small smile, hating the idea that she only wants me for my money, but knowing I deserve much worse. In an effort to smooth things over, I give her a kiss on the cheek before leaving.

LAUREN

A TALL FORM hovers in the doorway, but I continue with my task. If he wants my attention, he'll have to beg for it. I don't care how much he's paying me. It doesn't give him the right to dictate my every move.

He got home from his studio hours ago, and when he invited me to eat dinner with him, I lied and told him I wasn't hungry. I could see he wanted to ask if it was because I went out, but he knew he'd lost that right after our argument. And I refuse to give him the satisfaction of telling him I didn't go.

I've been ignoring him by pumping out videos in the most secluded room I could find in this giant house. Even now that it's dark out and the overhead lights make my skin look orange, I haven't stopped working, because I refuse to be anywhere near him until he apologizes. Without seeing his face, I know he's irritated. I feel it vibrating in the air between us.

It's satisfying.

"What are you working on?"

There's not much to the question, but I hear diffidence in his voice, which is unusual for him. He's sorry even though he doesn't want to say it.

It's not enough.

"Unboxing videos," I say without looking his way. "As you can see." I gesture at the array of open cardboard boxes on the floor.

"Those are my favorite. Of your videos, I mean."

I jerk my head in his direction. "What now?"

He stares at me for a moment before lowering his gaze to the wood floor. "Yeah, I watch your videos a lot."

"You *watch my videos*? Why on earth would you do that?"

He doesn't answer for a moment. "I don't know, Lauren." There's a touch of sarcasm in his tone. "Probably for the same reason I'm paying you over two-hundred thousand dollars to live with me for six months."

The words tug at me. Cam is so rarely vulnerable that it's hard not to be touched, even when I'm angry with him. "Yeah, but my videos are essentially advertisements. It's hard for me to understand why anyone watches them, even people who like makeup and skincare. Even I think they're boring, and I'm one of the vainest people in the world."

That familiar, affectionate smile forms on his lips, and when he lifts his eyes to meet mine, I have to look away to shield myself from it. I plop down on the small couch and grab a box from the floor. After setting it on my lap, I pretend to sort through it.

"I love watching them," he says. "You're so sincere. It makes me feel like I'm hanging out with you. You definitely don't seem like you're advertising something, which goes to show how skilled you are at what you do."

My stomach flutters, and my pulse starts to pound. I take a deep breath, trying to calm myself. I know I'm good at what I do. I don't need him to tell me.

"Do you mind if I watch you?"

My lips part. "You mean watch me make a video?"

"Yeah. I've seen so many of them, it'd be cool to see how you do it."

I stare at him, unable to speak.

No one has ever asked me that before. No one has ever shown the slightest interest in my work—even the people who love me the most—and it feels like the fleeting warmth of the sun on a cold, windy day at the beach.

I'm going to become a sad, pathetic person if I can't get this under control.

I force a smile. "I'm pretty much finished. I was mostly staying in here to avoid you."

His smile fades. "I'm sorry. I was out of line earlier."

"Yeah, you're a control freak."

He sighs heavily. "I know. Believe me, I know. People say it all the time. Everyone I work with, but Hunter and Janie especially, because they're affected by it the most. They're the people closest to me." He meets my gaze. "But now that's you, and it's going to take some getting used to."

"I can be patient, but you really need to work on it. I just left a dictatorship behind. I'm not going to live under another one."

"I don't want that, either. I want you to be comfortable here. I promise I'll try my hardest. Besides Hunter and Janie, I haven't shared a space with anyone since the first few months I lived in Brooklyn, and I was an asshole to him. Fuck..." He shuts his eyes. "I'm an asshole to everyone, and I don't mean to be."

A small smile lifts my lips. "I can meet you halfway. I'll try to stay out of your way as much as I can. It'll be easy since this house is so—"

"I don't want that." His voice is hard, and it makes my stomach flip.

"But that's what you said."

"It is what I said, but that was only because I thought you would distract me from my work. But I've found you distract me no matter what. Even when I'm not around you, you distract me."

Heat pools in my belly at the intensity of his dark gaze. "I'm sorry," I say, but I'm not sorry in the least.

"Can we... I don't know. Hang out right now. Watch a movie or something?"

I smile. "Of course. Full warning, I'll probably fall asleep. I'm a mom now. Movies and TV shows are nap time for me."

A fond smile touches his lips. "They were nap time for you even when we were younger, and I don't mind. I don't know what it is..." His smile fades, and his brow furrows. "I've always loved being around you, even when we aren't talking."

It's too much, and I can't stand one more second of it, so I lower my gaze to my lap. "That's strange since you've avoided me for years."

"You know why I did."

"Yes." I sigh heavily before meeting his eyes. "Cam, we need to talk about that night. It's this huge elephant in the room, and—"

"I don't want to talk about it."

I smile tightly. "Okay. Go put something on, and I'll come join you when I'm done cleaning all of this up. And please pick something brainless like *Real Housewives*. I don't like having to think when I watch TV."

He looks shocked, as if he expected me to press him.

Maybe he wanted me to.

ELEVEN

Lauren

EVEN CONTROL FREAKS CAN CHANGE.

Twenty-three years of living with my mother led me to believe otherwise, making this last month with Camden seem almost blissful in comparison. He ought to thank Helen Henderson for lowering my expectations.

He still has his high-handed moments, but I can see that he's trying. Instead of ordering me around when he's annoyed, he clenches his jaw and narrows those dark eyes, which does strange things to my insides.

I never could have imagined living with him would feel this natural, as if we've been sharing a space for years. He's hardly ever in his studio. Instead, he sits with his guitar and an open notebook at his side on the living room couch while I fold laundry or shoot my videos. And even though he still some-times says he doesn't like sharing a bed, he doesn't loosen his hold on me at the end of the night. When Cadence is at

Ryder's, it's become a given that I'll spend my nights in his room, even though we've never explicitly agreed to it.

I'd be perfectly happy with everything if I didn't sense his underlying unease about his relationship with Hunter. They've hardly spoken at all this last month. At least not when I've been around them, and I can feel it eating away at Cam.

My gaze drifts to Hunter. He stands near the kitchen counter, staring down into his green juice. He just spent the last five minutes purging Cam's fridge of vegetables and sticking them all into his probably unused juicer.

I avert my eyes. I can't explain it, but the health kick he goes on during sobriety always makes me uneasy. It doesn't seem like Hunter, like he's pretending to be someone else. Pretending to be sober. I try to shake off the thought, knowing it's presumptuous and unfair.

"What's going on with you and Cam?" I ask.

"What do you mean?"

"You only come over here when he's gone. And you always leave before he gets home."

The smile that tugs at his lips looks a little cynical. "I'm around him all the time."

"Yeah, but that's work. You never seem to want to hang out with him anymore."

He shakes his head. "We've never had that kind of relationship. Not like you and Logan have. I love him, but we don't hang out."

"No way. You used to hang out all the time."

His smile widens, and now there's no doubt that it's cynical. "No, I used to follow him around, and he tolerated my presence."

"That's not true at all, and you know it. I've never known anyone who adores his brother more. You guys barely even fought growing up, which is so unusual. There were times when I literally—no joke—considered murdering Logan. But Cam treated you almost like a son."

"Yeah." He raises his brows. "And that's not normal. I honestly don't think Cam is capable of real love. He has loving feelings, but only for people he sees as beneath him, which isn't the same thing."

My mouth drops open. "Do you really think that?"

He takes a big gulp of his juice. "I do."

I stare at him, unable to believe what I'm hearing. "Hunter, that's awful."

He shrugs, but it's a jerky movement, and for the first time, I sense the emotion behind his matter-of-fact tone. This isn't an objective assessment of Camden's ability to love. This is a deep hurt that Hunter doesn't want to talk about.

"Cam would be heartbroken if he heard you say something like that."

An emotion flashes in Hunter's eyes. Something I don't like. "Oh, no. You're not falling in love with him, are you?"

I scowl. "Of course not."

His piteous expression stays fixed. "Don't do that. Seriously, don't do it. Whatever you're feeling right now, just...push that shit deep down as far as you can for the next... How much more time do you have? Five months? Because if you love him, he'll have power over you. And he's a nightmare when he has power over you."

I'm somehow able to smile even while my heart is in my throat. "He already has power over me. I work for him."

He scoffs. "Yeah, but the power is entirely on your side. He doesn't even give our hottest fans the time of day. And not to brag, but our fans are top shelf. Way hotter than average. And you got him to pay over two-hundred thousand dollars for sex." He eyes narrow on my face. "And don't give me that look. You know that's what he's really paying for, no matter whatever bullshit he fed you about going to parties with him. He doesn't even go to parties. Not even when our publicist begs him. He never would have done any of this if I hadn't made him think you and I were going to have sex."

I roll my eyes. "I still can't believe you did that."

A lazy grin spreads over his face. "I don't regret it at all. I really just did it for fun, because he'll never admit he has a huge crush on you, even though it's painfully obvious to me and Janie. But still, I had no idea he'd do this. It's beyond my wildest expectations. All for you."

All for you. I hate how the words make my stomach flutter. I've been trying so hard to keep my hope in check, but if he wants me this much, maybe it means something.

"But you need to be careful, because he could throw you out at any moment." Hunter's words are like a bucket of ice water dumped over my warm reflections.

"And he would, too," he says. "He does shit like that all the time. We're now on our eighth banjoist. We've had *eight* in four years."

I look away from him, not wanting him to see the turmoil of my emotions. "God," I say in an effort at levity. "Who even plays the fucking banjo? He's going to run through all the banjoists in the world."

He chuckles, and I'm grateful for the sound of it. "So we're back to making fun of folk music. Even though you've basically become a River of Sight groupie."

I lift my head, smiling primly. "I'm a River of Sight *live-in girlfriend.* And even though folk rock isn't my cup of tea, I love it because you make it."

"Right." His smile widens. "Spoken like a mother who thinks her ugly child is beautiful."

"Exactly." I wink.

His smile grows tender as he walks in my direction. After

he disappears behind my chair, I feel the pressure of his hands kneading my shoulders. "If there's one good thing about this canceled tour, it's getting to be around you all the time. I really think it's good for me." He presses a hard kiss against my cheek.

"What's going on?"

I jerk back into my chair at the deep sound of Cam's voice.

Camden

HE'S TOUCHING HER.

He's *kissing* her.

It takes all my willpower not to march over to the kitchen table and shove him away. He's been coming over here at least once a week since she moved in—always when I'm out of the house. As much as I want to rush home every time I see his phone location next to hers, I tell myself a mature, non-control freak wouldn't intervene in what they've both always insisted is only a close friendship.

Of course, the one day I let my jealousy get the better of me and end my meeting with my agent early, I come home and find them like this. They touch and kiss all the time. I know this. It's a lovey-dovey friendship typical of affectionate people with poor boundaries, and I've been forced to witness it almost my entire life, even as it nauseated me.

But now that she's mine—or feels like she is—I don't think I can stand it.

"Hunter, I don't want you coming over when I'm not here."

"Excuse me?"

Surprisingly, it's Lauren's voice.

When I glance in her direction, those big green eyes are blazing.

My jaw clenches. "I don't think that's unreasonable. Not given our history."

Her nostrils flare as she places both hands on her hips. "Are you ready to talk about our history? Now seems like a good time."

I avert my gaze, wishing I hadn't brought up the subject. "No, there's no need—"

"There *is* a need." She's nearly shouting. "You've been blaming me for years for something that isn't all my fault." I hear her footsteps approaching me, but I can't bring myself to look up. Her voice lowers to a melodic hum. "Do you remember what you said to me right after we had sex?"

A cold sickness settles in my stomach. Of course I remember. Those words still have the power to make me wince. I've worked hard to push them away, but sometimes they rise to the surface when I least expect it, and the memory is so vivid, I can even hear the petulant lilt of my stupid twenty-year-old voice.

"Why don't you go find Hunter so you can fuck two brothers in the same night?"

"I don't want to talk about it." My words are rapid.

"I think you should, Cam," Hunter says.

My eyes snap open, and I glare at him. "You don't even remember any of it."

In his face, I see the same thinly veiled contempt that's been characteristic of all of our interactions in these last forty-eight days he's been sober. "Right," he says. "My opinion doesn't count because I'm an alcoholic."

I roll my eyes at his typical self-pity. This is why his sobriety never sticks. He's still not willing to own up to his mistakes.

It's why I live in a constant state of uncertainty.

"You guys," Lauren's voice is notably softer now. "This isn't about Hunter's drinking. This is really just between me and

Cam." She glances in Hunter's direction, her expression warming, and I wish I didn't hate him for it. I wish I could get this petty jealousy under control. "Why don't you go check on Cadence for me? She's been too quiet. She might be in Cam's studio destroying his fancy equipment for all I know." As she turns to me, her lips twinge. "I almost hope she is."

I roll my eyes as Hunter saunters away, his chuckle echoing in the hallway.

For several seconds, Lauren and I stare at each other in silence. I couldn't find the words if I tried. Now that I've lashed out, I'm living in a jealousy hangover. I recognize my irrationality but still feel the jealousy too acutely to apologize.

"So..." she starts.

"So..." I repeat, looking away from her.

"It's obvious you're terrified to have a conversation about what happened between us."

My throat grows tight, my pulse starting to race. "'Terrified' is a strong word."

"Okay, honey."

"I don't feel like talking about it. It's not a pleasant memory."

Her smile fades. "Don't you think that's even more reason to talk about it? How can we have a healthy relationship—"

"We don't have a relationship. Did you forget that?"

When she jerks back as if I hit her, I want to reach out and touch her, but then her gaze hardens, and I think better of it.

"Well, whatever we are," she says. "I absolutely cannot live like this. I cannot have you accusing me of cheating on you every time I'm in the general vicinity of another man. I can't have you trying to dictate my every move."

I clench my jaw. "That's not what I'm doing."

"Really? Because I've only hung out with two guys since I moved in—one of them I didn't even end up hanging out with.

So far, you're two for two. You just ordered my *best friend* to stay away from me, which is unacceptable." She crosses her arms over her chest. "I quite simply won't allow it."

My gaze snaps to her face. "I'm in charge here. You agreed to that."

Her eyelids flutter. "I agreed to be your mistress, honey. Not your little bitch."

Heat washes over my face, my nostrils flaring. She's always been this way with me—both sassy and dismissive—and it pulls up an ancient urge I remember from when I tried to boss her around in our childhood. I couldn't understand what it meant back then. All I knew was that I wanted to reach out and grab her, but not out of anger.

Now I know.

I want to fuck her into submission.

"I think we should settle this in the bedroom," she says, as if reading my mind.

My eyebrows shoot to my forehead. "What do you mean?"

"I mean, I think we could have an excellent Dom-sub relationship. I'll be a brat, obviously, because I just can't be anything else. It's not in my nature. But it'll be okay because you can punish me for it."

"How would I punish you?" My voice is breathless.

She shrugs. "However you want. You can bite me, flog me, spank me. I'm down for any and all of it."

Her words wash over me like a drug, making me almost dizzy. Oh God, does she have any idea what she's doing to me? As I imagine slapping her bare ass, hot shame creeps into my cheeks even as my dick grows hard. I shouldn't be repulsed with myself when she offered it up like it's nothing. She clearly wants it, but it's hard to wash away years of being taught not to lay a hand on a woman.

"Spank you," I say, my words just above a whisper.

She looks like she's holding back a smile. "Is that what you want to do to me?"

"Yeah."

Her eyes grow hooded, her smile slow. "I'd enjoy that."

"Do you really mean it?"

"Absolutely. I'm totally turned on by how domineering you are, even though I'll have absolutely none of it. As long as we keep it in the bedroom, it'll be perfect. I'll do nothing you say, and you can spank me for it."

My brows draw together when a thought occurs to me. "Have you done this before?"

Her smile grows enigmatic. "If I have, do you want me to tell you all about it?"

"No." My jaw clenches. "God, no. Don't tell me a damn thing."

She giggles. "That's what I thought. If you knew my sexual history, you'd never let me leave the house."

"Not a word." I lift a hand to silence her. "Seriously. I don't ever want to hear anything about...anything you've done in the past."

Her giggle turns into a cackle, and the sound of it warms me.

God, I love the sound of her laugh.

"Okay, honey. I won't say anything. Do we have a deal, though?"

"Yes." My eyes grow hard. "But not when you're out in public with me. You aren't allowed to openly disobey me. You agreed to do a job."

"I've hardly even had to do my job..." Her smile grows lazy. "Except the fun part of it. But so far, you've bailed on all the parties."

"Well, that changes tomorrow. We have that concert in Portland."

Her eyes grow wide. "That wasn't on the list."

"Yeah, but after I cancelled the other two, it seems fair for you to come. You won't have Cadence this weekend, and you haven't mentioned any other plans..."

She narrows her eyes, as if she's skeptical of my motives, and goddamn it, I wish I had the moral high ground. I wish I hadn't just decided out of the blue this morning that I want her to come with me because I can't stand the thought of being away from her.

If I had my way, she'd never leave my sight.

"I don't have any other plans." Still, that skeptical look doesn't fade.

"Good. Brayden is getting everything booked for you. We're playing with Isaac Belman for the first time in a few years. He's having a party after the show. It's going to be small and exclusive, because he knows I wouldn't stay very long if it wasn't. The whole thing is pretty special because he helped us get our start. He let us open for him back when we were still playing in Brooklyn dive bars." A smile rises to my lips. "He's one of my five people. I'm looking forward to you meeting him."

When she smiles warmly, my lips part. Did I really say that? *I'm looking forward to you meeting him.* I sound like her goddamn boyfriend. "But I'm going to need you on your best behavior." And just like that, the spell is broken. All the warmth in her eyes vanishes.

"As opposed to?"

Do I really need to explain this? "As opposed to getting drunk. Letting guys take shots between your tits. Giving lap dances. That sort of thing."

Her brows snap together. "Do I look like I'm seventeen fucking years old? What in my behavior this last month has made you think I still do that kind of stuff?"

"You haven't had a chance to prove me otherwise." I lift my

chin as I stare down at her. "The last time I went to a party with you was five years ago."

For a moment, I can see all over her face that she thinks I'm being unreasonable. And it would be unreasonable if she were any other woman.

But I have a lot of reason to mistrust her when she's been drinking.

When an enigmatic smile spreads over her face, I feel a prickle of foreboding at the back of my neck.

"I'll be on my best behavior, Master."

TWELVE

Camden

"I DON'T LIKE the EQ on my guitar," I say into the mic, and it echoes across the arena. "Roll off some of the bottom end."

"Got it," the sound engineer says.

I lower my guitar and pull my phone from the back pocket of my jeans.

3:23. God, will sound check ever end?

"She texted me a minute ago and said she's boarding her flight."

Hunter's voice makes me jump, but I keep my eyes fixed on my phone.

"What was *that* look for?" he asks.

Heat creeps into my neck when I realize I'm clenching my jaw. This is so incredibly stupid. A month with her, and I've fully reverted to the obsessed and horny teenage boy who's jealous of a fucking text. This isn't healthy.

She isn't good for me.

"Nothing," I say. "I'm just in a bad mood."

In the worst mood, actually. It occurred to me that I'll be introducing her to all kinds of people in our industry tonight, people who have a lot to offer a single mother. And while Lauren may not be the most conventionally gorgeous woman in the world, she's got something...

She sparkles.

And she's in danger of catching someone else's eye. How can I stop her? She's not technically my girlfriend. It's fair to expect fidelity for the next five months. It's not fair to keep her locked away from the rest of the world like I wish I could.

And what's going to happen when this is all over? It's been hard enough these last few years after moving away from Coronado knowing she was out there doing who knows what. I knew she'd be touched and kissed and fucked and maybe even loved by people who weren't me, and as much as I hated the thought of it, I was mostly okay because I knew it was for the best.

Now the thought is unbearable.

LAUREN

AN ELECTRIC THRILL runs through my body as I pull my suitcase from the overhead cabinet.

Though my anger will return in full force when I see my beautiful, jealous control freak, I can't help but enjoy this moment. Here I am exiting a first-class flight to visit my rich and famous sugar daddy, and he flew me out here because he couldn't go two days without touching me.

I feel like I'm floating as I walk along the endless conveyor belt, which is probably mostly thanks to the three flutes of champagne I downed on that two hour and twenty-minute flight. As soon as I make it to the arrivals lobby, I pull out my phone and text the driver Brayden scheduled for me. I have a driver. Not an Uber, but a driver.

Howard—the driver—texts back, telling me to meet him on the sidewalk near the Delta baggage claim. As I roll my suitcase outside, my phone buzzes again, and when I lift it up, a jolt of electricity shoots into my belly at the sight of Cam's name.

Cam: Where the fuck are you?

I smile slowly.

Me: There was traffic on the runway in San Diego, so it took forever to take off.

Cam: We're performing in an hour. Don't linger.

I gulp back a laugh. He's angry already, and I didn't even have to try. If only he knew what's in store for him tonight.

When I spot the black Audi, I wave at the man with the white beard in the driver's seat. He immediately exits the car and grabs my suitcase. "Hi there, Lauren." He pops the trunk and sets my suitcase inside. "Did you have a nice flight?"

"Hell yeah." I open the passenger door. "I drank the whole time."

He chuckles. "That's the only way to fly."

After I slide inside the car, I pull out my phone.

Me: I'll get there as soon as I can.

I smile to myself as I pull up the Google app and type "lingerie stores Portland" into the search bar.

BRAYDEN DOESN'T GIVE me his usual bright smile when he greets me at the entrance of the concert arena.

I wince, wrapping my arms around myself to fight the chill from the misty wind. "Is he being terrible?"

"No, he's fine, but we need to hurry. They're about to go on stage, and I think he wants to see you first."

I frown as I follow him through the long hallway and into the elevator. "He's being a dick. I just know he is."

Brayden only smiles awkwardly as he presses the button for the second floor. He wants this conversation to end.

"I'm sorry," I say. "I know you're not allowed to talk shit about him, but, oh my God, doesn't it suck to work for such a control freak?"

He licks his lips, his eyes fixed on the linoleum floor. "I actually really love my job."

I set my hand on his shoulder. "Honey, it's okay. I'm going to fix him for you. By the end of tonight, he'll learn that the only person he can control is himself." I smile slowly. "And he won't even be able to control that, because I'm going to drive him so crazy."

Brayden chuckles, but I can't help feeling that it's forced. I'm definitely making him uncomfortable, so I decide to keep those three glasses of champagne in check and shut my mouth. When the elevator pings, he guides me through another long, winding hallway. Just as we approach a doorway to a large room, Cam's scowling face appears in my vision. "It took you a fucking hour to get here. The airport is a fifteen-minute drive from here."

His dark voice sends a jolt of heat into my belly. I smile slowly. "Well, hey there, darling."

His scowl notably softens, but it doesn't keep the hard edge out of his voice. "If you made your driver stop somewhere, I'll fucking kill you. You did, huh? You probably forgot to pack something and made him stop at CVS on the way here. I know you."

"I did make him stop, but not because I forgot something. There was this cute little boutique in the Pearl District, and I wanted to get an outfit for tonight."

His lips part. "Are you *fucking* kidding me?" He says "fucking" with such angry emphasis that it takes all of my willpower to keep my laughter from bubbling out of my chest.

"No, and you're going to love it." I lift up the plastic bag in my hand. "Do you want me to show it to you?"

His nostrils flaring, he stares at me for a beat before speaking. "Why were you in the Pearl District? It's not even on the way here."

"If I'm being totally honest—" my lips twinge at the edges, "—I actually looked up this boutique beforehand."

His jaw ticks. "I told you we were going on in an hour." His voice is hushed and menacing, sending a tickling heat into my belly.

"I know, but..." I bite my bottom lip. "The dress I had picked out for tonight just wasn't right, and I really want to impress your friends."

"My friends won't give a shit..." He exhales a shaky breath through his nostrils. "I'm wound up right now. I wanted to spend time with you before we went on stage. I can't believe you went shopping. It's..." His eyes narrow. "It's so fucking like you to do something like this."

I put a hand on his shoulder and give it a squeeze. "Do you want to spank me?"

"Yes."

"Then do it."

His eyes pop open. "Right now?"

"Sure." I glance down the hallway. "There's a room some-where, right?"

I'm startled when he grabs me by the forearm. "Jeff," he calls out to the band manager, who happens to be walking in our direction. "Tell everyone I'll be right back."

Jeff scowls. "Fuck no. You're going on in five minutes."

Though Jeff's tone is commanding, I sense his fear, and it sends a wave of apprehension over me.

I'm getting people in trouble by doing this.

"I'll be back by then," Cam says.

"No, you won't," Jeff says. "Janie's going to kill me if I let you leave. I'm not letting you pull a Hunter."

"Then I'm firing you."

I wince, turning toward Cam. "I don't want to get anyone in trouble."

I plant myself firmly on the hard floor, but Cam continues to pull me, making my feet drag slightly. "No one's in trouble. Jeff knows I'm not serious."

I don't lift my feet, and I nearly stumble as Cam yanks me forward. "Yeah, but he might be in trouble with other people."

Cam groans. "He's fine. We're the headliners. We can do whatever the fuck we want, and he knows it."

I yank my arm out of his grip, and when he whips around, a dark frown forms on his brow. "We need to hurry." He finally seems to sense my distress, and his scowl softens. "Please hurry."

"Can we do it later?"

He shakes his head sharply. "No."

"What if you spanked me right now?" I grab the seam of my sweater dress and lift it to my mid-thigh.

"Right here?" he whisper-shouts, glancing down each direction in the hall. "What if someone walks by?"

"No one will care. You're a rock star. And if someone does walk by... Well, I'd like that even more."

His dark gaze bores into my face. "Would you really?"

"Yeah, honey, I told you already, I like all this kinky shit."

He glances down the hall and back again. "Alright, lift your dress."

My eyes must be saucers. I never expected him to agree. My belly flutters as I reach down and lift the hem of my dress over my thighs, exposing the leggings beneath.

"How hard can I spank you?" His tone is as gentle as I've ever heard it, and warmth stirs in my chest.

"Hard," I say. "Spank me as hard as you want."

"In that case..."

The sound echoes down the hall. It startles me into an upright position, and that's when I finally feel the heat of pain on my skin. When I twist around and glance at his face, his cheeks are pink and his eyes are glazed.

He liked that.

"Holy shit, Cam."

"Oh my God." His tone is frantic. "I'm so sorry. Was that too hard?"

His pleading eyes send another wave of warmth over me. "No, it was fine." I can't keep myself from lowering my hand to my ass, which draws Cam's attention.

"Oh my God," he says. "You're rubbing it. It was too hard."

"Go on stage, baby." I have a hard time keeping the laughter out of my voice. "I'll be just fine."

His jaw clenches. "You're not fine. I hurt you."

"Sweetheart, hurting me is part of it. Go perform. I'll be just fine."

The large notch at his throat rises and falls. "Are you sure?"

My stomach jolts when I think of what I have planned for him later. If I do everything right, he's really going to want to spank me after the party.

"I'm sure."

Camden

APPLAUSE ERUPTS as I lift my guitar, yet somehow my ears are drawn to the voice to my right. It floats through my insides, filling me with warmth.

I can't believe she's actually standing backstage. I've thought about her so many times when we've performed over the years.

I've imagined her there.

"Spank me, Camden Hayes!" she shouts.

I purse my lips to fight a smile.

"Choke me, Camden Hayes!"

I gulp back a laugh.

"Lauren, stop." It's Jeff's firm voice, and it draws my eyes to the right. He's holding her arm. "He doesn't like distractions. We have a room with a couch where you can watch them on the big screen. Come on—"

"Stop!"

Both Lauren and Jeff jump at my shout.

"Let her stay."

Jeff glances at Lauren and then back at me. He's looking at me like I've grown another head, and even without seeing their faces, I sense Hunter and Janie's surprise.

"Are you sure?" Jeff asks.

"Yeah, I'm sure."

This is the first time I've ever let anyone other than my last girlfriend stand backstage and watch us play, and that was years ago, at a much smaller venue than this. Not wanting to reflect on that further, I walk forward and speak into the mic. "How you doing, Portland?"

Applause breaks out. It never seems to matter that I'm stilted and unsmiling on stage. "I don't know why any of you live here," I say. "I haven't seen the sun in twenty-four hours. I'm not going to lie, I kind of hate all of you for buying tickets and making me come here."

Unsurprisingly, the crowd cheers again, even louder this time. My grumpiness is well-known now after four years of touring. Our fans expect it.

"He's had a bad day," Hunter says into his mic. "Plus, he's just an asshole."

Distantly, I hear a rumbling mixture of cheers and laughter, but my attention is drawn to Hunter. His face is soft and smiling, which doesn't match the venom in his tone.

This is our thing. Something we do at almost every show. I say asshole things, and Hunter makes fun of me for it. Janie sometimes jumps in with her stern voice and tells us to stop fighting like children. It's become part of our performance now, which would make me cringe for its inauthenticity if I gave it too much thought.

But something is different this time.

My eyes roam Hunter's face. His expression gives nothing away, but I know I heard it. He's angry. It's the same anger that's kept him silent whenever we're in the same room, but every once in a while, it bubbles to the surface.

I take a deep breath and try to let the thoughts float away when I exhale. It's not good to be in my head during a show. Surprisingly, it doesn't take a lot of effort to get out of it, not when I remember the dark-haired girl standing not too far away. Her presence has its usual effect, making me feel like I'm floating in warm tropical water. Before I know it, my mind is quiet, my fingers gliding over the strings, and words are flowing out of my mouth as if of their own volition.

Why is this heaven when giving into it would make me weak of will and sick at heart?

THIRTEEN

Lauren

"I WAS REALLY HOPING we would have a driver," I say quietly as I turn to the passenger window. Misty rain sputters over the glass, making the image of Portland streets opaque and muddled.

I wish we didn't have to rush off so quickly after the concert ended. Everyone seemed to be curious about the "girlfriend" Cam liked enough to invite backstage. I was enjoying the attention, but Cam is eager to get to this party.

"The sooner we get there, the sooner we can leave," he said after he came off stage, his cheeks flushed and his skin glistening with sweat.

Heat pooled in my belly, because I know the source of his impatience is more than his hatred of people. He's eager to get me back to the hotel.

Cam frowns, his eyes fixed on the road ahead. "What do you mean?"

"I mean, I had a driver from the airport, and it's the only time in my life I've ever felt like a rich person."

He smiles. "So the chef I hired for New Year's didn't do it for you? Or what about your first-class flight?"

"Oh my God," I shout, whipping around to face him. "Can we talk about first class for a second? Like seriously, what the hell? It's not nearly as fancy as it is in movies. I mean they gave me champagne and the seats were a little bigger, but that was basically it." I shake my head. "I'd been fantasizing about it since yesterday."

A wide smile spreads across his face. "It's not much on most domestic flights, especially when they're that short. But just wait till you fly international."

"Will I be flying international?" I nearly shout the question. "Are you guys doing concerts in other countries during your touring hiatus?"

His smile vanishes. "No." He shifts in his seat. "We won't be doing anything like that. And before I forget, I need to talk to you about something."

"And what's that?"

"I don't want you mentioning you're an influencer."

I frown. "I'm sorry, what?"

"Influencer is code for groupie in our industry. Everyone will think that's what you are. I don't do groupies, literally or figuratively. I don't want other *influencers* to get ideas after you and I part ways."

My stomach sinks at the thought of parting ways, but I try to keep my head in the present. "That's so stupid. All they'll have to do is search my name and find my videos."

"I don't want you telling them your last name, either."

My jaw clenches. "Should I adopt a fake Russian accent, too?"

He rolls his eyes. "It's not that big of a deal. I only want to stay for an hour anyway. Which reminds me, I'm not letting you have any more than two drinks. Two drinks in an hour is more than enough. Especially since you're technically on the clock."

Heat washes over me, making my skin prickle. "Are you fucking kidding me?"

"No." His tone is almost bored. "Like I said, I want you on your best behavior." He lifts a hand from the steering wheel and squeezes my thigh. "I think even you can be a good girl for an hour."

His dismissiveness raises my hackles, even though I would like it if he called me a good girl under different circumstances. I turn away from him, crossing my arms over my chest. "Fine. I'll be a good girl, Daddy. But don't be surprised if someone recognizes me. My 'Drunk Girl Makeup Tutorial' got five million views."

"I really like that one."

His response startles me. There's something in his voice... Wistfulness, almost. I know if I looked his way, I would see that affectionate smile that's now grown so familiar, and as always, my insides will turn to mush. I keep my eyes fixed on the foggy window. I can't let anything steer me from my purpose tonight.

He wants a good girl? He's going to get one.

After we arrive at the bar, I grimace up at the worn wooden sign. "Why is this party at an Irish pub? Why would anyone spend money to rent a place like this out?"

"I don't do clubs anymore. I'm too old for that shit, and Isaac wants me to stay longer than twenty minutes."

My eyelids flutter. "Here I thought I would be dancing tonight. I hate your hatred of people."

"It's not only that. I also asked him to avoid any place where Hunter might..."

The door swings open, and the murmur of voices from

inside grows suddenly much louder. Janie appears at the entrance. "There you guys are." She reaches out and grabs our hands. She shoots Cam a probing look. "We have a dark booth for you, and Isaac is saving you a corner seat. People will hardly be able to see you."

"Eww, Janie," I say, as she guides us inside, and I find I have to raise my voice once we cross the threshold. "I don't want to sit in a cramped booth all night because he's a sociopath."

She smiles. "And you shouldn't have to. You should mingle. There are plenty of people here in the beauty industry."

"No, she's not doing that." Cam's voice is somehow able to boom over the crowd noise, though he's hardly shouting. He shoots me a stern look before lowering his head to my ear. "Remember." His warm breath tickles my skin. "Be a good girl."

This time, his deep voice makes liquid heat stir in my belly. If only he knew...

Though the pub is crowded, we hardly have to push through it. People step aside of their own accord, and when I glance around at the faces, I see all of their eyes are fixed on Cam. Many of their expressions are slightly wary, as if they know it's not a good idea to approach him.

As we walk up to our booth, a tall, willowy form appears in front of us.

"Cam," a sweet voice says, and when I glance up at the face attached to it, my jaw drops. This woman is spectacularly beautiful, with high cheekbones, wide-set eyes, and a perfect heart-shaped mouth. I'd bet my last dime she's a beauty influencer. She probably reps for brands I'd kill for, like NYX or Boxy-Charm. Hell, she might even have her own brand.

"Remember me?" she asks. "I'm Mina. We went to a real Irish pub when you guys played in Dublin last year." She grins, lifting her pint glass in the air. "The beer was a lot better there."

"Yeah, that was great." With that, Cam turns to our booth and gestures for Hunter to scoot out of it.

My mouth is hanging open as my gaze shifts from Cam and back to Mina. She shoots me a knowing smile, as if she expected his rudeness.

"Get over here, Lauren."

At the sound of Cam's voice, I'm finally able to draw my gaze away from Mina.

"Are you telling me that's the type of woman you get to sleep with on tour?" I ask as I slide into the booth next to him.

"I don't know if I slept with her. She doesn't look familiar." He glances down at his water glass. "Maybe I did, though."

I can't even be jealous. It's all too surreal, as if I'm realizing for the first time that Cam and Hunter are actual rock stars, when up until now it felt like they were just playing at it. I shake my head slowly. "I can't believe it."

I glance around the table until I find Isaac. From the moment we were introduced after the concert, I knew in my gut that he understands Cam in a way other people don't. "How are you guys not worried about his sanity? He's paying me to be his arm candy when he could get *her* for free."

"Keep your voice down." Cam's voice intrudes, but I keep my eyes fixed on Isaac.

"I don't know." Isaac's smile is enigmatic. "He's never really been into the whole influencer or model scene. He's always preferred...*normal girls*."

Something about the way he says normal girls tells me it contains hidden meaning, like there's some kind of story behind it.

"So he has a normal-girl kink?" I ask, and no one at the table answers.

When I turn to Cam, I see that affectionate smile. Thankfully, I'm still stunned enough that it doesn't affect me. "Do you watch amateur porn, too—with jiggly, cellulite thighs like mine, and dad bods, and weird-shaped penises, and stuff?"

That smile grows—his eyes crinkling at the edges—and something starts to stir within me. "Yep, it's a kink." He lifts his hand and strokes a strand of hair behind my ear, sending tingles from my scalp to my neck. "You know me so well."

I look away, not wanting to crave more of his tender gaze and second-guess my plan. I glance around the area until I find the hallway entrance to the bathrooms.

I'll give myself ten minutes.

Let him get comfortable first.

I SMILE as I crumple my sweater dress into a ball and shove it into my purse. So far, the party has been a delight for a vain attention whore like me. I can feel the intense curiosity about who I am radiating from everyone I talk to, even though so far no one has been bold enough to ask me anything beyond, "So how did you and Cam meet?" And *he* thankfully hasn't forced me to sit at our dark booth all night, though anytime I've drifted too far from his sight, he's called out my name.

I find that I like it. I like his tight leash.

It turns me on.

As soon as I step out of the bathroom, someone yanks me by the arm and pulls me against a hard chest.

"Janie said you told someone your last name rhymes with Shmenderson." Cam's warm breath tickles the inside of my ear.

My stomach flutters at the menace in his tone. I repress the smile tugging at my lips. "It does. Henderson, Shmenderson."

"And you also told Isaac's brother that you take videos of yourself putting on makeup and post them on YouTube. In the two minutes I went to piss, you said both of those things."

"Yes, but when he asked me if I'm an influencer, I said no."
I smile lazily. "I got you, honey."

His jaw goes rigid. "Can I ask you something?"

I fight laughter at his obvious distress. Sucking my lips inside my mouth, I nod.

"Are you six fucking years old?"

The ache at the pit of my belly has turned to fire. I love taunting him.

And he doesn't even know what he's in for yet.

I smile sweetly as I lift my hand to the lapels of my peacoat. For greater effect, I remove the coat slowly, enjoying the spread of emotions over his face—shifting from confusion to surprise to terror—as he takes in what I'm wearing underneath. His wide eyes fixed on my chest, he nearly shouts, "What the hell is that?"

"A dress."

His gaze darts from my nearly exposed tits to the lace at my hips and back to my tits. "That is not a dress. That's fucking lingerie." His tone is frantic, and it sends heat into my groin.

"No, it's cocktail dress."

Finally seeming to compose himself, his jaw hardens. "You are *not* wearing that. Go in the bathroom and change back into that grandma sweater."

"I don't want to look like a grandma tonight."

He takes a step toward me until my tits are an inch from his chest. He lowers his chin to stare down at me. "And I don't want you looking like *that*. Go back into that bathroom and change, or I swear to God, I'll drag you out of here. *After* I cover you with that coat."

I raise challenging brows. "Honey, this isn't really fair. So far, I've *technically* followed all of your rules. You never said anything about what I'm allowed to wear, and to be honest, it sounds a lot like you're slut-shaming me for wanting to show off my body."

I want to howl in victory when his mouth snaps shut. He doesn't like the idea of slut-shaming me.

Especially given our history.

He stares at me for a full five seconds—his eyes roaming my body frantically—as if in indecision. Suddenly, his gaze snaps up. "We're staying for thirty more minutes, got it? And during that time, you're not leaving my sight."

When my mouth opens to protest, he lifts a hand to silence me. "That's your job. You agreed to it. You agreed to stay by my side at parties."

When I finally nod, he looks like he's ready to turn around and walk back into the bar, but then he hesitates, and his stern expression softens.

"What?"

"Please change." The words are soft.

I smile sadly. "No."

"You..." He shuts his eyes. "You're a fucking asshole, Lauren."

I lift my hand and place it softly on his cheek. "I know."

Even in his frustration, he leans into my hand. The sweet sight of it sends a pang of guilt into my chest.

Camden

SHE STANDS with her back to the bar, her eyes wide as she talks to a group of people, and even as I want to wince every time a small movement reveals yet more of her barely covered skin, I can't help but feel this eerie calm.

How is it possible to feel two contradictory emotions at

once? Teeth-grinding irritation and cool, quiet peace. It's always been this way with her.

She makes me crazy.

And at the same time, she feels like home.

I love watching her talk. I love watching her expressive eyes as they light up, her big gestures, her head motions making those long earrings swing wildly around her jaw.

I could watch her forever.

"I can tell she makes you really happy," Janie whispers into my ear.

I whip around to face her. "Are you high? This is *Lauren*..."

She smiles wide. "I know, and I'm glad you're doing this. I'm glad you're finally admitting what Hunter and I have known all along."

I shake my head. "It's not like that. I can't help that I'm obsessed with her. She was the first girl I ever saw naked. You don't just get over that. But even if I had deeper feelings, it wouldn't be healthy to indulge them."

"Why do you think that?"

"Because she makes me insane. You and Hunter think I'm a control freak? You should see me with her. I'm an absolute lunatic. I make myself cringe daily, and yet I can't keep myself in check no matter what I do. And it's only with her. I was never like this with any of my other girlfriends."

Janie stares at me for a moment, her expression thoughtful. If she noticed my slip up in putting Lauren in the category of "girlfriend", she doesn't show it. "Yeah, but to be honest, you never seemed like you were that in to your other girlfriends."

"What do you mean?"

"I don't know..." Her eyes grow unfocused, her lips pursing to the side. "You never seemed that invested. And you were still watching Lauren's videos when you were with Norah. I know because I saw you do it several times, and that's only when *I* caught you."

When my cheeks warm, I avert my gaze from hers. I search the room and find Lauren not far from where she was a moment ago. When our eyes meet, she winks, and my insides soften. I try to steel myself against the feeling.

"She's not good for me. I could never trust her."

"I don't know. I think she's changed since we were teenagers."

I snort. "Look at that fucking dress. Just look at it."

She places a palm over her mouth and gulps back a laugh. "I can't believe she put that on."

My smile doesn't reach my eyes. "She said it's a cocktail dress."

"No, it's not. That's lingerie. It might have even come from a sex shop. It looks it came with a whip."

"If it did, I'm going to use it on her tonight."

Janie's lips part into an open-mouth smile. "Oh, damn! I think she might be a good influence on you. She's your opposite, and I think that's a good thing."

"Absolutely not. I've never believed in that bullshit. We might be drawn to our opposites, but we should only be in relationships with like-minded people."

She looks in Lauren's direction. "Well, maybe she should be with Matt then, because he's a little wild too, and he seems to be really into her..."

My head snaps in Lauren's direction, and even though I know Janie's chuckle is at my expense, I don't care. Sure enough, Lauren is giving Matt that heavy-lidded look she gives when she knows she has someone under her thrall. I slide out of our booth, hell bent on separating them and not caring in the slightest what it looks like to anyone.

As I get closer, I see she's holding a phone that isn't hers and looking down at it. Matt has his eyes on her tits, and even though I kind of want to kill him for it, I can't blame him. How could anyone around her look at anything else?

Now that I'm a few feet away, I'm finally able to make out their conversation. Curiosity makes me stop for a moment and listen before interrupting.

"Lighting cannot be underestimated," she says. "People will scroll past something with bad light without even giving it a second thought, especially on TikTok. It doesn't matter how pretty the music is. I can tell you have a really dark house."

Matt smiles. "Naw, I just live in SF, and it's always overcast."

Lauren purses her lips, her eyes still fixed on the phone. "You need to invest in some professional lighting. And you can't have any dead space in your videos, especially at the beginning. And by that I'm not only talking about actual dead space, which you have in quite a few. I mean no starting a video with a greeting or a filler word. On TikTok, you have like one to two seconds to grab their attention. You have a little more time on YouTube, but not much. It's all a matter of..."

When she glances up at me, I realize I've now drawn so close I'm nearly touching her. "I was telling Matt how he can get more views on YouTube and TikTok," she says. "I didn't tell him what I do for a living."

Her self-consciousness makes my stomach hollow. God, I'm selfish for making her keep her mouth shut about her job. It never even occurred to me that she might be able to use this party for networking. But of course I only thought about myself and what people would think if they knew she was an influencer. I unflinchingly told her I didn't want other influencers to get any ideas about *me*, when I knew without a doubt that I really didn't want any of the other musicians to get any ideas about *her*.

Goddamn it, I'm a bastard.

"Are you ready to go?" she asks. "It's been thirty minutes."

Her question startles me, and as I look down at her, tenderness fills my chest so full I could burst with it. She looks so ridiculous standing there with that serious—could I call it contrite?—expression while wearing that shear black lace dress that barely covers her beautiful skin.

Suddenly, I'm dying to get her back to the hotel.

I smile. "Let's get your coat so you don't die of pneumonia."

FOURTEEN

Lauren

CAM'S EXPRESSION is blank as we pull into the hotel parking lot. He barely said a word on the drive here, and my stomach churned the whole time as I wondered what he might be thinking.

Why do I do this?

Why do I take my childish antics so far when I'm always filled with self-loathing afterward?

As I crawl out of the car, the scratchy lace of my dress cuts into my tits, and instead of feeling the delight of earlier, I want to cringe. I deliberately embarrassed him in front of all his closest friends. Why did I think it would be fun?

As we walk through the lobby, the hotel clerk greets Cam by name. When he doesn't even look her way, my anxiety only increases. That was rude, even for Cam. He must be so lost in thought he didn't even hear her.

We walk into the elevator, and as soon as the door shuts, I

nearly jump at the sound of his deep rumble of laughter. When I turn around, his head is pressed back against the wall and his shoulders are shaking.

I'm so frazzled from nerves, my first thought is that he must be drunk, even though I know I didn't see him drink at all at the pub. "Are you okay?"

He doesn't even look my way. His laughter is almost maniacal now. My lips part as I stare at him. His laughter finally subsides when we make it to our floor, which seems to snap him into action. He grabs me by the arm and guides me out of the elevator. We've barely stepped into the hall when he grips my shoulders and shoves me against the wall. He presses a hard kiss against my neck before pulling away and staring down at me with heavy-lidded eyes. "I can't believe you wore lingerie to an Irish pub."

I smile faintly, his laughter and affection making me almost dizzy with relief. "It's a cocktail dress."

"Sure it is." His eyes crinkle at the edges. "Where did you get it?"

I suck in my lips to fight a smile. "I think the shop was called Oh Baby. I only picked it because it was the furthest out of the way, and I wanted to be especially late after you told me to hurry."

His lips brush against my forehead. "It's exactly the type of thing you would have done when you were twelve and I tried to boss you around. Except much more sadistic."

"I've gotten more innovative with age."

"I underestimated you, Henderson. Or should I call you Shmenderson?"

His smile softens as he reaches out and touches my cheek. He runs the pad of his finger down to my chin, sending a tingle through my spine. "I'm going to punish you for it."

He presses soft kisses from the base of my neck to my jaw,

and I make a low hum at the back of my throat. "Why do you think I did it in the first place?"

By the time his lips make it to my mouth, his pace has become more frantic. He kisses me so hard his teeth click against mine, and his fingers cut into my ribcage, sending a pleasurable pain into my core. I gasp as he lifts me into the air and presses my pelvis into his belly. I wrap my legs around his hips as he walks down the hall. Just as we make it to our room, I remember the missed call I saw I had when we were driving here.

"Cam." My voice is husky.

"What, baby?"

He's never called me baby before, and it makes my hips involuntarily grind into his. "You're going to have to give me a few minutes to do something before we get the night started."

He throws his head back and groans. "What the fuck? Why do you always do this to me? I swear, you do it on purpose to torture me."

"Not this time. I need to call Cadence."

His body grows still. "Oh."

"Yeah." I swallow. "She tried to FaceTime me when we were in the car. My guess is she was expecting her bedtime story. I almost never miss it, even when she's at her dad's."

Camden

SHE LOOKS down at her phone, a wide smile spreading across her face. A small stack of books she pulled from her suitcase now sits at her side. "I can't believe you're still awake," she says. "Your dad's going to pay for it, because you're going to be a crank tomorrow."

I stare at her, unable to move.

I knew she did this. I knew she disappeared around eight o'clock every night to put Cadence to bed and read her a bedtime story. But knowing it happens and witnessing it are two entirely different things.

"Daddy says I can have cupcakes for breakfast. He bought the Oreo ones at Vons."

Lauren rolls her eyes. "It's almost midnight, you're still awake, *and* he's letting you have cupcakes for breakfast? Tell him Mommy said only one cupcake, or else he's in trouble."

"You can't get Daddy in trouble. He's a grown up, and he's bigger than you."

When I snort out a laugh, Lauren's eyes dart up to meet mine, and an emotion fills them that I can't quite interpret. But in a flash, the look is gone, and her gaze returns to the phone. "We need to get to your story, honey, because Mommy needs to go to bed soon. I brought *Where the Wild Things Are—*"

"No," Cadence interrupts. "I want *Brown Bear.*"

When Lauren's eyelids flutter dramatically, I smile. The look reminds me so much of when she was a kid—so expressive and sassy. "I didn't bring *Brown Bear.*"

"Then Daddy can hold it up and you can read it. Daddy!" Cadence calls out.

"No, no, no. Don't call him in there." Lauren's groan is almost a growl. "I lied, okay? I did bring *Brown Bear*, but I was hoping you would choose something else. We've literally read it every night for the last two months. Can we please read *Where the Wild Things Are?*"

"No, I don't like it. The monsters are ugly, and it's boring."

"Cade, *Brown Bear* is literally the definition of boring. It's the same sentence on every page with one word swapped out."

I chuckle at Lauren's genuine dismay, and the sound of it draws her attention. "I know I sound the like worst parent ever right now, but you have no idea how mind-numbing it is to read the same book every night for months and months at a time." She looks down at the phone, a smile tugging at her lips. "Cadence knows it, too. She doesn't really love *Brown Bear* this much. She just loves bossing her mommy."

When Cadence giggles, a smile spreads over Lauren's face that makes my breath catch. Her eyes alight with so much warmth, my chest seizes with such a powerful ache of longing, it takes effort to breathe.

I never could have imagined this when I first got the news that she was pregnant. When I first heard, I went out with a group of friends I'd just met in Brooklyn, got drunker than I'd ever been in my life, and woke up on an ice-cold bathroom floor with a bar receipt stuck to my face. Whenever I've thought of her since then—even knowing she's a mother—I still imagined the same wild party girl Lauren.

What could have happened if I hadn't avoided her? Would watching her read to Cadence be a mundane daily activity?

Lauren starts reading the book, and as usual, the lull of her voice draws me into almost a state of hypnosis. Before I know it, she's looking at me with questioning frown, and I realize she's no longer reading, and the phone is on her lap.

"What's wrong?" she asks.

Caught off guard, I say the first thing that comes to mind. "You're a good mom."

Her eyes flash with that same emotion I saw a moment ago. It looks like shock and something else... But I don't get the chance to figure it out, because she averts her gaze from mine. "My mom thinks I'm too casual with her. I treat her like a friend instead of a daughter. She says that isn't healthy."

I shake my head sharply. "You're so yourself with her. So open and sincere and warm. Your relationship with her is easy, like neither of you have anything to hide. That's how it should be. And who is your mom to define a healthy relationship? Your mom is fucking awful."

"Is she?" Lauren smiles faintly, her eyes growing unfocused as she runs a finger along the threading on the edge of the couch armrest. "I don't know... She can't help the way she is. She loves me and Logan more than anything. And Cadence probably more than either of us. I really believe that. But she shows love by controlling people. It's like she thinks she knows what's best, so she tries to force it, and since she fully believes she's right, she doesn't feel bad manipulating or shaming people into doing what she wants. It's a shitty way to love, but it's who she is. I don't know if that's really her fault."

An uncomfortable thought rises at the back of my mind, making my skin prickle and my throat grow tight. I lift a hand and run it through my hair.

"What?" she asks.

"I think maybe..." I pause for a moment. "I think maybe I do that with Hunter."

A notch forms between her brows.

"His addiction has been really hard for me. I know I need to let go. The first thing you learn in any recovery program is that trying to interfere—trying to keep your addict loved one safe—is actually worse for them, but I still find myself doing it. I still find myself interfering in his life, trying to make things better for him. He probably already told you it was my decision to cancel the tour. He didn't want to do it. He said he was fine, and I think he meant it. But I was worried about what would happen when the parties started—having to be around people drinking and doing drugs when he was so fresh out of rehab— and ultimately, it's my call. So I cancelled it." I take a deep breath. This is the first time I've even fully admitted this to myself.

"So what?"

Her words startle me. I search her face to gauge her serious-ness, and her expression matches her blasé tone.

I frown. "So it's bad for his recovery if I try to control him."

"Yeah, but it's not like you have an ankle bracelet on him or keep him locked in a basement. You just love him... What?" she asks when I avert my gaze.

"I have his location on my phone." When her eyes widen, heat washes over my face.

Good God, if she only knew I have hers, too.

"I mean, it's not like I forced him to share it with me. It was something we all agreed on—my mom, dad, and him—probably two or three rehabs ago. All three of us have it." My lips close, and the heat creeping into my cheeks intensifies when I realize none of these defenses apply to my behavior with her.

"So if you all agreed on it as a family, why are you stressing about it?"

"Because it's another way for me to control him. If I ever see that he's in a suspicious place, I'd hunt him down in a second, and I'd prevent him from facing the real consequences of his actions, which is exactly what recovery programs tell you not to do."

"So what?"

I stare at her, unable to believe what I'm hearing. She's unabashedly ridiculed me for being a control freak for as long as I can remember.

"I'd do the same thing," she says. "And I wouldn't feel at all guilty about it, because of course I would. I love Hunter. And your love for him is like nothing I've ever seen in a sibling rela-tionship. You're more like a dad to him than your own dad. Of course you'd go out of your way to protect him. It's completely natural. Who are the people in these recovery programs, anyway? Are they superhuman? Are they Jesus?" She shakes her head. "I don't trust people like that."

A smile rises to my lips. "You don't trust Jesus?"

"No." She smiles lazily. "I don't trust noble people. I never have. I only trust selfish and petty people. At least their choices make sense to me, because I can relate to them."

Something loosens in my chest. I love how she accepts her own flaws. How she accepts the flaws of others, even selfish control freaks like me.

She dazzles me.

When she gives me an odd look, I realize the warmth and intensity of my feelings must be all over my face. I look away, schooling my face into a blank expression. "They aren't noble people. They know it's hard to let go, but their information is based on what works and what doesn't. Trying to control Hunter isn't good for him. It's probably not good for me, either."

"If you're so worried about it, work on it. Treat it like an addiction. Take steps...or whatever. The first step is admitting you have a problem, right? You just did that with me. Your next step can be removing his location from your phone."

I swallow, the thought alone making my pulse race.

If I did that, I'd need to remove hers, too.

"I shouldn't be talking to you about this," I say. "It's too personal." Without even looking at her, I feel the warmth between us diffuse in an instant, and I wish I could pull it all back. I wish we could be in harmony always.

"You're right." Her voice is tight. "And I guess you flew me here for a reason, huh?" She stands up from the couch, lowering her hands to the seam of her ridiculous dress. In one swoop, she pulls it over her head and tosses it onto the floor. "We should get to it."

I know I need to apologize, but the sight of her naked body after I've been so starved for her makes my need for her too urgent for words. I stand up and walk in her direction, my gaze fixed on her brown nipples.

I grab her by the waist and yank her against me. "I've been waiting a fucking eternity for this."

When I look down at her face, her eyelids are heavy. All trace of her earlier hurt are gone. I pull her in the direction of the bed, lowering my head and kissing her with all the hunger I've felt these last twenty-four hours.

After pressing her down on the mattress, I run my fingers along the seam of her pussy lips, groaning when I feel how wet she is already. Without thinking, I lift my fingers to my lips and suck them clean.

She moans. "Oh my God, it makes me crazy when you do things like that."

I raise my hand high in the air and bring it down to the side of her ass with a resounding smack. "This isn't about you. This is for me only. You're being punished."

When she whimpers, my heart seizes with panic. "Shit! Did I hurt you?"

She curls forward and grabs my shirt, yanking me in her direction. "Absolutely not." Her eyes are wild. "I loved it. Do it again."

I exhale, shutting my eyes. "I'm sorry. I've never done...this kind of stuff before."

"I can tell." I hear a smile in her voice.

"I'm going to have to get used to it."

"Oh, honey, it shouldn't take you long at all. You were born a dom."

When I take in the look on her face, I realize in an instant she really means it. "You think so?"

"Absolutely. It's pretty much what you do all the time. You boss everyone around, and they're all so afraid of you, they do exactly what you say. God, I could see it all over their faces tonight. Jeff looked like he was going to have a heart attack when you told him you weren't coming out on stage. Even Hunter is terrified of you."

I lift a hand to halt her, my cheeks warming. "Alright, I got it. No need to go on and on about it."

A slow smile spreads across her face. "Maybe you should punish me for sassing you."

My dick twitches. I could get used to this. Just before I raise my hand again, a realization dawns that nearly knocks me off my feet.

For the first time in my life, I have what I've always wanted.

This is what I wanted from her. Even as I told myself I couldn't stand her, I secretly loved her wildness. Even when I told myself I wished she'd change, I didn't really. Because I wanted it to be like this. I wanted us to be at odds and in harmony at once. I wanted her to taunt me. I wanted to taunt her back. I wanted to chase and grab her and kiss her and...

Love her.

"What's wrong?"

Her question jerks my attention into the present. She's looking up at me expectantly, and I can't let her see what I'm feeling.

"Nothing." I lower my chin, narrowing my eyes at her. "Turn over. I need better access to your ass. You said I can bite you, right?"

"Yes," she answers, breathless.

I nod once before gripping her hips and roughly tossing her onto her belly. She releases a high-pitched giggle. "Oh, Cam, I told you, didn't I? You were born for this."

A smile tugs at my lips as I stare down at those white cheeks, tan around the edges. She has a beautiful ass. Plump and round and jiggly when she makes even the slightest movement. I raise my hand high in the air and hold it there for a moment. As expected, the muscles in her ass clench, and the sight of goes straight to my dick.

"Oh my God," she says, "you're killing me."

My smile widens, but I don't give in. Not yet. I want to enjoy this. When I finally bring my hand down across her ass, the sound is so loud and crisp, it startles me. My eyes roam her plump cheek, and as expected, a pink handprint starts to form. I can't help but panic yet again, but I force myself to wait for her reaction.

"Holy shit."

"That wasn't too hard, was it?"

She flips over and props herself up with her elbows, glaring at me. "Stop fucking apologizing. Seriously. If you're going to be a dom, be a fucking dom. It's an instant turn off when you spank me like that and then act like a little bitch afterward."

My lips part. "Did you just call me a little bitch?"

She bites her bottom lip. "I said you were acting like a little bitch."

I want to smile, but with effort, I keep my face blank. I hold her stare for what feels like an eternity. With each passing second, I sense her apprehension grow. Without warning, I jerk forward and grab her by the hips.

"I take it back!" she squeals as I flip her over.

I yank her body to the edge of the bed. "You can't take it back."

She giggles, the sound muffled against the comforter.

"I wouldn't be laughing." I lower my head to her ass and lick the soft, smooth skin. Her sweet little hum makes my balls tingle. "That's only going to make your punishment worse."

I open my mouth and take a hard bite. Her soft, squishy skin between my teeth makes my whole belly clench, hunching my body forward. I can't help but groan when I finally open my mouth and release her.

Even in the midst of my erotic haze, I want to ask if I hurt her, but I keep myself from opening my mouth.

"Holy shit, Cam!" she finally shouts, and I instantly exhale, because I can hear in her voice that she's not in pain. Or if she is, she likes it.

She twists her body and looks up at me, her eyes so wide I can see the whites around her green pupils. "I always had a hunch you were kinky as fuck, but I seriously can't believe you took a bite out of my ass. It was probably a mistake, because I'm going to be bratting like crazy now."

My brow furrows. "What does that mean exactly?"

"I mean, I won't do a thing you say and will sass you constantly. I'm going to drive your control freak ass crazy."

I look at her incredulously. "You do that already."

"Oh, it will get much worse."

"It couldn't possibly be worse."

She lifts one of her dark brows. "I don't think you understand who you're dealing with here."

The words were meant to be playful, but still, they stop me in my tracks. An overwhelming tenderness washes through me. I do know what I'm dealing with. I know exactly what I'm dealing with.

And I wouldn't change a thing about her.

I lean forward and grab her face. Her eyes widen, as if she's startled by the change in my mood, but she doesn't stop me. After pressing my lips softly against hers, I run my tongue along the seam of her mouth. She releases a sweet little sigh as I pull away.

"I'm starved for you," I say, lowering my head to her belly, my eyelids nearly shutting when I catch the sweet, earthy scent of her wet pussy. Just before my lips touch her clit, she grabs me by the shoulders.

"No." Her tone is frantic. "I really want you inside me. I

can't believe I'm turning down oral right now, but that bite out of my ass really did something for me. I need your cock. Now."

I release an involuntary groan. "Say that again."

"I need your cock right now."

This time, I whimper, so aroused I can't move. My head buried between her thighs, I inhale deeply, my cock so hard I'm afraid I might explode in my jeans.

"Jesus Christ, Cam!"

Startled out of my erotic haze, I jerk back, and I see that she's scowling at me. "Who do I have to blow around here to get you to fuck me already?"

Unexpectedly, I burst into laughter. She stares at me while my shoulders shake, her expression shifting from indignation to anger, which only makes me laugh harder.

"Is my sexual frustration funny to you?"

I crawl forward and press my lips against hers, my throat still tight from laughter. "That's what you said that night in my car." My smile softens at the memory of those big green eyes as she straddled my lap. I felt the same way, too. Even though my cock was so hard it was almost painful, I couldn't help but laugh.

Her whole body freezes, and my smile fades as we stare at each other. She looks as stunned as I am. This might be the first time I've been able to even think about that night without pain, let alone talk about it. I rub my lips softly against hers before pulling away. "I don't want to be angry with you anymore."

"Me, neither. I want..." Her eyes flash. "I want this to be more. I want it to be a real relationship."

Her words send a fire though my veins. In a quick motion, I yank down my jeans and press into her in one plunge. I shudder as her warmth clenches around me. "God, you feel like heaven."

When I start moving inside her, she grinds her hips frantically against mine, as if searching for her orgasm already. She mumbles something that sounds halfway between a nonsense word and a moan, and I smile against her neck. "The sounds you make are my favorite."

She stares up at me with heavy-lidded, confused eyes. "Sounds?"

I chuckle, and the movement makes me sink even deeper inside her. I groan so loud it echoes across the room. As I brush my fingers across her cheek, I stare down into her wide, dazed eyes. A small smile tugs at my lips. "I think this might be the first time I've ever made a woman lose the ability to comprehend language."

"What?" Her eyes grow even more confused, and a familiar feeling seizes my chest.

I can't deny it any longer.

This feeling is love.

I've always loved her.

I slip my hands around her hips and cup her soft bare ass. After gripping firmly, I press my hips upward. She whimpers, and the sound of it combined with the pressure of her pussy stretching over my dick makes me hiss.

When I move harder and faster, the world around me blurs, though her face is still sharp and clear. Her eyes grow wide, and I force myself back into the present. I know her well enough now to know that she's very close to coming, and I love watching her come.

"Touch my clit," she begs. "Touch my clit now."

Even in the midst of my erotic haze, a chuckle erupts from my chest. She's so undeniably herself, even in a moment like this.

"Okay, I guess I have to do it." She slips her hand between our slick bodies.

Glaring down at her, I reach around and slap her so hard on the side of her ass, she shrieks.

"No." I yank her hand away. "That's mine." I place two fingers on her clit and rub back and forth in the motion I've learned she likes. She jerks back so hard that her head hits the wall behind us. I grip the back of her neck to cradle her in place. When her cunt starts to pulse around my cock, I have to clench my teeth to keep myself from coming with her. I don't want to lose myself.

I want to watch her.

Her eyes glaze over, and she starts to whimper. She sobs when she comes, and it still marvels me. I never imagined it, even in my countless fantasies. The sight of it touches me deep inside. Her brows draw together and her lips pout as she cries out.

She releases one last whimper before going still and limp. I lower my head and press a kiss against her cheek. I whisper words into her ear that I know I'll regret tomorrow, but I'm too overwhelmed to care. I thrust harder and faster, and when the electricity shoots through my body, I say the words aloud this time.

"I love you."

FIFTEEN

Lauren

I'M WARM.

Hard arms are wrapped around my body. I pull them closer and wiggle my hips. My eyes pop open at the sharpness of his hard cock against my lower back, and memories of the night before rush over me like warm water.

I love you.

I wiggle my hips again, hoping to wake him, relishing the fact I'm locked in his arms in the morning hours. We rarely get to have morning sex—only when Cadence is at Ryder's—and it makes me feel like we're just another couple, taking advantage of our precious kid-free moments together.

Like our relationship is real.

When his body starts to stir, I reach my hand under the blankets, slip it behind my back, and grab his cock. I soften my grip as I rub up and down. Cam releases a groan that vibrates at the pit of my belly.

"Looks like someone didn't get enough last night," I say.

I'm startled when my hand is suddenly empty. I twist around as he rolls out of bed and starts marching toward the bathroom. "I don't have time. Isaac wants to get brunch in an hour."

He leaves the door open as he walks into the bathroom and pulls out a toothbrush from a small black case. When he squeezes toothpaste over the bristles, a notch forms between my brows. This is the first time I've ever seen him brush his teeth, and it's strange to watch him do something so hauntingly domestic while he's pushing me away.

"An hour sounds like plenty of time," I say.

He shakes his head as he spits into the sink. "I won't have enough time to shower, and I can't show up at brunch smelling like pussy."

My whole body grows cold, and I try to retreat into my head to shield myself.

This is what he does. When things get too intense, he puts up his guard.

I swallow before speaking, keeping my voice even with effort. "So I'm not going to brunch with you?"

"No," he says, his voice notably softened. "It will only be Hunter, Isaac, and Janie and her husband. So three of my five people will be there. I won't need you to talk to people so I won't have to."

Of course I wouldn't go to brunch with him and the closest people in his life. Because this isn't a real relationship.

Summoning every ounce of bravado I have, I throw the comforter open, exposing my bare body to the cold air. After hopping off the bed, I march to the bathroom. Cam's head snaps in my direction as I walk through the door. When I plop down on the toilet, his eyebrows shoot to his forehead. His eyes snap to my hips at the sound of liquid falling into the toilet.

"You're peeing in front me." His voice has a faraway quality to it.

I smile cheekily. "Yep."

Broken-hearted girls don't pee in front of the boys who crushed their hopes.

He doesn't say anything, but his eyes stay fixed on my hips. A smile rises to my lips.

"I pee in front of everyone. I have no boundaries. If it bothers you, I won't do it. But most of my friends don't mind."

"I don't mind." His voice is hushed, and he looks almost mesmerized.

"Oh my God! Do you have, like, a thing for pee?"

His smile vanishes, his eyes growing wide.

"If you do, it's totally fine. Not my kink, but I can work with it. I don't think I could go beyond that though. If you have a poop thing, you're going to have to contract out. But I won't judge you."

He continues to stare at me with wide eyes, and I nearly jump when he bursts into laughter. He lowers his head, his shoulders vibrating. "I can't believe you," he says in a strained voice. "You were really serious."

I frown at him. "Forgive me for misunderstanding when you were staring at me while I peed. You looked like you were into it."

He shakes his head, his shoulders still shaking with laughter. "You thought I had a defecation kink." His voice is strangled. "And you were okay with it."

"Yeah, I don't kink shame."

"I know you don't." He smiles down at me, his eyes hooded. After walking over to the toilet, he kneels in front of me and presses a hard kiss against my lips. When he pulls away, he raises his hand and strokes a strand of hair behind my ear. "I think you might be the least judgmental person I've ever met."

I swallow, lowering my gaze. "That's funny, because I've always thought you're the most judgmental person I've ever met."

He stiffens, but he doesn't pull away. "I'm sorry."

My heart starts to race. I take a deep breath in through my nose and release it slowly out of my mouth. "For what?"

When he doesn't answer right away, my stomach sinks. I know what he's going to say.

I just know.

"I can't do this longer than six months. I can't make this a real relationship."

The air leaves my lungs as suddenly as if he hit me in the chest.

"I just can't do it." His eyes are pleading. "I already feel like my life is spiraling out of control. Like I'm losing a handle on...everything."

"And that's my fault?" My voice is small and tight.

He doesn't respond, and that's all the answer I need.

"You do this a lot, don't you?" I ask.

His brows pull together. "What?"

"Whenever things are good, you push people away. Things were good between us that night. The first time we had sex." I shake my head slowly. "And then you slut-shamed me. Why did you do it?"

His eyes grow wide, almost fearful. In an instant, he's standing. His spine is rigid as he walks out of the bathroom. "I need to shower," he says. "Let me know when you're done in here."

As he disappears from sight, I clench my teeth to fight the rising tears. If he really cared about me, he would talk about it. He would explain himself.

My heart is breaking in two, but I can't fall apart. I wipe, stand up from the toilet, and rush to the bedside table. After grabbing my phone, I walk right back to the bathroom and shut the door.

I pull up my contact list and press the name of the only person I know who can fully understand what I'm going through.

SIXTEEN

Camden

"WHAT'S WRONG?" Janie's voice is soft, and when I glance to my right, I see that Hunter, Isaac, and Janie's husband, Jeremiah, are still engrossed in conversation about a local Portland guitar maker. I exhale, relieved that she waited until this moment to ask.

I look down at my plate and rub my fork along the barely touched lobster omelet. Fuck, I don't even like lobster. Or omelets.

"Lauren wants this to be more than it is. She wants a real relationship."

She stares at me steadily. "And how do you feel?"

I lift a hand and run it through my hair. "I wish I had never done this thing with her in the first place."

Janie's quiet for a moment. "But you don't really feel that way."

I sigh heavily. She's right, of course. I don't regret it for a second, because it gave me what I've always wanted.

The problem is I might not be able to let go.

"No," I finally say.

"Why don't you just do it?"

"Because I can't trust her." It's hard to keep the accusation out of my tone. Janie seems to be forgetting all my justified misgivings. "She's impulsive and unpredictable even when things are good between us. What's going to happen when they aren't? What is she going to do the next time she's angry with me, like *really* angry?" My jaw clenches. "We know what she did last time."

"Yeah, but she was eighteen."

"And she still does the same kind of shit she did back then. You saw her last night. She wore that dress because she was mad that I tried to give her rules on how to behave at the party. And I'm fucking paying her to go to parties with me."

"I don't think resisting your tight leash is the same thing as..." Janie doesn't finish that sentence, because she understands better than anyone why it's so hard for me to talk about that night.

The shame and regret are too overwhelming.

"I don't keep her on a tight leash. She's doing a job for me, and I'm paying her thousands of dollars at the end of this."

Janie's lips quirk. "Yeah, but do you only tell her what to do at parties?"

"Yes." My answer comes so rapidly that it sounds insincere even to my own ears. I shut my eyes for a moment, not surprised when the sound of Janie's laughter hits my ears.

"Okay, listen to me for a second," she says. "I understand your situation a lot better than you think. I may be a people pleaser with the rest of the world, but with Jeremiah, I'm every bit as much of a control freak as you. I hate being away from him when we tour. It gives me so much anxiety. And I make him text me constantly throughout the day. I am not kidding when I tell you he is on a texting schedule with me, and if he ever forgets, I go out of my way to make him feel terrible. Like, I'll bring up old stuff—times he messed up in the past—to make it really hit home." She smiles faintly. "It's not healthy at all, but he puts up with it because he knows where it comes from."

I look away, apprehension rising at where I think her story is going.

"You care about Lauren. And you want to control her because you're scared. You're scared of losing her."

My jaw clenches. "I have a lot of reason to fear what she might do."

"I don't know if that's true anymore." Her voice is hushed. "I think this might be something you need to work through. It's definitely something that I've had to work through, and I'm still not there. Jeremiah has given me no real reason not to trust him, and yet it's so hard for me. But that's because trust is an action, not a feeling."

"That's bullshit therapy talk. Trust is earned."

She shakes her head as she lifts her mimosa and takes a small sip. "I don't agree. Because for people like you and me— and by that I mean people with anxiety—the people in our lives could never do enough to earn it."

"I don't have anxiety." My voice is so loud, I draw the attention of the other three.

"No, you're just an asshole," Hunter says with a smile.

My brows draw together at the coldness in his tone. I can't ever remember him being this snarky with me.

"We're talking about how Cam and I are both control freaks," Janie says.

A goofy grin spreads across Jeremiah's face as he turns to Janie and sets a hand on her thigh. "I married Larry David."

"Eww." Janie cringes. "I'm not that bad."

"Controlling people is Cam's love language," Hunter says.

I whip my head in his direction. As expected, he has that same coy smile I've seen so many times in the last month and a half since his relapse. It's a malicious smile, I realize now.

"That's a fucked-up thing to say." As soon the words are out, the whole table goes quiet. Hunter's smile fades, his eyes widening. I sense the discomfort of the others, but I'm too riled up to care. His words are too hauntingly similar to what Lauren said about her mom last night. I may have my issues, but I'm no Helen fucking Henderson.

"I was joking," Hunter says, his voice small.

"No, you fucking weren't." I'm practically shouting now, but I don't care. "You've been acting like an asshole since you relapsed, constantly making passive aggressive jabs at me. If you have something to say to me, say it directly. You're a fucking grown-ass man. I don't care if you've struggled. We all have our shit. It's not an excuse to treat people like garbage."

The hurt in his eyes sends a pang of guilt into my chest.

"You have no idea what I've been through."

I roll my eyes, sick to death of this conversation after years of having it over and over again. "I know exactly what you've been through. I know what you've been through probably even better than you do, because I was actually sober for it. *You* have no idea what *I've* been through. You have no idea what it's like to love someone who's been to rehab six times, and to the hospital eight. You can't even understand the panic—"

"Cam." Isaac's stern voice summons me out of my head, and I realize that I'm not only nearly yelling at Hunter, but I'm also jabbing my finger at him.

Good God, who am I? Why am I yelling at my baby brother for his chemical dependency, something he literally can't help? Why am I calling him an asshole for understandably resenting that Mother Nature dealt him a shitty hand when it comes to brain chemistry?

"Maybe you should table this for now," Isaac says, reaching out and patting me hard on the back. "Wait till you can talk somewhere private."

"I agree," Janie says, her eyes wide. "People are looking at us. I think I even saw someone with their phone in the air. I don't want anyone to post this on Instagram or YouTube or something."

"I'm sorry," I say on an exhale. "I'm having a bad day."

"Yeah, Lauren told me."

Startled, my gaze darts to Hunter.

"As a matter of fact," he says. "I should probably call her back. I told her I would so she could finish venting about what an asshole you are." The words were said breezily, but I know it took effort.

He's hurt. He's hurt, and he's trying to hide it.

Still, his movements are light as he stands up from the table and starts walking in the direction of restaurant entrance. I feel like utter shit after everything I said, and I wish I could reach out and hug him like I used to when he was a little boy—squeezing his shoulders and pressing my cheek against his—but I can't stifle this familiar feeling of jealousy. It makes my skin hot and my chest tight.

Of course she would turn to him.

She always does.

SEVENTEEN

Lauren

AS I PULL the chicken nuggets out of the oven, my phone rings, making me jump. A nugget at the edge of the baking sheet flies into the air, but before it hits the floor, I catch it with the top of my foot.

"Look, Cadence," I shout.

She glances up from the kitchen bar, kneading a clump of play dough in her hands. "What?"

"I caught the nugget with my foot." I lift my leg higher to give her a better view.

She glances at my foot, grimacing. "I don't want it now. I don't like foot nuggets. And I wanted ten, so you have to make another one."

After turning from her view, I roll my eyes. She's been grumpy all morning since I picked her up from her dad's. Apparently, Ryder promised to take her surfing with him and his buddies this morning, because he's a man-child and forgot that Monday is my day to pick her up, even though we've had a nearly identical schedule since she was an infant.

Cadence hasn't missed an opportunity to make it clear that she likes it better at her dad's. It's stupid that it hurts. It's stupid that I'm so petty and take it personally. This is what kids do. I know this.

I blame it all on Cam. My emotions have been chaotic these last few weeks since he rejected me in that hotel bathroom. Even though he's tried to make up for it, I can't shake the hurt. I should be overjoyed he's now offered to use his connections to help find me a social media job, but I can only see it as a confirmation that he doesn't want me around four months from now.

To top it off, he's in Oakland now, probably getting ready to leave his hotel to go to sound check. This is the first time since we moved in that he's left town without me.

He's pushing me away.

"Good thing I made fifteen," I say tightly, bending down and picking up the foot nugget.

"I don't want fifteen. I want ten."

I mouth, "I want ten" as I turn to the trash compactor. I know I'm being stupid. But somehow, I can never control myself when I'm hurt.

"Who called?" she asks.

"It was the Darth Vader ringtone." I grab the ketchup from the fridge. "It was Grammy."

"Uncle Logan has the Darth Vader music, too."

I smile at her impeccable memory. "I guess he does, huh? I forget because he never calls me. And he has the Darth Vader music for a different reason than Grammy."

"Can we go to Grammy and Papa's house today?"

Her tone is completely guileless—all of her earlier sass a distant memory—and it makes my stomach sink with guilt. I've been avoiding my mom since we moved, and it's taking a toll on Cadence.

Steeling myself, I walk over to where my phone sits on the counter. I smile brightly at Cadence as I press the name on the call list. "I'll check and see if they're free." When Cadence smiles wide, I know I did the right thing, and I wish I were noble enough to dread this call less.

As the phone rings, my pulse speeds up. How does my mom still have the power to make me feel this way, even now when she no longer rules my life?

"I haven't seen my granddaughter in over a week," she says as soon as she picks up.

I can't help but smile cynically at her non-greeting. "Hey, Mom."

"This isn't healthy," she says as if she didn't hear me. "Your dad and I were part of her everyday routine. She's used to seeing us. Just because you live in a fancy house now doesn't change that. She needs her grandparents."

"I agree with you."

The phone goes silent. I must have surprised her with my ready assent.

"Then when are we going to see her?"

"I was actually going to see if you're free this afternoon."

"I can't this afternoon. I have a hair appointment and my book club after that." Her tone is full of self-pity, and a smile rises to my lips when I think of how similar she sounds to Cadence whining about the foot nugget. "But this isn't about this afternoon. We need to see her more in general. Your life-style may have changed, but it shouldn't change hers. You should be putting her needs above your own. That's what it means to be a mother."

As usual, that familiar rage starts as a small flame, making my skin prickle and my stomach flip. If I'm not careful, it will grow like a wildfire. I want to lash out. I want to say something that will hurt her back, but something stops me. Maybe it's that Cadence is sitting right across the room, and she understands so much more than she can articulate. Maybe it's that I've been brought so low after making myself vulnerable recently, that I don't feel like I have anything left to lose.

I try my best to sound reasonable when I speak. "How do you not see the irony of telling me what it means to be a good mother when you're trying to make me feel shitty about myself? *You* are trying to make *your daughter* feel shitty."

The phone goes quiet for a moment, and then she sighs. "I wasn't trying to make you feel shitty."

"Then why would you say that?"

She pauses for a beat. "I just want to see my granddaughter."

I ought to applaud her for her honesty, because manipulation and shame are tools Helen Henderson uses to get what she wants. Even when what she wants is love.

"And I tried to arrange it so you can see her. It's not my fault you're busy."

"I don't like any of this, Lauren."

Ah, now we've gotten to it. The real reason she's upset. Her loss of control over my life.

"I don't like this...*relationship* you have with Cam. I don't think it's healthy for Cadence, but I especially don't think it's healthy for you."

I grit my teeth, heat washing over my face. "You know literally nothing about it. I haven't talked to you about it for a reason."

"Honey, I know more about it than you think."

Her tone is full of hidden meaning, and it makes my spine go rigid. "If you use my relationship with Cam as an excuse to tell me about some eighties celebrity who hit on you once at a bar, I will literally throw up in the sink right now."

"He didn't hit on me once. We had a much longer relationship than that. Very similar to the one you have with Cam. He was a very wealthy man."

I grimace. "Oh my God, are you talking about the news anchor guy? Mom, I'm sorry, but a San Diego weather reporter is not a celebrity. And there's no way he was wealthy. He lied to you. There's literally an entire movie about how pathetic those guys are, and every time you mention him, I picture Will Farrell with a mustache."

She sighs heavily. "I'm not talking about Dan. I'm talking about a man I've never told you about."

My eyelids flutter at the smugness in her tone. She thinks she's titillating me with these oblique references to her past. "Either way, I don't want to hear about him. I'm not going to be impressed."

"Goodness, Lauren. You think I'm trying to impress my own daughter with my sexual conquests? This man rejected me. It was nothing to brag about. I was heartbroken, and it took me years to get over it. I think that's probably why I've never told you about it. Even after thirty years, the wound is still fresh."

My shoulders relax a little at her uncharacteristic vulnerability. Still, I don't want to hear about it.

"Well, I don't need any details. I've heard enough of your stories to last me a lifetime."

"And I don't want to tell you about it." Her tone is defensive. "But I will tell you one thing. That experience taught me a lot of life lessons, especially about men. Men of a certain status are all the same, and Cam is one of them. Just because we've known him his whole life doesn't change it. When men achieve a certain level of power, and Camden has with his fame and wealth—"

"*Moderate* fame," I cut in, my cheeks growing hot. "And *moderate* wealth."

"Compared to whom? Justin Bieber? You can minimize it all you want, but it doesn't make it any less true, and I know men like that. I know them better than you do, because of... what I used to look like."

I roll my eyes at her not-so-humble brag.

"They're a product of our patriarchal society," she says. "And they feel like they can have whatever they want. Even good boys like Camden. Having that kind of power changes them. They feel entitled to a certain type of woman."

My heart jumps into my throat at the implication, my hands growing cold and numb.

A certain type of woman.

I take a deep breath, an unsteady breath. "And I'm not that type of woman."

"Honey, you know you aren't."

The answer comes so quickly, and I'm ill prepared for it. I shut my eyes tightly, my chest seizing with an ache so acute it takes effort to breathe.

"Of course, you have your own unique beauty. And you have that feisty personality that draws men in. You can tell them off and still make them eat out of the palm of your hand. You've always had that quality—even when you were fourteen years old—and it's a rarity. I never had that. But you know what I'm talking about, honey, right?"

It's only when I feel a trickle down my cheek that I realize how much she got to me.

"Camden has all kinds of women throwing themselves at him now, and while he may still have a little bit of a crush on you left over from your teenage years, it won't last. And I'm not saying that to hurt you. I'm really not. I'm saying this because I'm worried about you, and I want you to protect yourself. I want you to guard your heart from him. I wish I had done that all those years ago. Do what I was too smitten and too much of a pushover to do. Make Camden work for you. Make him still think about you years from now, long after this fling between you is over."

I take another deep breath, but it does nothing to calm my rage. I straighten my spine, clenching my teeth. "I thought you were jealous before, but now I'm convinced."

"Mothers can't be jealous of their daughters. You should know that. Our daughters are extensions of ourselves. Their joy and their pain is ours, too."

"If my pain is yours, why are you going out of your way right now to make me feel like shit about myself? Why remind me that you used to be objectively gorgeous, while I only have my *own unique beauty*? For that matter, why are you so obsessed with what you used to look like? You aren't beautiful anymore. You're old and wrinkly, and no one cares how beautiful you used to be. When you tell your stories, when you show off your old modeling pictures, people think you're pathetic. I feel sorry for you when I see it in their faces." As soon as the words are out, I inhale a shaky breath, and another trickle of liquid falls down my cheek.

"I can see that I hurt your feelings, and that wasn't my intention." Her voice is just above a whisper. The hurt in it is plain, and even in my agony and rage, I still hate myself for coming unleashed. I can't do this anymore. If I don't gain some self-control, I'll be alone for the rest of my life.

And my impulsivity has already cost me enough.

EIGHTEEN

Camden

AS I WALK through the door, their chattering voices echo from the kitchen. My chest seizes with that familiar, bittersweet pain. Home never felt like this before the two of them moved in.

It wasn't home.

I forced myself to go to the Oakland show without Lauren in an attempt to prove that I don't need her with me all the time. But I ached for her the whole trip. I'd reach out across the bed in the middle of the night, my stomach sinking when I found nothing. I checked her phone location throughout each day like it was my job to know where she was.

There's no denying it any longer. I can't let her go. Even when it's dangerous to keep her. Because as much as I fear what she'll do when she's out of my sight, when I'm with her, my normally racing mind is hushed. She makes me feel like the whole world is soft and cool and quiet, like a walk on the beach before sunrise.

Nothing else has the power to make me feel that way, not even music.

I need her.

I need both of them.

When I walk into the kitchen, Cadence jumps up from her seat at the table. "Uncle Cam!" she shouts before rushing over to me and wrapping her arms around my legs. "I'm so happy you're here. My mommy's making ice cream with your ice-cream maker. I wanted her to make it yesterday, but the bowl thing wasn't frozen, and I cried a lot."

"Yes, she did," Lauren cuts in, her tone accusing. She glares at me, holding what looks like a metal bowl in the air. Her face is strained, her shoulders tense, and it makes me want to reach out and take her into my arms. "You need to keep this piece in the freezer at all times. Or else you can't make the ice cream for twenty-four hours, and let me tell you, to a four-year-old, that's a fucking eternity." She winces before turning to Cadence. "Sorry, Cade. I shouldn't have used that word."

Cadence frowns up at me. "She says that word all the time."

I fight a smile. "Not all the time."

"No, I do," Lauren says, her speech rapid. "Because I'm a hot mess of a mother, which is what you were really thinking, and you know it."

After patting Cadence's back, I walk over to where Lauren stands at the counter. "Well, hello to you, too." I grip her by the waist and pull her in for a kiss.

As soon as her lips touch mine, I know. I know that moment in the hotel bathroom is still between us, like it has been for the last few weeks. I find myself frantically searching my mind for a way to fix it.

She turns away from me. "I'm sorry." She opens the fridge and pulls out a carton of milk. "I don't mean to bite your head off when you just got back. But my mom came over to see Cadence earlier, and she was acting like a raging..." Lauren glances at Cadence and then back at me. "C-U-N-T, and I—"

"I know what that means!" Cadence shouts.

Lauren's brow furrows as she looks at Cadence. "No, you don't." She looks back at me. "She really doesn't, I promise. I'm not that much of a hot mess. Anyway—"

"Yes, I do," Cadence says. "It means..." She puts her hand over her mouth as she whispers, "Bitch."

Unable to help myself, I burst into laughter, and Lauren's strained expression finally begins to soften. A small smile rises to her lips. "Sort of, honey." Lauren's voice is tight, as if she's holding back laughter. "But it's a naughtier word. A word Mommy really shouldn't call your grammy."

When my laughter eventually subsides, I see that Lauren's mood has lightened, and it sends a thrill down my spine. I need the harmony we've found these past two months.

I can't live without it.

Elated at the change in her mood, I grab her by the shoulders and yank her in for a kiss. "Have you guys eaten? Let me make you dinner."

Her eyes widen. "But you just got home, after traveling, too. I should be the one making you dinner."

"I'm used to traveling, and it sounds like you had a rougher day than I did." I turn to Cadence. "How do you feel about spaghetti? It was your mom's favorite when she was little. She ate it three meals a day, and she used to pour Taco Bell hot sauce all over it." I cringe dramatically.

Cadence grimaces. "I don't like spaghetti. Or hot sauce."

I smile as I turn back to Lauren, about to ask her what I should make instead, and I'm arrested by the look on her face.

She looks utterly shocked. God, she's probably wondering how the hell I remember her favorite food from over fifteen years ago.

She still doesn't understand the full extent of my obsession.

"What else does she like?" I ask, surprised by my lack of embarrassment.

As if snapping out of her head, Lauren's brows draw together. She waves a dismissive hand. "I'm not going to make you cook for two people. I'll make her some Dino nuggets."

"No." I grab her shoulders and dig my fingers into the tense muscles at the base of her neck. "You've had a rough day. Why don't you go take a bubble bath or something, and I'll finish making the ice cream for Cadence?"

She looks almost bewildered. "Are you on something?"

"Am I that much of a dick that you can't imagine I'd give you some time to yourself?"

"I never thought I'd hear the words 'bubble bath' come out of your mouth."

I smile sheepishly. "Our bath is incredible. Have you used it yet? The jets feel like a massage."

She gives me a strange look before assenting and walking away, leaving me alone with Cadence. It's only after she disappears that it dawns on me that I called it *our* bath.

Because this is our home.

LAUREN

MY TREK down the long wooden staircase is slow, my body soft and limber from the hot water. It's the most relaxed I've been in years, and goddamn it, why did it have to come right now? Why does he have to be so wonderful right after that awful conversation with my mom? Just when I think it can't get any worse, I catch sight of him in the kitchen, and my whole body grows still.

Cam and Cadence sit side by side, each with a small action figure in their hands. A tall toy tower sits in front of them, one I've never seen before, and Cam's look of earnest concentration in whatever they're playing makes my throat grow tight.

When Cadence glances up, a wide-eyed smile spreads over her face. "Mommy, he got me the Iron Man headquarters!"

As I walk closer to the table, I recognize the toy. Cadence wanted it for her birthday this year, and it's the only time I haven't been able to give her exactly what she wanted, because even my parents weren't willing to spot me five-hundred bucks for a plastic toy. I shoot wide eyes at Camden. "Where the hell did you get this?"

"I think Brayden found it on eBay. Cadence told me she wanted it." He smiles at her, and that deep aching tug pulls at my heart once again. I wish I could shut my eyes and make it go away.

I don't want to see this.

"Uncle Cam put it together for me, Mommy." Cadence looks up at him. "My mommy always needs help from my papa because she's not good at building things."

Cam smiles. "Well, your mom is good at other things."

"Yeah, she's good at everything, like makeup and hair. I'm really good at makeup and hair, too."

His smile lingers. "I'll bet you are." He tugs at the end of her fishtail braid. "I really like whatever you did here."

"My mommy braided this, but I can braid my own hair, and I do my own eye shadow. Here!" She reaches out her hand. "We forgot to put the stickers on the tower. Let me do it."

Cam smiles as he grabs the sheet of stickers.

"When my mommy builded my Barbie Dreamhouse, she spilled wine on it. It turned the stickers red."

The abruptness of the statement stops Cam mid-movement. He jerks his head in my direction, a wide grin spreading over his face. "You just got called out, Henderson."

A smile tugs at my lips. "That damn Barbie Dreamhouse. It's the one toy I've ever messed up, and she never lets me forget it. And that thing came in like five-hundred plastic pieces unassembled. It took me at least an hour to put together. Wine was a necessity."

"I cried a lot," Cadence says.

"Yes, she did, and it made me want to drink even more wine. You should see her when she cries. It rips your heart out."

Cam glances at Cadence. "I would have cried, too. I got my first guitar when I was your age. It wasn't a real guitar—just one for kids—but man, I loved it. And then one day, I found it floating in the pool. The wood was soaked through, and it was ruined."

Cadence looks up at him, her dark brows drawing together. "Why was it in the pool?"

"Your Uncle Hunter threw it in."

When her mouth drops open, Cam smiles at her. "He didn't do it to be mean. He was only two back then, so he was a baby. He was the sweetest little guy, too, so I couldn't even be mad at him, but I was so sad. I cried for probably a whole day."

When my eyes mist over, I clench my teeth, willing the tightness in my chest to go away.

I don't regret the choice I made five years ago.

I don't regret that I didn't even consider the remote possibility he might be her father, because I never could have known he'd be this easy with her when he was the complete opposite with me.

I clear my throat. "Did you decide what you're making for dinner? I'm getting hungry."

It's a lie, but I can't watch this anymore—not in the vulnerable state I'm in since the conversation with my mom. Hopefully, I can work up an appetite while he cooks.

A guilty expression flashes across his face. "I actually ordered Thai Kitchen on GrubHub, and I got our usual. Cadence wanted me to put the headquarters together, and I wasn't sure if you were too hungry to wait for me to cook. Plus, she wanted McDonald's."

My eyes snap to Cadence. "I already told you no McDonald's. You tricked Cam."

"No, I didn't! You said we couldn't go to McDonald's, and he got McDonald's on GrubHub."

I lift a brow. "You know that's cheating."

"No, it's not!"

Cam touches Cadence's shoulder. "Hey, why don't we play some songs on my guitar now that your mom is out of her bath?"

Cadence's indignant expression vanishes, replaced by a big smile. "Yes! Mommy, Cam knows how to play Ariana Grande on his guitar."

Cam smiles warmly at her. "Why don't you head to my studio and pick out your favorite guitar. Your mom and I will come soon."

Cadence jumps from her seat and rushes out of the kitchen. Her bouncing footsteps pound across the hallway tile, and when I turn back to Cam, he's wincing. "Sorry about the McDonald's thing."

I wave a hand. "It's not that big of a deal, but I'm trying to set boundaries with her. I'm too indulgent and casual most of the time, and it's not healthy." I glance at the floor. "My mom certainly thinks it isn't."

"Well, your mom isn't half the mother you are." His tone is firm and certain, and I feel the air leave my lungs in a whoosh.

It's too much. It's too much for one night.

"Let's go," I say, my voice quivering.

He looks a little surprised by the abrupt change in my mood, but he doesn't say anything. He nods once before getting up and walking over to me. As I turn toward the hallway, he grabs me by the waist and pulls my back flush against his body. His breath tickles my cheek before his lips press against my skin. "I missed you."

I shut my eyes tightly, letting the words wash over me. Against my better judgment, I lean back into his hold.

I don't want my mom to be right, but maybe I should be working harder to protect myself.

NINETEEN

Camden

"OH MY GOD, I *actually* love this!"

I suppress a smile as I pick the mandolin strings. I can't help but notice how she emphasized the word "actually", like I should be flattered she'd deign to praise my music. Her insistence that she hates folk rock has always amused me, because I know exactly what it means.

You won't get anything from me, Cam. Not when you treat me like shit.

I applaud her for it, because I deserve it.

After I play the last few chords of the outro, I look down at her, and I'm inordinately pleased with the rapt expression on her face. If she's going to like any song of mine, it ought to be that one, since it's about her. Though if I'm being completely honest with myself... I suppose they all are in a way.

We've spent almost the entire evening in my studio, a place I've kept so private since I bought this house, even

Hunter and Janie tend to stay out of it. Somehow, everything Lauren, Cadence, and I have done these past few hours felt as natural if it were a daily routine. I sat on the couch and played my guitar while they sang and danced. I was somehow able to keep up with Cadence's requests, relying on my reflexes when I played songs I haven't heard in well over a decade, like "Sunny Days" from *Sesame Street*. Cadence seemed almost inexhaustible, but when I switched to slower songs, she eventually plopped on the couch and fell asleep. I felt like a father as I held her in my arms and carried her to bed, and after I came back, Lauren didn't want me to stop playing.

Even in the depths of my obsession when I was young— back when I had hope we could be something someday—I couldn't have even imagined spending an evening like this. I have a family now, and the thought of losing it in four months makes me want to die.

I need to find a way to keep them.

I just wish I knew how to keep Lauren and my sanity at the same time.

"I seriously love that," she says as I finish up a song. "It's... achingly beautiful. Like it hurts right here." She places her hand on the center of her chest. "It feels kind of like nostalgia. But not for the past. For right now." She wrinkles her nose. "Do you know what I mean?"

I smile warmly. "I do. That's why I love writing music. It gives me the power to manufacture that feeling."

She shakes her head slowly. "Nothing usually makes me feel that way. And definitely not folk rock. I literally wish the banjo could be outlawed." She points to my instrument. "But you made it sound beautiful."

I'm somehow able to keep from laughing. "It's a mandolin."

"Really? It sounds like a banjo."

I gesture with my head to the corner of the room. "That's a banjo."

She twists around for a moment, and when she turns back, her whole face is scrunched in disgust. "Oh God, they even look stupid. Like you should have a straw hanging out of your mouth when you play it."

I gasp out a laugh. "It's always the banjo with you. Ever since I started playing it in high school. We probably only use it in half of our songs, and yet it seems to be the number one reason you don't like our music. I don't know how one instrument can inspire so much hatred."

"The banjo sounds stupid. And your voice is so pretty, so the banjo sounds so much stupider in comparison." She smiles ruefully. "I'll admit, I almost changed my mind when I watched that interview where you were talking about the history of folk and Americana music. It was all super interesting, and you even made the hillbilly banjo sound important. I thought maybe I wasn't giving it a fair chance, but then as soon as you got it out and played a few chords, I was like, nope. It's as bad as I remember."

"That must have been the PBS interview." My brow furrows. "You watched that? It was like two hours long. I don't even think my parents watched it."

Her face lights up. "Oh, I've watched *so many* of your interviews. I type in 'Camden Hayes interviews' and go down the list on YouTube." Her lips spread into a toothy grin. "You're such an asshole to the people who interview you. The PBS one was an exception. Normally, you give one-word answers, and these poor journalists are literally sweating, trying so hard to get you to talk."

My stomach flips at the thought of her watching me from afar—like I watch her. I look away to hide the bashful smile rising to my mouth. "Yeah, well... I can't help that I have terrible social skills, and those journalists are rarely musicians themselves. They're always trying to get these wordy, eloquent answers, and the truth is that writing music isn't an intellectual exercise. It's almost purely instinct, which makes it so hard to talk about. And I don't like talking to strangers as it is."

"Well, you definitely don't talk much in your interviews, even though technically the whole point is sitting down and talking. Oh my God, they're hilarious." Her big smile makes her eyes crease at the edges. "It's so you. So Cam."

She looks startled when I set my hand on hers. "Did you only watch them because they're funny?"

Her smile softens, and my pulse speeds up as I wait for her answer.

"Of course not. I watched them for the same reason you watched my makeup tutorials."

The tenderness in her eyes makes me lightheaded, even though she can't remotely comprehend the full implication of her words. I watched her videos because I love her. Because I've loved her for as long as I can remember, and even when I tried my hardest to stay away, I couldn't get by without a piece of her, however small.

I lean in to kiss her, but she pulls back. "I also watched them as research," she says.

My stomach sinks at the flatness in her voice, such a contrast to the warmth of a moment ago.

Maybe this isn't the time to tell her how I feel.

"Research?" I ask absently.

"Yes." She sets two hands primly on her lap, straightening her posture. "I've known for a long time that I should be making content for you guys. I have better marketing instincts than whoever you have now. Your fans love what an asshole you are. Why hasn't your social media manager capitalized on these interviews? I would have been on that shit immediately.

My guess is whoever you have now is part of some huge company, and they have a big enough clientele to know that celebrities like you—who already have a blue checkmark on all their platforms—don't have a clue what it takes to be successful on social media. So they flatter you into thinking your music will sell itself, which is bullshit. The only people listening to your music on YouTube are people who already like twangy banjo music. I know how to reach a larger audience." She leans back into the couch and crosses her arms over her chest. "I should be working for you guys."

When she raises both brows in challenge, I'm pulled out of my daze. It's my cue to tell her she's right.

But goddamn it, her timing makes me want to throw something. I'm ready to give her so much more than a job. I'm ready to give her all of myself even though it terrifies me. Why does she have to remind me that she's mostly here because of my money? If I hadn't swooped in and offered her an obscene amount of it, she'd be with Hunter at this moment, doing who knows what?

Unable to stand the thought, I grab her by the waist and lift her onto my lap. Her eyes grow wide, her lips parting in surprise. Not wanting to give her a chance to speak, I grab the back of her neck and yank her mouth against mine. I kiss her frantically because I can't help myself, even as I recognize that seeking reassurance in this way isn't healthy. I shouldn't be looking for signs that she loves me as much as I love her. If I'm going to make this a real relationship, I need to accept the risk that she could destroy me.

Like she did before.

When I pull away, she's breathless, her chest rising and falling rapidly. She stares into my eyes, narrowing her own in skepticism. "Was that your way of shutting me up? Are you trying to tell me there's no way in hell you'll hire me for anything but—" she glances pointedly down at my hips, "—*this*."

"No." I place both hands at the sides of her head, my gaze boring into hers. "That was my way of telling you I'd rather talk about this another time. That I've missed you so much in the last forty-eight hours..." I press my forehead against hers and shut my eyes, hating how this vulnerability makes me want to sink into her and never come out again. "I need you right now."

When I'm brave enough to open my eyes and look up at her face, I finally see what I've been searching for all evening. Her eyes are wide and full of tenderness. "I need you, too."

Her words light a fire in me. I reach for the hem of her tank top and try to pull it upward. I fumble around for a moment before I notice my hands are shaking. I look at her sternly and pat her on the ass. "Take off your clothes. Now."

She grins, wrinkling her nose. "Yes, Sir. Are you going to spank me if I make you wait too long?"

"I'm not playing. I can't be gentle right now. If you don't take off all your clothes in ten seconds, I'll rip them off." I narrow my eyes. "That's a promise."

She giggles as she slips from my lap and stands in front of me, pulling her tank top slowly over her head. "I love it when you're like this, boss." Her eyelids grow heavy as she peels down her yoga pants, revealing her long, beautiful legs. "Or should I call you Daddy?"

I reach out and slap her hard on her bare ass, the sound as crisp as a firecracker in my insulated studio. She squeals, but I've learned not to question it. I understand now that she likes it.

"Not Daddy," I say. "Not boss. Call me Camden."

"Camden?" Her nose wrinkles. "The 'den' feels so weird."

She hisses when I grab her by the waist and yank her between my legs. I take one of her nipples into my mouth and clamp my teeth down softly. As I pull away, I blow on the glistening skin. "Camden," I repeat. "Say it."

"Camden." Her voice is breathy. "Can you call *me* Daddy, then?" She lifts her legs onto the couch and straddles my lap, her lips forming a cheeky smile. "Please, Camden?"

"No." The word is sharp. I pull her neck to my mouth and take a bite. She shrieks and tries to pull away, so I squeeze her waist. When I tug at her skin with my teeth, she whimpers. "I don't want to play right now," I say against her neck. "Say my name, and I'll say yours."

"Okay," she whispers, and I can hear in her voice that she finally understands my mood. "Camden."

"Lauren." I whisper the word, and it feels like a plea.

Go easy on me, Lauren. Don't put me through what you did five years ago.

I press my lips against hers, slipping my tongue into her warm mouth. She matches my fervor, wildly rubbing her tongue against mine as she digs sharp fingernails into my scalp. Her frenzied pace reminds me that, in her mind, we're on a limited timeline. She's supposed to be out of my house in four months. I have no permanent claim on her.

The thought makes me want to burst out of my skin. Unable to wait a moment longer, I unbuckle my jeans and slip them down just far enough to free my cock. I grab her, pressing my thumbs against her sharp hipbones as I raise her into the air. I guide my cock inside her. She so wet already, I'm able to press her all the way down in one plunge.

"Camden," she says, and I'm so consumed by the beautiful whisper of my full name on her lips, the first swivel of her hips makes my eyes roll back into my head.

"Tell me you love me." The words leave my mouth as if they have a will of their own.

When her whole body grows still, my head jerks up. I

search her face for reluctance, but I find only surprise. Her eyes are wide and maybe a little fearful. I can't blame her for doubting me. Why wouldn't she be confused after all those times I've pushed her away?

I wish I could be sorry. I wish I weren't so selfish, but goddamn it, I'm scared. And I need reassurance before I leap over the edge with her. My eyes grow hard, my thumbs pressing into her skin. "Tell me, Lauren."

She swallows. "You know I love you."

The words crash over my body like a wave, and as they echo in my head, I feel like I've been swept out to sea. I've been waiting my whole life for her to say those words.

Nothing will ever be the same after tonight.

I pull her body against mine and squeeze her, wishing I could consume her. Wishing I could own her. Keep her locked away and never release her.

Wishing I never had to feel this skin-crawling uncertainty.

When she whimpers, I cover her mouth with mine, as if I can swallow the sound. She starts rocking faster and harder, and the pleasure that radiates through my body makes me hiss. I let her maintain the pace she needs to get herself off, but when she reaches a hand between our bodies and starts rubbing her clit, I grab her arm and yank it away.

"No, that's mine." I place my finger on her clit and flick up and down.

Her laugh sounds almost like a sob. "I love it when you say dom things like that."

I clench my jaw as a pleasurable wave radiates from my core to the tips of my fingers and toes. "I'm not playing."

"I know." The rasp of her voice tells me she's close to coming.

She presses both hands on the wall behind the couch, pulling her chest wide and exposing her beautiful tits. She starts rocking her hips rapidly, throwing her head back. Her eyes glaze over as her pussy clenches around my dick in pulses, and it's too much. My whole body grows taut with electricity, my hips jerking so hard I lift her into the air.

Minutes later, we're both still breathing heavily. Her head rests against my shoulder as I cradle her in my arms. I trail my fingers up and down her back. When her breathing grows rhythmic, I grab her shoulders and shake her. "Don't fall asleep. I'm not done with you."

She hums quietly. "It's your fault I'm sleepy."

I smile. "No way. You could always fall asleep anywhere. I don't think I've ever seen you watch a movie all the way through. You usually fell asleep in the first twenty minutes, or you're on your phone the whole time."

She sighs, a sweet little sound that I fear will echo on loop in my head in quiet moments if I don't make sure that she's mine for good. "I've just always had a hard time...being still. Do you know what I mean?"

I do, surprisingly. I know exactly what she means. It's why I started writing music.

"I don't like being alone with my thoughts," she says as she shifts from my lap, and I grunt when my dick slips out of her. "I don't like reflecting, to be honest. And I know this is a hot take, but I don't think anything good comes out of it. I think we always need to be moving forward."

The vulnerability in her tone tugs at me. I keep my voice hushed when I speak. "I tend to be the opposite of you. I fixate on my mistakes, and the mistakes of other people, and all it does is make me unhappy. It's not productive."

She snorts as she slips from the couch. After picking up her tank top, she pulls it over her head. "If I dwelled on my mistakes, I'd fucking kill myself."

Rage flares so suddenly that the world around me starts to

buzz, and I have to keep myself from reaching out and grabbing her. I don't care that her tone was light. I don't care that she didn't mean it. "Don't you ever say anything like that again. That's a fucking awful thing to say, and I'll throw your ass out of my house if I ever hear it again."

She glances up as she slips on her yoga pants, her expression utterly incredulous. "Jesus. I didn't mean it literally."

"I don't care. It fucking pisses me off."

"Oh, chill out."

Her dismissiveness makes my heart pound against my throat. "Your self-pity irritates the fuck out of me. You didn't have to make these mistakes. You're completely in control of what you do. You do it all deliberately because you can't stand it when people try to corner you."

Her nostrils flare. "Are you talking about you trying to control my every move?"

"No, I'm talking about how you think you have the right to behave like a child because you have a parent who's hard on you. We all have our shit. I've been terrified my brother is dead multiple times. I'm always waiting to hear the bad news, but it doesn't give me an excuse to treat other people like shit."

"Excuse me?" She grits her teeth. "I don't just have a parent who's hard on me. I have a vindictive, miserable bitch who constantly reminds me of my worst mistakes. And I've made mistakes. I've been really careless with Cadence…" Her voice breaks, her eyes widening as if she's surprised by her own rising emotion.

Guilt washes over me suddenly. I reach out and pull her close. She lets me cradle her in my arms, but then again, maybe she's still so bewildered by her emotions that she's forgotten she's mad at me.

"I'm sorry," I whisper against her hair.

"When Cadence was a year and a half, I fell asleep in the bathtub with her."

I force my body to go very still, not wanting to spook her out of what she's about to tell me. I get the feeling she wouldn't be telling me at all if she hadn't been caught off guard.

"I wasn't drunk," she says, and I detect some defensiveness in her tone. "I know that's what you're thinking."

"No, it's not."

"But I was hungover." Her voice sounds faraway. "I used to take baths with her all the time back then. It seemed easier because she always wanted to stay in there forever playing with her little water toys, and I'd get so bored sitting on the toilet waiting for her. But I really shouldn't have done it that time. I had just gotten home from a seriously wild Vegas weekend. I mean, like constant drunkenness kind of weekend. It was the first time I partied after I had her, and I went all out. I vaguely remember letting a random guy go down on me in a hot tub. God, he was so old, too."

My jaw clenches with that familiar jealousy. It shows how irrational it is, that I would feel it even in a moment like this, but for some reason, I can never seem to help it. Thankfully, she's too lost in her head to notice how my body stiffened.

"When I got home, all I wanted to do was sleep, but of course, my mom wanted to punish me because she had been stalking my Instagram the whole weekend. I know because she viewed every single one of my stories. So she basically dumped Cadence off on me and disappeared into her bedroom..."

When she trails off, I know she's in the past right now, because I've been there, too. Those heart-stopping moments when I found Hunter on the floor or with his head facedown on a couch are so vivid that I can even smell the stale, sweaty stench of vodka radiating from his skin.

When I stroke my finger along her cheek, she resumes talking, her voice hushed. "I never thought I would fall asleep. I really didn't..."

"Of course you didn't."

"No, but... I should have known, because I'm always falling asleep—like you were saying—especially since I became a mom. And this time I was seriously exhausted."

"No one ever thinks something like that will happen."

"It was almost like blacking out when you're drunk. One minute I was sitting there watching Cadence splash around in the water, and the next I was jerking awake at the sound of my mom yelling. She told me we had been in the bathroom for an hour—" Her voice is choked.

I tighten my hold around her, stroking the side of her arm with my thumb.

"I knew she wasn't exaggerating because the water was cold." She shivers. "I'll never forget that part of it. It makes me sick to my stomach, because I can't stop myself from imagining..."

Her little inhale is so unsteady, she must be either crying or trying to stop herself from crying. "Don't think about that. Nothing happened. Cadence was fine."

"She was crying because she couldn't get out of the tub, and I didn't hear her. I kept sleeping."

When I hear the first sob, a chill runs through my whole body. I haven't heard her cry since she was a little girl. I graze my lips over the top of her head.

"I think she still remembers," Lauren says. "I think she does subconsciously. And she'll never really trust me."

"That's crazy, and I think you know it. People don't remember things from that early in life."

She shakes her head vehemently, and I feel it against my chest. "Maybe we don't have any conscious memories, but I think experiences like that stay with us. There's no way she could forget a betrayal like that."

I keep my voice very soft, not wanting to sound condescending. "I think you're speaking more for yourself than for her. I think you can't forget it, and you're projecting those feelings on to her. That little girl adores you. And she fully trusts you."

"How do you know?"

The hope in her voice—her unflinching trust in my opinion —makes my pulse speed up. A lot is riding on my answer. This is an opportunity to prove my value to her. I take a deep breath before speaking.

"Hunter never liked it when my parents went out of town. When he was really little, I mean. He would cry and cry, and I remember, even as a seven-year-old, being perplexed by it. I remember thinking it was almost like he was worried they wouldn't come back. Or he didn't trust them to leave us with people who would treat us well."

"And?" Her tone is skeptical, but I still sense that she's eager to be convinced.

"And I think I was right about that. I don't think Hunter trusts our parents, even now, and it's because, as much as they love him, they've never known how to give him what he needs. Once I got a little older, and I mean not even much older, like maybe eight or nine, it was like he suddenly replaced my parents with me. If he was sad or scared, he would come to me instead of them."

"I always noticed that."

"It's because I knew how to meet his needs. I knew how to make him feel safe." My eyes bore into hers. "And that's exactly what you do with Cadence. That confidence she has in herself —the way she'll tell you what she thinks, as if her opinions are as valid as any adult's—that comes from you. You listen to her. You validate her."

She nods slowly, her brows drawing together. "I don't know if I can take credit for that. I think that's all her." The ghost of a smile touches her lips. "Sometimes I think I got really lucky. I don't know what I would do if I had a shitty kid. I think I'd be a terrible mom. Do you remember the other twins on our block? From like ten years ago? Callum and Connor? One time I caught Callum throwing rocks at a stray cat. God, he was a fucking psychopath. I'll bet he's in jail now. And Connor whined all the time. I'd be a really shitty mom if they were my kids."

After I kiss her head, I smile against her hair, the soft strands tickling my lips. "I don't think that's true. I think you'd rise to the occasion, but she is a pretty amazing little girl."

For the first time, she looks up at me. Her cheeks are glistening since she hasn't bothered to wipe her tears away.

"You're really sweet to Cadence. I never thought you'd be so nice."

"She's a great kid. She reminds me so much of you at that age." I smile. "She thinks she knows everything."

When I lift my hand and tuck a strand of hair behind her ear, a small smile tugs at her lips. "I never thought you would like kids, since you don't like people."

"I don't normally, but I adore her." My eyes grow unfocused as an inchoate thought starts to form—something that sparked the day I found Cadence in my kitchen and has been steadily growing beneath the surface ever since. "I think some primitive part of my brain knows she isn't just any other kid."

The moment the words escape my lips, certainty fills me. Certainty I've never felt before, not even on that day I took Lauren to Denny's and made my accusation. A strange exhilaration rushes through my veins, something akin to victory.

A notch forms between her brows. "What do you mean?"

I settle hard eyes on her face, my nostrils flaring. "You know what I mean."

When her gaze darts from mine, I grab her chin and force her to look at me. "She really is my daughter, isn't she?"

TWENTY

Lauren

A COLD SHIVER runs down my spine. I shut my eyes for a moment to collect myself, taking a deep breath in through my nose and releasing it slowly out of my mouth. When I finally feel like I have control over myself, I lift my head and meet his gaze. "It's much more likely that Ryder is her biological father."

"According to the DNA test, right? The DNA test you told me you got? The results came back and said it's *much more likely* that Ryder is her biological father?"

His sarcasm makes me want to shrink into myself. He's again hard, controlling Cam, and it makes me ache for the tenderness of moments ago, when he held me against his chest and all but forced me to accept that I'm a wonderful mother. But now he wants something, and that makes him ruthless.

I raise my chin, forcing myself to stare at him without flinching. "I never got it done."

He shakes his head. "I can't believe you lied to me. Do you have any integrity at all? This is a big fucking deal, Lauren. I may have lost four whole years of *my daughter's* life." His dark eyes look almost hateful, and it makes the last few magical hours we spent together feel like a fading dream. "You're reckless and careless."

His words make my skin prickle with apprehension. It's a visceral reaction I can't help after so many years of hearing similar things from my mother. I know Cam isn't a monster. I know he wouldn't threaten to take her away from me, but coparenting with him might be difficult.

Especially if we lose this harmony between us.

I narrow my eyes on his face. "I was eighteen fucking years old, and you were a complete asshole to me. You had already cut me out of your life by the time I found out I was pregnant. Is it really so hard to understand why I was more inclined to believe she belonged to someone who cared about me? Someone who was ecstatic about having a baby even after I had broken his heart a few months before?"

He opens his mouth as if he wants to argue with me, but then his face shutters. "But you didn't know for sure that he was her father, and you didn't even give me a chance."

"No, but it was so much more likely she was Ryder's. I had sex with him multiple times that month..." I'm surprised when he flinches, as if the thought is unpalatable. How the hell could he be jealous of my high school boyfriend after all these years? "And only once with you. But either way, I don't care about DNA. I'm an IVF baby. If it were up to nature, Logan and I wouldn't even exist. What makes a father has nothing to do with biology. Ryder is her father, and he's a good one."

Cam's eyes grow a little bewildered. "And I wouldn't be a good father?"

When I hesitate, the hurt look only grows, and it makes something twinge in my chest. I soften my voice. "It's not that. It's just... Everything was so complicated between us back then. And..."

"And what?" His look is eager, probing, which means my next words are very important. I don't know how to tell him the truth without hurting him. "I didn't think you would want her. You were so invested in the band. You moved across the whole fucking country. I was sure if you found out I was having your baby, you would feel like she was this huge burden, dragging you back to your boring hometown. And even back then—even when she was a little thing growing in my belly—I hurt for her. It hurt me to think of her having a parent who didn't really want her."

"Well, I do want her." He stares down at me, his face growing hard. "We're getting that DNA test done. Tomorrow, if I can arrange it."

"No, we're not." I lower my chin. "And if you think you can scare me into doing it by taking me into your lawyer's fancy office, think again. I've researched the hell out of this. You have no rights, even if she really is yours biologically. You can't make me do anything."

He huffs, shaking his head. "I can't believe you. How could you do this to me? How could you do this to her? You might be keeping her real father away from her."

The hurt in his voice compels me to place my hand on his. Surprisingly, he doesn't pull it away. "It's because of her that I'm putting my foot down. Think of how confusing this will be at her age. How would we even explain it in a way that she could understand? She loves Ryder. He's her daddy..." I swallow when my throat grows tight. "You've become part of her life, and she's bonding with you, but she still doesn't really know you. I can't suddenly tell her you're her real father. That would rock her little world."

I can see all over his face that he doesn't agree. "It would only rock her world because of *your* irresponsibility. If you had done the right thing years ago, we wouldn't be in this predicament." His eyes narrow. "Think of everything I could have given her. Think of the life she could have had."

The implication that I haven't given her enough makes rage flare through my veins, making me almost dizzy. "She's never gone without!" My mouth snaps shut when I realize I shouted in his face. I make an effort to soften my voice. "I've been getting help from my parents—even when it meant living with my asshole of a mother—so I could give Cadence everything you and I had growing up."

"And I didn't even start thinking she might *possibly* be yours until very recently, like the last few months. How would you have reacted if I called you up three months ago and said, 'Hey, Cam, remember when you asked me if Cadence might be your baby, way back before you had money? Well, now that you're a multimillionaire and I'm still living with my parents, I think we should finally get that DNA test.' What would you have done?" I can't keep the accusation out of my voice.

He stares at me for a moment before speaking. "We'll never know, will we?" His voice is hauntingly soft, and it makes my skin prickle.

He leans back into the couch, shaking his head absently. He looks so lost I want to reach out and touch him.

Was I a coward? Was I so terrified of his rejection that I'd willfully ignored the possibility that he might actually want her and be a good father?

But then a long-forgotten memory rises to the surface. The look in his eyes as he grabbed me by the forearm and dragged me out of that laundry room, and what he said to me afterward...

"You repulse me."

I had every reason to fear his rejection.

"This isn't over," he says, snapping me out of my daze. "Don't think I'll let this go. It changes everything."

TWENTY-ONE

Lauren

"CAN I GET YOU ANYTHING ELSE?"

When I glance up from my iPad, I see the pretty flight attendant staring at Cam. His eyes are glued to his phone, and he doesn't respond.

I would laugh if I weren't so emotionally exhausted. At least the flight attendant is getting the same treatment I have for the last week. He's barely said a word.

And he hasn't touched me once.

I'm surprised he let me come to Omaha for this concert, but lately he's hardly let me out of his sight, even though it seems like he can't stand my presence. I wish I weren't so crushed by his coldness. I know he's hurting, and with each passing day, I'm more convinced this isn't an attempt to quench his righteous indignation.

He really wants to be Cadence's father.

I told him a few days ago that we could ease him into a

fatherly role. He can start taking her on ice-cream and park dates. They can spend time together just the two of them, and let her get used to the idea that he could be *a* father to her. Not *the* father. But my offer clearly wasn't enough for him. He turned around and walked out of the kitchen without saying a word. And for the last few days, he's been cold, distant, and hollow-eyed when he looks at me.

"While you're here," I say to the flight attendant, desperate for a distraction, "I'll take another champagne." I pick up my half-full glass and guzzle it down before handing it to her. "To save you the trip."

"You have to get a glass," I say to Cam as she walks away. "I think it's actually good champagne."

"No, it's not." His eyes are fixed on his phone as he types what looks like an email. "It's the ten-dollar shit you get at the grocery store."

I shoot him a bright, sarcastic smile he doesn't see. When he has spoken to me this past week, he's been the old Cam—stiff and judgmental—and now that I've experienced his warmth, the absence of it feels that much colder. I'd almost forgotten that this is how he used to treat me all the time. "Well, it tastes good to me."

"Because you don't have any idea what you're talking about. You'd never even tried real champagne until a month ago, and you said it was bitter."

"Are you sure I wasn't referring to the company?"

Cam whips around to face me. "Can you stop talking please? I'm trying to write an email, and your nasally voice is distracting me."

"Sure." I plant a tight smile on my face. When I see the flight attendant coming our way with a champagne flute in her hand, I turn to him. "Let's order you a drink. You need some-thing to help you...not be a complete fucking asshole."

His mouth quirks slightly at the corners, like it usually does when I insult him, but he doesn't look the least bit sorry. "Cheap champagne won't help, and besides, I never drink when I'm around Hunter."

A notch forms between my brows as his meaning registers. I glance up at the back of Hunter's head two aisles up. He's so still, and my heart clenches at the sight of it. I never even thought about how he must hate to fly now that he's sober. He's never liked cramped spaces. He never even really enjoyed clubs unless he was wasted.

"Shit," I mumble.

As the flight attendant starts to hand me my champagne, I send her an apologetic look. "I actually decided I don't want it. I'm so sorry for being annoying." I glance pointedly at the glass. "You should just down it when no one is looking."

"Oh, it's not a problem." She smiles politely as she turns around and walks down the aisle. I don't look at Cam, but I sense his gaze on my face.

"You didn't have to do that." His voice is softer than it's been all week. "The no-drinking rule is my own thing—something I decided when he first went to rehab—but you don't have to worry about it. Hunter is around people who drink all the time. He can't help it in our industry. He'll be fine if you have some champagne."

"I don't need it." I shrug, keeping my eyes on my phone as I absently check my YouTube notifications, not wanting to show him how much his softening makes me feel warm and fuzzy.

I refuse to feel this way.

I refuse to gobble up his crumbs of affection. Impulsively, I unbuckle my belt and launch from my seat.

"Where are you going?" The apprehension in his voice is a balm to my frazzled, insecure nerves.

"To pee. And then I'm going to sit by Hunter."

"Don't do that. You'll have to trade seats with Jeff. He'll want to talk. I don't feel like making conversation right now."

"Well, I *do* feel like making conversation. With someone who's not going to ask me to stop talking."

As I start to walk, he grabs my wrist. When I look back at him, his eyes are pleading. "I'm sorry I've been such a dick. Don't ditch me, please. I like having you next to me, even when we aren't talking." His brows draw together. "You calm me."

I fight the warmth rising to my chest. "I think you mean especially when I'm not talking...with my *nasally* voice."

He flinches. "I'm really sorry I said that. You can talk all you want. I like hearing you talk, even when I need to work." He stares at me for a beat. "Please stay with me."

The desperation in his voice tugs at me, but I can't give in after I've worked so hard to resist him. I smile softly. "I just want to hang out with Hunter for a little bit, and then I'll come right back."

His jaw stiffens, but he nods.

After peeing in the cramped bathroom, I make my way to Hunter. He glances up from his phone, his golden-brown eyes lighting up. "You need a break?" He turns to Jeff, who has his eyes shut. "Can you do Lauren and me a favor and go sit by Mr. Sunshine?"

Jeff's eyes pop open. He glances at me and then back at Hunter, and then his whole face falls. "He won't like that. He'll feel like I took Lauren away from him, and he'll take it out on me."

"Well, Lauren's put in her time, and she needs a break. It's your turn. Keep napping, and he'll be happy."

"No, he won't. He's going to be an asshole to me for the next three days. At least," Jeff says.

Hunter frowns. "How is that any different than normal?"

"I already told him I'm forcing you to switch. He knows it's my fault." I pout. "Can you do this for me? We have a few hours at the hotel before rehearsal. That gives me enough time to make him forget all about it." I wink.

Jeff groans as he unbuckles his seatbelt. "If he's still an asshole tonight, I'm blaming you, Lauren."

As Jeff starts plodding down the aisle, I glance back at Cam, and even though I can barely see his expression as he stares at his phone, I can feel his annoyance all the way from over here. It's almost satisfying.

I plop on the seat next to Hunter. "Does it suck having to fly and not being able to drink?"

He smiles faintly. "It does, but I'm getting used to it. I used to get so hammered on our flights—especially when they were international. I'd be so wrecked afterward, I couldn't perform without muscle relaxers, which made my hands sluggish, so I used to play pretty shittily. Cam hated it."

My brow furrows. "He says he doesn't drink when he's around you."

Hunter's smile doesn't reach his eyes. "Isn't he so responsible? What a great guy."

I glare at him. "He *is* a great guy. What the fuck is this? Why are you so mad at him all the time?"

He rolls his eyes. "Because he isn't *not* drinking because he loves me. He thinks by being a self-righteous prick, he can shame me into never relapsing again."

I can't only stare at him, stunned by the venom behind his words.

Hunter rolls his eyes. "Don't look at me like that. I love him to death. I'm just done with his bullshit." His jaw grows hard. "I won't put up with it anymore."

I set my hand on his. "I know he can be tough with his controlling ways, but it never used to bother you this much. You used to joke about it. What's changed between you guys?"

He shakes his head slowly. "I don't know. I've been seeing things differently since I've been sober this time around. I realized something when he cancelled the tour. He didn't let me have any part in that decision. He wouldn't even hear me out." His jaw hardens. "He loves me, but he doesn't respect me, and I'm fucking sick of it. You of all people should understand."

"Are you saying he loves but doesn't respect *me?*"

"Of course. It's how he is with everyone he loves..." He keeps talking, something about how Cam has a god complex, but I hardly hear him.

He's right.

He's absolutely right.

I've always had Cam's love, even on that beautiful, miserable night five years ago. That's why he was so upset over what I did with Hunter, even though I didn't owe him fidelity. That's why he's spent so much money to have me do so little for him these past few months. That's why he's treated me with so much tenderness.

But I've never had his respect.

I've craved it desperately. Craved it enough to fear his rejection as if it might burn my skin if I got too close. Enough to form an invisible wall around myself.

"Do you think he would be a good father?" The words are out before I have a chance to think about what I'm asking.

Hunter's jaw drops. He stares at me for a full five seconds before speaking. "Holy shit, are you pregnant?" His gaze immediately drops to my stomach.

"No... Sorry, that was out of nowhere. But... I think Cam wants to be a father to Cadence. And I think I should let him. Along with Ryder I mean."

"I wouldn't, Lauren."

His answer is so sudden it startles me. "Why not?"

"I think he's probably looking for a way to keep tabs on you after your six months are up."

"No, I really don't think it's that. You haven't seen him with Cadence these last few months, and there's something I never told you before about my pregnancy..."

Hunter stares at me for a moment before grimacing. "Jesus Christ. She's not his kid, is she?"

"No, no... I mean, I don't think so, but she could be."

"But you said you were positive she was Ryder's. I think your exact words were 'I'm one-hundred percent sure'."

A shameful heat creeps up my neck. "I was more like ninety-five percent sure, or... I don't know. Maybe I was scared. But it's not about that. I don't care about biology. I really don't. Cam wants to be a father to her, and I'll let him, because I think it's the right thing to do. She can have two fathers."

Hunter's concerned expression fades, and he looks at me with urgency. "Just be careful. You don't want him to have leverage over you. When you need him for something, Cam can be fucking terrifying, especially if he ever feels like you crossed him."

I wish I could dismiss his words, but he's right. Even with all the kindness and affection Cam has shown me these past few months, he's ruthless when he wants something.

How can I do what's best for my little girl and still protect my own heart?

TWENTY-TWO

Camden

"CAM," she calls from the hotel bedroom. "I want to talk to you about something."

I have to keep myself from running to her. Everything rides on her decision, and she knows it. I already contacted Chris earlier this week, and while family law isn't his expertise, he knows enough to know I don't have a shot in hell. Even with the best family lawyer in the state of California, I wouldn't be able force a paternity test. With Ryder's name on Cadence's birth certificate and the fact that he's had joint custody almost since she was born, I have nothing.

And all the while I can't stop thinking about how this little girl might really be my daughter. I don't know how to feel. I love her. I know this aching tenderness—this desire to be close to her, to care for her—must be love because it's so similar to what I feel for Hunter. Yet I don't really know Cadence. I don't know her the way a father should know his four-year-old daughter. And I can't be sure if this gut instinct that she's mine is real or just another twisted excuse to keep her mother close.

I hate this itching uncertainty. I hate being adrift.

I take a deep breath before setting my guitar down and walking toward the bedroom. Apprehension churns my stomach, making me resent Lauren that much more when I finally walk inside and catch sight of her placid expression. She has no reason to be anxious.

Not when she holds all the cards.

Her gaze roams my face, and whatever she sees makes her calm expression grow ever so slightly wary. "I decided you can be Cadence's father."

The relief that descends over me makes me dizzy. My eyelids grow heavy, and my body sways forward.

"*One of* her father's, I mean, and we're not getting a DNA test. And we're going to have to ease into this whole thing, because it's a big change for her. I've already thought about how we might explain it to her without having to...you know, tell her Mommy was a ho." A faint smile twinges her lips, but when I don't return it, it quickly fades. "I was thinking we can tell her how all families are different. You know, the usual story that some families have two mommies, some have one mommy and one daddy, some have one mommy and two daddies."

"But that's not true in this case."

"What do you mean?"

I walk in her direction, my expression growing harder with each step. "I mean, she has one father in this case. We just don't know who it is."

Something that looks like fear flashes in her eyes, but it's quickly gone. "I'm not going to jump into getting a DNA test. It's not fair to Cadence. Would you want to know if your dad —the man who raised you your whole life—wasn't your biological father? I wouldn't, and I'd be really upset if someone took that choice from me. This needs to be her decision."

My eyes narrow. "She's four years old."

"Right." Her nostrils flare. "So it's going to be a long time before we'll know what she wants to do. And you'll need to be okay with that."

She looks up at me with those big green eyes, and somehow, even with the hardness in her voice, the rigidity of her spine, and those willowy arms crossed over her chest, she's never looked more vulnerable in all the years I've known her. My throat grows tight.

She's scared.

For all of her insistence on knowing her rights, she's terrified of me, because she knows I could fuck her. Maybe not with the law, but with money. I have it, and she needs it. And I could use it to manipulate her. But if I did, I'd have nothing left.

I'd lose her forever.

"I can respect that." My voice is soft.

Her eyes widen at first and then narrow on my face, as if she's not sure she believes me. "So you'll be okay never knowing for sure, if that's her choice?"

"No," I answer right away, and she looks even more skeptical. "But I understand your reasoning. I can see..." It's hard to admit this, because once I do, I can never take it back. "I can see how it might be harmful to Cadence...to find out that Ryder isn't her biological father."

"Yes." Lauren nods vigorously. My answer seems to have increased her confidence. "We need to put her first."

I nod slowly. On impulse, I reach out and graze her cheek with my hand. "You're a good mother."

When she presses her face against my hand, I rub my thumb across her cheekbone. "You've said that so many times since we started this thing," she says. "I don't know if I'd ever heard anyone else say it before."

"It's the absolute truth. Lauren." My throat grows tight, and I'm not sure if I'm brave enough to say more. But I have to. There's no other way.

"I want to revisit the discussion about maybe...not ending this after six months."

"You do?"

I clear my throat. "Yes."

She narrows her eyes. "Because of Cadence?"

I lift my other hand to her chin and hold her face. "No." My tone is firm. "Not because of that. I've been thinking about this for a while, but I can't..." I glance at the clock on the wall. "I can't talk about it right now. I have to leave in fifteen minutes for rehearsal."

My gaze returns to her face, and hope rises behind her eyes.

"We'll talk about it tonight." My tone is firm.

I WROTE a love song when I was sixteen.

It was every bit as melodramatic and sappy as you'd expect from a teenage boy who considered himself cursed by unrequited love, which makes it that much more embarrassing when I remember playing it at San Diego coffee shops with almost brazen earnestness.

It's a terrible song, like most of what I wrote back then. The lyrics are flowery, the melody simplistic and derivative, and yet it's the most honest thing I've ever written. It's maybe the one time in my life I was brave enough to accept my feelings as they were and turn an unfiltered version of them into music.

I knew I loved her back then. It was only after she broke my heart that I tried to rationalize it away.

Both Hunter and Janie's mouths drop open when I tell them I want to add my sappy song to our setlist for tonight. And even as I sense their cringes while we rehearse it, even as I want to cringe myself, I know it's the right decision.

It's time to finally be honest with myself.

It's time to finally be honest with her.

"I'll show you my tits, Camden Hayes!" Lauren shouts from backstage a few hours later, and warmth rushes through me. God, I love how ridiculous she is.

I'm surprised I'm even able to make the words out. The roar of the crowd is so loud, I can barely hear my own thoughts. But in these last few months, I've become attuned to her every move.

"Lauren." It's Jeff's irritated voice. "Don't make him laugh."

"He's not laughing."

"He's smiling. That's the same as laughing for him. It means his attention is over here, and he needs to engage with the audience."

When I lift up my guitar, the roar grows so loud my ears start to ring, but I can still hear her voice.

"I'll let you come on my face, Camden Hayes!"

I gasp out a laugh, and even though I'm standing three feet from the mic, the sound resonates through the arena.

"Goddamn it, Lauren," Jeff says. "I'm about ready to ban you from being out here. Why don't you go ask Jade to make you a cocktail? She can make you a pure vodka, extra dirty martini. Come back after you've found your chill."

"Alright fine," she says.

"No!" I shout.

Lauren twirls around, her eyes wide, and Jeff's face falls.

"I want her out here."

When her eyes fill with hope, I'm propelled away from the

mic. As I walk in her direction, I know what I'm going to do, even if I'm not quite ready.

It's time.

No more procrastinating.

"I want you out here every time we play," I say, and I'm immediately rewarded for it. Her smile grows, lighting her whole face, and something clicks into place in my chest. Something I've known since we were children, but never admitted aloud.

"You make me feel..."

Her eyes grow even wider, shining with a mixture of anticipation and hope. Oh God, I can't fuck this up. I have to tell her the truth, no matter how hard it is to say. No matter how it might irreparably change everything.

"Like..." I shut my eyes tightly, struggling to find the words.

"Cam, you need to get back out there," Jeff says.

When I shoot him the look of death, his face doesn't change. He's long accustomed to my surliness, but then a warm hand touches my shoulder, and I instantly relax.

"Don't be mean to him," Lauren says. "He's absolutely right. You can tell me after the show."

"No. I need to tell you now," I say. "You feel like home."

Her eyes widen.

"And I've never understood it, because you also drive me insane, especially when I'm away from you, but when I'm in your presence, my mind goes quiet, and I feel... I don't know... Warm and happy. It only happens with you, and I think I've been chasing that feeling ever since we were kids. I think it's why I've never been able to let go of you, even after everything that happened." My voice quavers. "I love you."

She looks stunned, and I know I should turn around and get back on stage. If I wait here, she'll feel pressured to say the words back, and I want her to really mean them. I don't want it to be like last time when I all but begged her to say them. But I find I can't move.

Her daze clears. "I love you, too," she says, and my head grows heavy, my eyelids nearly falling shut.

"And I want to be with you for real," she says. "And you do, too, and we need to talk about it. We need to finally talk about everything, even what went down that night."

Even in my euphoria, I can't fight the gnawing anxiety creeping into the back of my mind. I've avoided thoughts about that night for so long, I've grown to fear them.

"You're right," I say, because there's no other way. "We can talk about it tonight. Talk about everything."

"Alright." She squeezes my arm and pushes me in the direction of the stage. "We can do that, but you need to go back out there so your fans don't hate you. I don't want you to lose your career." She smiles lazily, lifting a single brow. "I want to be able to keep spending your money, boss."

As quick as I can, I grab her by waist and press my lips against hers. At first, her kiss is all fire, but then her pace begins to slow, and I can feel all the tenderness she just confessed in the languorous movement of her tongue. By the time I make it back to the mic, I hardly hear the crowd. I'm too exhilarated.

"What's up, Omaha?" A wide grin spreads across my face. "Normally I'd insult you, but I'm in too good of a mood right now. My apologies."

In my periphery, I see both Hunter and Janie's heads snap in my direction. I can't see their faces, but I sense their shock.

I grin at the crowd as I lift my guitar. "Okay, this is a really old one. I wrote it for the girl next door."

"I SAW you dancing a little bit backstage," I say as I turn out of the venue parking lot. "You seemed to like the song."

"I loved it. I can't believe a sixteen-year-old wrote it. It was really beautiful, and I'm not just saying that because it was about me." Out of the corner of my eye, I see her smile. "I noticed it didn't have the banjo in it."

I smile. "I would never insult you like that."

I reach my hand across the center console and set it on her lap. She slips her little hand underneath my palm and interlocks her fingers with mine. We sit in silence for the rest of the drive, and I know she feels it, too.

The future is overwhelming.

When we pull up to the hotel lobby, I turn to her. "I have to go meet with Jeff about something and...think about some things before we talk." When apprehension flashes in her eyes, I give her hand a tight squeeze. "Nothing bad."

Her hand softens in my grip, as if she's reassured. Still, she lifts her other hand and tucks a strand of hair behind her ears, a sign of lingering nervousness. "What kind of things?"

I exhale heavily. "The night we had sex for the first time. The whole thing is really hard for me to think about, let alone talk about. I don't think I've ever talked to anyone about it except Janie, and that was right after it happened. Since then, I've pushed it as far away as I could. It's so... God." I take a deep breath. "Lauren, what I said to you after we had sex... It was reprehensible, and I deserved everything I got for it."

"I wouldn't say you deserved everything you got." Her voice is soft.

"No, I did, and I've been blaming you for years for something that deep down I know was my fault. The whole thing is so painful for me. What I said... What you did..." I shake my head. "All I can think about is how it could have been different."

Her gaze is fixed on our joined hands. "It wasn't all your fault. I definitely overreacted, like I always do, but..." She lifts her gaze to meet mine. "Why did you slut shame me?"

"Oh God." I look away from her, unable to bear her reaction, knowing my excuse is going to sound that much more paltry and childish when I put it into words. "I'm not trying to justify what I said. I hope you realize that. I'm only trying to explain what my idiot twenty-year-old brain was thinking..." I shut my eyes, shaking my head. "I was upset because... In a way, I had kind of..." I lower my voice. "Saved myself for you."

"You mean, like, your virginity?"

Her voice is so full of disbelief, I can't help but smile, even as my palms sweat and my pulse pounds. "Yeah, I was a virgin."

When I'm finally able to look at her again, I see only surprise on her face. "Really?"

I smile faintly. "Really."

"We had sex in your car. I was straddling you. I can't believe that was your first time. You didn't seem inexperienced..." Her nose wrinkles. "I mean you did come pretty fast."

I gasp out a laugh. "I probably would have no matter what." I squeeze her hand. "Either way, it would have been my first time with you."

"So you really liked me a lot, huh?" The question is timid. "I mean...you wrote that song for me. You saved yourself."

I snort, shaking my head at the understatement of the century. *Liked her a lot.* "From the time I was about fourteen until the moment you straddled my lap, I thought about almost nothing but you. I thought about you every hour of the day. That's not an exaggeration."

Her pursed smile looks almost bashful, and my chest twinges. I'm not sure if I've ever seen her look this way. "I thought about you a lot, too. I kind of knew you were attracted to me, but I had no idea you wanted me that much."

I lean in closer. "It would have terrified you if you knew how much I wanted you."

All of her timidity fades. "I don't think so. I would have liked it."

My throat grows tight. "I wish I had just told you. I wish I wasn't always such an asshole."

She frowns. "Why were you an asshole when you wanted me so much?"

The answer once felt so complicated, but it's strangely simple now. "Because you owned me, and I resented you for it. I don't like it when...my life feels out of control."

Her brow furrows. "It doesn't feel out of control anymore, does it?"

"It feels more out of control than ever." When she starts to look hesitant, I give her hand a reassuring squeeze. "But I'm starting to think it's worth it."

She looks like she wants to say more, but instead, she smiles warmly and exits the car. My pulse finally starts to slow as I watch her walk into the hotel lobby. I meant those words. Her power over me is terrifying, but there's nothing to be done about it.

I need her.

If she destroys me again, so be it.

TWENTY-THREE

Lauren

MY PHONE RINGS.

Camden must have finished his meeting early. My stomach flips as I leap for the bedside table and grab my phone, but when I see the name, my buoyant mood deflates.

Hunter.

My brow furrows, a shapeless fear rising at the back of my mind. Hunter never calls me this late at night. I pick up the call, unable to keep the apprehension out of my voice as I ask, "What's up?"

"Hey, love."

My anxiety eases a bit at the lightness in his voice, but something is off. He sounds different than he did an hour ago when we left the concert venue.

"Is everything okay?"

"Of course it is."

My anxiety grows. The words were enunciated too slow and clearly, the consonants too precise...

He's drunk and trying hard to sound like he isn't. Now that I've had a moment to think, I recognize the ambient noise in the background—the muffled conversation and occasional shouts—and my stomach twists. "Are you at a bar?"

There's a pause. "Where's Camden? Is he right next to you?"

My brow furrows. "No, he had a meeting with Jeff. Why?"

He's silent for a moment, and when he speaks again, his words are thick and slushy, the earlier effort to sound sober now a distant memory. "Perfect. That's just perfect. I want you to come out with me."

"Oh, no." I say the words mostly to myself.

"Oh, yes." I hear a smile in his voice.

"Where are you? I'm picking you up."

"No. You're coming out. We're dancing tonight."

I sigh heavily. "Hunter, where are you? Tell me now."

"That's my bossy girl." He chuckles, and the sound gives me chills. I've grown to hate the sound of his laughter when he's drunk. It's so oddly foreign—high pitched and nasally—completely unlike his real laughter. "I'm at the diviest dive bar in all of Nebraska. You would seriously love this place. It reminds me of that bar we used to go to in high school—the one in Banker's Hill that never used to card. I think I'm the only person here under the age of sixty."

"Just tell me where you are." I wince after I say it. Sternness is the wrong approach with him right now.

"Only on one condition."

Changing tactics, I soften my voice. "Okay?"

"Number one, you can't tell Cam I'm here, and number two, you have to promise to have a drink with me."

My eyelids flutter. "So two conditions?"

"What?"

"You said you had one condition, but that was two."

He chuckles. "I didn't go to college. I can't do math. What do you say?"

"I say Camden's going to know where you are because he has your phone location."

"He told you about that?" Hunter makes a deep grunt at the back of his throat. "Well, I turned it off before I took the Uber out here, so he won't find me."

"He's going to notice you turned it off." My heart aches for Cam. After what he confessed several weeks ago, I can only imagine the panic he'll feel the moment he notices Hunter turned it off. He may even be feeling it already. But I can't think about that now. "Alright, give me the name of the bar."

After he tells me, I launch from my seat, repeating the name under my breath as I walk to the chair and grab the hideous neon-pink snow jacket Cam had Brayden buy me before this trip.

I need to get to this place as soon as possible. I can't trust Hunter's word that he'll stay at the bar. Nothing he says is reliable when he's in this state. Depending on the company he meets, he could disappear before I even get there.

"Okay, I'll be there ASAP. Do not—I repeat—do not leave that bar. Don't even get up from your seat."

"What if I have to pee?"

"Pee your pants."

He cackles, a high-pitched, artificial sound that pulls up cloudy memories—the pressure of his arms around my shoulders as I tried to carry him out of clubs when I was wasted myself. God, I'm so glad I don't do that shit anymore.

The drive to the bar is interminable, every stoplight feeling like an opportunity for Hunter to slip away. And it's agony keeping Cam in the dark. What if he's back at the hotel already, wondering where I am? I ought to just call him and tell him everything. Hunter probably won't even remember that I promised him I wouldn't, but for some reason, I can't bring myself to do it. Maybe it's because I'm dreading his reaction.

He's going to be devastated.

As we pull into the small parking lot, I turn to the Uber driver. "Can you wait a minute? I want to make sure he's still here."

He nods, and I practically leap out of the car and run to the entrance. I halt in place when I take in the sight in front of me. "What the fuck, Hunter?" I say to myself.

The building is so old and poorly maintained that it almost looks abandoned. If not for the murmur of voices coming from the doorway and the abundance of wet cigarette butts all over the icy concrete, I might actually think that it was.

When I press open the wooden door, my nose is assaulted by stale cigarette smoke mixed with even staler sweat. It takes me no time at all to find Hunter, and immediately my shoulders relax.

When I march over to him, a lazy smile spreads across his face. Thankfully, he doesn't have that faraway look that comes with pills and alcohol, which fills me with determination to get him back to the hotel.

As soon as I get close, Hunter yanks me against his chest, pressing his cheek to my head. "I'm so happy you came."

I shove him back. "Well, I'm not."

He hesitates for a moment, his heavy-lidded gaze roaming my face before a little pout settles on his lips. "Don't be grumpy. I promise tonight will be fun. Just look at this dive." He gestures around the area. "Isn't it amazing?"

I frown. "No, it's not. It's beyond a dive bar. It's a my-life-is-in-the-toilet bar. An I'm-drinking-here-because-I-have-nothing-left-to-live-for bar."

A slow smile spreads over his face. "You'll like it better in a second. Wait till you try one of their drinks. They're like pure alcohol and only four bucks. God, I love the Midwest."

I scowl at him. "What do I look like to you? Seventeen years old with my first fake ID? For the last two months, I've been drinking French wine from your brother's cellar. I'm not getting one of their nasty drinks." I glance around the area. "Someone will probably slip a roofie in it."

My phone chimes, and my stomach sinks. When I pull it from my purse and flash the screen, I find exactly what I feared.

Cam: Where did you go?

"Shit," I mumble.

"What?" Hunter asks.

"Cam is asking where I went. He must be back at the hotel."

"Ignore it."

I lift my head, glaring incredulously. "Do you know your brother at all? He'll probably send like four hundred more. And then he'll call the police."

"God, he's a psychopath," he says under his breath. "I don't know... Tell him you went out to get tampons."

I roll my eyes. It's a sign of how drunk he is that he thinks there's a chance in hell he can pull off our little night out without his brother finding out. "We have sex regularly. He knows I'm not on my period, and anyway I'm not lying to him."

His eyes grow hard. "Well, you promised me you wouldn't tell him where we are. Were you lying to me?"

I huff, shaking my head. "Don't pull that shit with me. I didn't promise I'd point blank lie to him."

"If you make up an excuse, I promise I'll only have one more drink, and then we can go back to the hotel together. But if you tell him where we are, I'm calling my own Uber and finding another bar."

When I narrow my eyes, he smiles lazily, and it makes me want to hit him. "I fucking hate you right now."

His smile widens. "It's your choice, babe."

I shake my head as I lift up my phone. My stomach sinks as I think of plausible excuses. Ultimately, I send something I know will lead to more questions, but at least I feel like less of a liar.

Me: Just stepped out for a bit. Be back soon.

After setting my phone down on the bar, I jab a finger in Hunter's face. "You only ever pull shit like this when you're drunk."

His smile widens. "Yep. Because I'm more fun when I'm drunk."

"No, you're not. You're annoying and manipulative and whiney... And you're even mean when you're really drunk. I'll have one drink with you because I promised, but after that, I'm never drinking with you again. Not ever. Not even when you try to bullshit me by saying things like you've been sober for six months, so it's okay if you have a beer now."

His smile vanishes. "So you've become just like him, huh?"

I roll my eyes at his drunken melodrama. Even given his recent anger at Cam, he would never say something like that sober.

"No, it's okay," he says, his tone biting. "I knew it would happen eventually. I knew once he brought you over to his side, you'd become a judgmental bitch just like him."

I raise my hand in the air and gesture at the bartender. "Make me an extra-dirty martini. As a matter of fact, give me straight vodka and an olive."

Hunter claps his hands, and I wince at the sound. I'm not in the mood for this. I want to be back in my hotel bed, waiting for Cam to come home so we can finally start our new relationship.

"That's my girl," Hunter says. "Let's get you good and drunk."

I turn sharply toward him. "No! I didn't order that for you. I ordered it for me, because if I hear one more second of your whining, I'll literally throw up right here on this bar."

His smile stays fixed, though it no longer meets his eyes.

"You have a brother who loves you like crazy, and he's going to be devastated when he finds out about this. Think about how you're breaking his heart when you order your next drink."

The smile fades, and his usually warm eyes grow cold. "When did you become such a cunt?"

Rage flares so suddenly that I have to keep myself from reaching out and slapping his face. "Call me a cunt one more time, Hunter. Do it! I dare you." I grit my teeth, shoving my face forward until it's inches from his. Hunter is so startled he jerks his head back. "I'm only here because you're an absolute shitshow when you binge. You'll probably pass out in the snow when they kick your wasted ass out at closing time, and I'm not going to risk that. But if you keep calling me names and whining like a self-pitying little bitch, I will beat your ass down to the ground, and I'll enjoy it!" My face is so strained, it feels like my forehead might burst open.

But the angry high fades quickly, and I wish I could suck the words back in. Why do I lash out like this?

Thankfully, his eyes no longer look hurt like they did a moment ago. He almost looks dazed. "Shit," he mumbles. "You're really pissed off."

I exhale, plopping down on the stool next to him. "Yes." My throat so tight I can barely get the word out. "I love you, but I hate you when you're like this." Now my voice is completely choked, and belatedly I realize that tears are rolling down my cheeks. "Shit," I whisper, lifting my hands and wiping under my eyes with the pads of my fingers.

"Aww, honey."

When his arms wrap around my waist and his chin rest on my shoulder, I relax into him. But then my dirty martini is set in front of me, and I stiffen, my stomach sinking with shame. Here I am drinking pure vodka at a slimy dive bar in Omaha with a recovering alcoholic.

What a disaster.

"Uh-oh," Hunter says. "Looks like we have company."

TWENTY-FOUR

Camden

WHY IS SHE AT A BAR?

Even more alarming, why didn't she tell me she went to a bar? Why did she say she stepped out for a bit? The questions repeat over and over again in my mind as I drive down the dark country road.

Checking her location has become a habit. It's a comfort to know where she is. And most of the time, she's exactly where I'd expect her to be. In my house. At her parents'. Or in our hotel.

But not this time.

And what peculiar timing when we just had one of the most important discussions of our relationship. If our situations were reversed, if she told me she needed time to think about our future, I'd be at this moment pacing the hotel room floor waiting for her to get back.

What does it mean? Did she get cold feet?

Logic tells me I'm jumping to conclusions. I'm always assuming the worst. I've done this with Hunter, too. Any time something seems even slightly off with him, I imagine only the bleakest scenarios. Finding him facedown on a hotel-room floor or getting a sobbing phone call from my mom or opening the door and seeing a morose-looking police officer on the other side of it. Ninety-nine percent of the time the truth is far less grim.

I needed to get away to think. Maybe she did, too. But that doesn't sound like Lauren. By her own admission, she doesn't like to reflect. She doesn't think anything good comes out of it.

Waiting is hell, an unbearable anxiety that makes my skin hot and my stomach sick. I know it well after so many agonizing hours after Hunter disappeared, dreading the state he'd be in when I finally found him. Out of survival, I've learned how to disconnect from my fear. To exist in a meditative state of mindfulness.

Mostly.

With effort, I take a deep breath. The flat, endless road ahead. The smooth steering wheel, now damp from my clammy hands. The prickling heat at the back of my neck. The coldness at the pit of my stomach. Before I know it, I'm standing in front of a bar. The queasiness in my stomach makes it hard to breathe. Somehow, I know in my gut that when I enter this place, everything will change between us.

My gaze finds her the moment I walk through the door, and the sight of her has the usual calming effect, but it's short-lived. When I process the full sight in front of me, my body grows so stiff I can barely move. Hunter steps behind her and wraps his arms around her shoulders. Her green eyes are bright and glistening, and she sits with...

A martini in front of her.

I shut my eyes tightly, forcing myself to breathe deeply.

She's here with Hunter.

He's relapsing. And she's with him.

Not only that. She covered for him.

She lied to me.

When I finally feel like I have a handle on myself, I open my eyes and run my gaze over Hunter. I can tell in an instant that he's drunk. His eyes are hooded, and even his smallest movements are sluggish. He's only been sober eighty-three days, and he's drinking again. And she's his accomplice.

God, is possible to die of a broken heart?

As I walk in their direction, a guilty expression flashes in Lauren's eyes. I look away, unable to stand the sight of her. "What the fuck are you doing?" I ask Hunter

"Having a drink with my girl." Hunter's voice is both light and shrill, as if he's trying to pull off levity but can't muster it. "How the fuck did you find us?"

"I have your phone location."

He narrows his eyes. "I turned it off."

I hold his stare, though my cheeks warm. She's going to find out. She's going to know that I've been tracking her location behind her back. Though I suppose it doesn't matter.

It's over between us.

"Cam, I'm sorry I didn't tell you where we went." I must be feeling nostalgic already, because her sweet voice floats through me, warming my insides even when I can't stand the sight of her.

"Hunter made me promise." She sets her soft hand on my arm, and I keep my gaze on Hunter, still unable to look at her. "He said he'd have only one drink, and then we could leave..."

I'm about to snap. About to tell her to shut her fucking mouth, about to ask her what kind of person takes a recovering alcoholic out for a drink when Hunter steps forward.

"Stop talking about me like I'm not even here, like I'm your fucking kid. I'm so sick of this shit."

My eyes pop open, and I pin Hunter with a hard stare. "Then maybe you should stop acting like a fucking kid."

A cynical smile spreads over his mouth. "Don't act like you don't like it. You know you like that I'm a fucking mess—that I have no life skills—because it means you get to take care of me. You get to keep tabs on me and tell me what to do. You like having me at your mercy." He nods in Lauren's direction. "Just like you like having her at your mercy."

I force myself to look at her, and her big green eyes are pleading. She's protecting Hunter, and the coldness that runs through my veins sends a shiver down my spine.

"Go get in the car, Hunter." My eyes are fixed on Lauren.

"Don't fucking tell me what to do."

"Go now." My voice drops to a low rumble. "I need to talk to Lauren."

Hunter must catch the threat in my voice. He looks like he's about to leave, but then he hesitates. "Don't blame her." For the first time all night, he sounds like the real Hunter. "She only came out because I made her."

"Go."

His face falls. "Fine, I'll go." He lifts a plastic cup from the bar top. "I'm taking this with me for the drive."

"Enjoy it. It will be your last. You're calling Dave the second we get back to the hotel. And you'll be sleeping in my hotel room tonight."

Hunter sighs heavily as he walks away, and I take a step closer to Lauren, staring down at her in cold silence. "This is over."

She jerks back as if I hit her. As those long, beaded earrings flutter like frightened birds around her jawline, the faintest pang of regret punctures my cold rage. But I can't let it soften me.

"I'm taking you to the airport now. When you get back to San Diego, I want you to start packing immediately. I'll be back tomorrow evening, and I want you out by then. Do you understand?"

Her expression is blank, as if in she's in shock, but then her eyes start gathering moisture. When my first instinct is to reach out and pull her against my chest, all the air leaves my lungs in an instant.

This is what it feels like to be given what you've always wanted, and lose it.

To lose what you've always loved.

But I can't think about that now. I can't let anything steer me from my purpose.

I look down at her, about to tell her she won't be able to sway my decision, when she startles me.

"Yes, I understand." Her face is a placid mask. "Let's go."

LAUREN

HIS EYES WIDEN MINUTELY, as if he was expecting me to argue with him. We stare at each other for several unending seconds.

He doesn't trust me.

He doesn't respect me.

I hold his stare, not wanting him to see how my heart is shattering, how the pain in my chest has grown so tight I can hardly breathe. I knew he'd be upset by my text, but I never anticipated this. I never understood the depth of his mistrust until this moment.

Oh God, why does this have to hurt so much? Why does it have to make me feel so small and worthless? He thinks I'm a child. A wild, reckless child, like the eighteen-year-old girl who dragged his brother into a laundry room and shattered any hope of a future between us. He'll never let it go.

There's no hope for us.

I'm pulled out of my head when Cam's eyes drift to my right. A slight, humorless smile rises to his lips. "So I guess the no-champagne thing this morning was something you did for show?"

My stomach stirs with sickness. Was my stupid martini the culprit? Maybe he would have made the correct assumption if he hadn't seen this drink. Maybe he would have guessed the real reason behind my evasive text...

But no.

It wouldn't have mattered.

He's predisposed to think the worst of me. Just like he was five years ago. Even after I begged him to believe that I wouldn't have actually had sex with Hunter. That I was coming to my senses right before he found us. That I only dragged Hunter into that room in the first place because I was desolate and hurt. He didn't believe me then, like he doesn't believe me now. Because he doesn't trust me, and it's not fucking fair.

I glance down at my drink, and that familiar rage courses through my veins, that malicious thrill that makes my belly flip over with giddiness even in my despair.

What would he do if I picked up that drink and downed it in one gulp?

My stomach plummets.

I can't do this anymore.

I stand up from my barstool and drift past him, willing my lips to stop quivering.

Don't cry, Lauren. Wait until the airport, at least.

When we get into the car, Hunter is already snoring, and it's a relief. I couldn't bear it if he came to my defense right now. It would be too much. I'd lose this weak grip on my emotions and fully break down.

After slamming the driver's side door, Cam hands me his phone. The United app is already up. "Don't worry about the cost," he says. "Just get the soonest flight you can. I want you to have plenty of time to pack."

My throat constricts at the ice in his voice. I scroll through the app, instinct drawing my eyes to the most expensive flights. Childish Lauren would click on the one that's over a thousand dollars more than all the others, probably because it leaves in an hour, but I refuse to do it. Instead, I reserve the one that leaves in the wee hours of the morning, even though the wait will be agony as I sit alone with my thoughts and my watery airport Bloody Mary. "You're being irrational," I say softly. "You'll realize it in the morning."

He doesn't respond, but his hands clench over the steering wheel, his knuckles growing almost white. The sight of it is satisfying. He may look and sound cold, but a molten rage is brewing underneath the ice.

"Did you even think about Cadence?" I ask. "Tomorrow is my day with her. Ryder is set to drop her off at your house in the evening. I'm going to have to tell her that she won't have her big room anymore. Without any warning."

"Of course I thought about her," he says, but I suspect he's lying. He's so myopic in his rage that all he sees is me. "And she'll still have her room. We're getting that DNA test. I won't pay off your student loans if you don't agree to get it done. You can try to call me out, say I'm breaking our agreement, but I consider what you did tonight infidelity. You lied to me. You took my alcoholic brother out to a bar."

My lips quiver, and I hold my breath to keep the sob from coming out. It's only when I feel the cold drop on my arm that I realize I already lost the battle.

"But if you get the DNA test, we'll call it a day. We both know she's mine. She looks more like me than Ryder. So we'll get the test and confirm it, and moving forward, we'll work out some kind of custody agreement. I'll even support you from here on out, assuming you can prove to me that you can be responsible enough—"

"You're out of your fucking mind if you think you can manipulate me like this."

The car goes quiet. Even Hunter has stopped snoring.

The words feel like they came from outside of me. Even as they echo in my head, they sound like someone else. Rage has made the world around me buzz, the ambient road noise sharp and crisp.

"I'll let you be a father to her. Like I said I would. But if you think you can use my student loans to get exactly what you want from me, think again. I'm not a stupid teenager anymore."

His nostrils flare, his jaw clenching. "Tonight proves otherwise."

The humorless laugh wrenched from my chest feels almost like a sob. "And what about you? What about you tracking my phone location without even telling me? I know that's what you did. I know that's how you knew where we were."

His expression doesn't change, though his jaw clenches.

"What in God's name is wrong with you? Do you really hate me this much? Why has it not occurred to you that I showed up at the bar tonight because I was worried about him?"

"That explains your martini, doesn't it?"

I flinch, but I refuse to cower. "Yeah, I shouldn't have ordered that. I shouldn't have let him manipulate me. I was pissed off and not thinking straight, but it still boggles my mind that you would think I came out here to party with him. What in my behavior these last few months would make you think I would do that?"

He opens his mouth but then closes it, and it feels like an eternity before he finally answers. "I saw him put his arms around you, and the way you—" His mouth snaps shut, but I can fill in the rest.

The way I leaned into his arms.

"Oh my God." My voice grows breathless from rising hope. "Is this about the laundry room? Are you... Are you jealous of Hunter? Because you know I only did that to lash out at you. You have to know that, right? I was hurt, and I do stupid things when I'm hurt. It's never been like that between Hunter and me. We're almost like brother and sister. I mean, he did used to try to kiss me sometimes when he was drunk, and sometimes I'd let him just because—"

"Jesus Christ, stop talking!"

I flinch, realizing the euphoria of hope is making my tongue loose.

"Cam." I try to adopt a reasonable tone. "If this is about jealousy, we can work through it. At first I thought you were blaming me for his relapse—"

"This isn't about jealousy." His tone is almost bored. "This is about the conditions of your employment. What you did tonight was a betrayal. Maybe not a physical betrayal, although..." He huffs out a humorless laugh, but it doesn't sound right. It's too brittle, almost like a cry. "Who knows with you?"

"You *are* jealous." I grunt, turning away and shaking my head. "You're acting like you caught me fucking him."

I'm startled when he pulls off to the side of the road and slams on the breaks. He whips around to face me. "You mean caught you fucking him *again*, right? And if I hadn't caught you guys tonight when I did, you would have fucked him. Just like you would have fucked him five years ago!"

He's shouting now, and I welcome it. This is the rage that I knew was there all along, and it feels so much better than his icy contempt.

"I know you. I know you better than anyone. You may not have set out to fuck him, but you would have. If you had enough to drink. Or if you got a text from me that made you angry. Or if we got in a fight..." He looks away, his eyes growing unfocused. "Maybe not tonight, maybe not even him, but something like that would happen eventually..."

He looks so lost right now. His unseeing eyes are intently focused on the steering wheel. Impulsively, I reach out and touch his face. He flinches in surprise, but he doesn't pull away.

"I love you," I say.

His head snaps in my direction, his eyes wide and dazed. He looks like a trapped animal, not knowing which way to run. But then cynicism enters his eyes as he yanks away from my touch.

"You don't have to worry about your two-hundred grand. I'll give it to you either way. I'm not that much of a monster that I'd deprive the mother of my child of her income."

"I didn't say I love you because I'm worried about the money. I said it because I'm sick of being childish. I'm twenty-three years old, and I think I'm finally growing up."

He grunts. "I'll believe that when I see it."

"You won't see it, because I'll be out of your life."

An emotion flashes in his eyes. Something that almost looks like fear.

"And that's for the best," I say.

He clenches his jaw so tightly it looks like it might snap in two. "Glad you recognize that."

I nod slowly. "I do. All my life I've craved respect and validation from people who withhold it from me—people like you and my mom. I resent it, and I haven't dealt with that resentment very well. I've done some childish things, but I'm done with all that. I don't need your respect or your trust. Not if you aren't willing to give it to me freely. I won't jump through hoops to earn it." When I place a hand on his arm, he flinches. "Tomorrow, you're going to realize what a stupid mistake you've made."

His nostrils flare. "I won't."

"You will, and when you call me, I won't answer." I pull away from him, settling back into my seat. "Just go ahead and get me to the airport. My flight leaves in a few hours. I'd like to get at least some sleep."

His eyebrows shoot to his forehead. "You booked it already?"

I only nod, and the bewildered look in his eyes makes me wonder if somewhere deep down he'd hoped I wouldn't do it. That I'd be childish Lauren, throw a tantrum and refuse to do his bidding. He really will regret this tomorrow, maybe even sooner. But it doesn't matter.

By then, I'll be gone.

TWENTY-FIVE

Camden

MY GAZE STAYS FIXED on her retreating back as she saunters through the wide automatic door. When she finally disappears from sight, it feels like the whole world went with her and I'm the biggest sap who ever lived, because I would take it all back. Even after everything, I'd take it all back and live in this constant state of uncertainty, never knowing what to expect from her, if it meant I could keep her close.

And here I was thinking I really loved her.

This isn't love. It's obsession—the need to make her mine at all costs. The need to keep her entirely to myself because I could never trust her enough to let her roam free.

If this is love, I'm a masochist.

I nearly leap out of the car the moment I pull into the hotel parking lot, and the icy air hits my lungs. When I open the back door of the car, I give Hunter a pat on the face, realizing only after the fact that it was harder than I'd intended and I'd nearly slapped him.

Shit. I need to get my temper under control. This isn't his fault.

After another pat on the cheek, Hunter's eyes pop open. "Shit." His voice is breathless. "We're here already? Did I fall asleep?"

I roll my eyes. "No, you've been awake the whole time. We teleported from the bar to the hotel."

He blinks a few times before jerking up and glancing around, seeming to absorb our surroundings. "Where's Lauren?" The apprehension in his voice tells me he can probably guess.

"I dropped her off at the airport."

His gaze snaps to my face. "She's supposed to fly out with us tomorrow."

And her suitcase is still sitting in our hotel room, while she's probably at this moment sleeping on an airport bench.

My throat grows tight at my lack of forethought.

"I decided to send her home a little early."

"You blamed her," he mumbles and then laughs—a shrill, humorless chuckle that sends a chill down my spine. "You blamed her like you always blame everyone except me."

He jumps out of the car, startling me by grabbing me by the shoulders. "Have you not learned a goddamn thing? Is your little Al-Anon group thing just something you do so you can look like the responsible brother?"

I stare at him dumbly, unable to believe that he's asking me this.

"No one can make me do anything. How do you still not understand that? She only came out because she was worried about me. And I blackmailed her into sending that text. I told her I'd stay out and drink more if she didn't." He narrows his eyes, shaking his head. "It never even occurred to me I'd get her in trouble. I thought you had more sense than that."

A cold sickness settles over me. "It's not about that. She—" I swallow. "She and I have a lot of issues. This has been building for a long time. It's for the best."

It's true. So why does my stomach sink with the weight of my injustice? I had an inkling she was telling the truth in the car. It does seem unlike her recent behavior to go out and party with a relapsing addict.

So why was it my first assumption?

"You're a fucking control freak. I'm so sick of it. You can't stand it when other people aren't perfect. People like me and Lauren. You try to force us to be something that's acceptable to you. That's not love, Cam. Love is unconditional. I should be able to expect that from you as your fucking flesh and blood."

My mouth drops open. "Is that what you really think?" I take a step in his direction. "I *do* love you unconditionally, and if I'm a control freak, it's because I'm fucking worried all the time. Do you have any idea what that's like? I love you so much it's fucking torture, because I'm constantly worried I'm going to lose you. I worry about you like it's my job. I worry about you as if worrying about you will protect you from harm. Like if I worry enough, the universe will understand that nothing can ever happen to you. That I would die..." When my voice cracks, I take a deep, shaky breath.

Hunter's eyes are saucers. "Shit," he mumbles. I'm startled when he spreads his arms open wide and wraps them around me, squeezing tightly. "I'm sorry," he says against my shoulder. "I'm sorry I'm such a fucking mess. That I've been such a shitty brother to you."

I wrap my arms around his shoulders and press my cheek against his head, like I used to when he was little. "You haven't been a shitty brother. I wish you didn't struggle so much. I wish it were me. I wish I could take away your addiction and make it mine."

"No, don't say that. I need you the way you are. I need you strong and together. You're my rock. You always have been."

Moisture gathers in my eyes. "I'm sorry I'm such a controlling prick."

He pats me hard on the back before pulling away. "Don't apologize for it. I understand why you do it, but you got to let go. I know it's hard, but you've got to do it. I need to start figuring out my own shit. You have no idea what it's like for me. I know I have an amazing life—getting to do what we do —and I'm not trying to be annoying and complain, but the only reason I have any of it is because of you. And that feels really shitty. I feel like a fucking baby. Sometimes it's like..." He shakes his head, his eyes growing unfocused. "It seriously feels like I've been in a coma for the last several years, like everyone around me has moved forward, and I'm still a teenager. It's such a shitty feeling. It makes me want to drink."

I step forward, setting my hand on his shoulder. "You need to go call your sponsor. Right now. I'll even fly him out here tomorrow morning if you want."

A knowing smile forms on his lips, and heat creeps into my cheeks. "Shit, I'm sorry. I don't mean to be like this, I promise. It's a reflex."

His smile grows. "Take it one day at a time."

I shut my eyes, nodding.

"With Lauren too"

My eyes pop open. "What do you mean?"

"Obviously, you need to work on letting go with her, too."

I avert my eyes from his. "It's different with her. She's proven she's not trustworthy." When shame for my earlier behavior makes my skin prickle, I clarify. "In the past, I mean."

He sighs heavily. "Why is it always on her? Why haven't you ever blamed me?"

"You were so drunk you didn't even know what you were doing."

His smile grows piteous. "I'm not only talking about that night at the party. I'm talking about my whole relationship with her. I know you've always been jealous of how close we are."

"That's not true."

"It is." He sets his hand on my shoulder. "And it's okay. You love her. And it's totally reasonable for you to want to keep me away from her, because to be honest, if I were drunk enough, I probably would fuck her. Even now."

When I flinch, he presses his thumb into my collarbone. "And you ought to be mad at me for that."

"You're only responsible for that first drink."

He makes a deep grunting sound at the back of his throat. "Stop treating me like a baby. I'm a grown ass man. And I was a grown-ass man when I almost fucked her in the laundry room..." I try to pull away, but his grip tightens. "Why haven't you ever tried to talk to me about it? Why is this the first time?"

I shut my eyes. "It was easier... And you didn't know..."

"Easier to blame her," he fills in. "And I *did* know. I knew you had a crush on her. I think I maybe even liked your jealousy a little bit. I always felt like you had everything—you were smarter and better at school, and way better at guitar than me—and I liked having something you didn't."

"I don't like talking about this."

He chuckles. "I know, but we have to. Cam, look at me."

With effort, I force my eyes to meet his. Surprisingly, there's not an ounce of resentment in them. I hated myself for my petty jealousy. I pushed it deep down as if it could sever the bond between us if I ever let it rise to the surface. And he knew all along.

"You need to start treating me like an adult. Let me make my own decisions. Let me spend my money on stupid shit. Let me drink myself to death..."

When I wince, his grip on my shoulder softens.

"And if I almost fuck your girl in a laundry room, punch me in the face for it."

"I don't want to talk about this."

His smile is a little sad, but then he abruptly pulls me in for a hug, giving me a hard pat on the back afterward. "One day at a time, big brother."

TWENTY-SIX

Lauren

HUMANS ARE RESILIENT.

My heart is shattered, and yet here I just packed up an entire bedroom in less than an hour. And I didn't cry once. Not even when I found the LED light Cam had apparently bought and set up in my usual video room. Or the *Frozen Castle* he bought Cadence.

I grit my teeth, willing the tension in my throat to go away. I can't think about this now. I need to keep moving.

I thought we were going to have to move right back in to my parents' house, which felt like a prison sentence. Not only would I have to deal with my mom's I-told-you-so smugness over the demise of my relationship with Camden, but I'd also be a couple hundred feet away from his parents' house. I'd be in danger of seeing him while I'm still fragile. I almost cried out of gratitude when Armaan offered us an alternative.

Together, we arranged a two-week vacation at his parents' beach house in Corona Del Mar, where we'd do nothing but strategize a social media plan for his new company and take Cadence on beach picnics. It will be a nice distraction.

Just as I shove the last high heel into a black garbage bag, my phone rings. My skin prickles when I think of who might be calling. I've yet to hear from Cam.

When I see Ryder's name, I lift the phone to my face, unsure if the slowing of my pulse is from relief or disappointment. "What's up?"

"I'm around the corner."

I release an exhausted sigh. "I'm not quite done, and I don't want Cadence to see my empty room. Take her to my parents' house, and I'll pick her up later."

He doesn't say anything at first, and I hear the static murmur of road noise through his Bluetooth speaker. "Do you want me to beat him up?" he eventually asks.

I throw my head back, smiling to myself even as my lips quiver. "Tempting, but I'd rather he suffer emotionally."

"And he will." His voice is soft. "You're one in a million, Lauren. If I could have married you—"

I grimace. "Honey, I've had a rough twenty-four hours. Please don't make me feel sorry for you."

He chuckles. "Alright. I'm already on my way to your parents'. Take all the time you need."

MY ARMS and legs feel leaden as I walk through the door of my parents' house. My mom is curt and stiff when I greet her, but there's nothing new about that. It's not until I drop off the last garbage bag of clothes that I realize this is beyond her normal bitchiness.

"Where are you taking my granddaughter?" Her tone is full of accusation.

I roll my eyes before I turn around and face her. "What did Ryder tell you?"

She places both hands on her hips. "He told me you're going out of town for the next several weeks. *Several* weeks, Lauren? How can you uproot her life like that? What kind of mother are you?"

The question makes me grow still, sending a surge of rage from my scalp to the tips of my fingers and toes, electrifying my whole body, clenching my hands into fists.

It almost feels good, like a high. Wow. This is it, I guess. I should have known it would all come back to Helen.

It surprisingly doesn't take that much effort to speak calmly. "I'm not putting her in danger, so there's no reason to lose your shit. I'm staying with a friend for a bit because I need some time to myself. Cadence will be fine."

My explanation clearly doesn't appease her. Her jaw clenches as she steps closer to me. "You're probably whoring yourself with some new guy now that Cam doesn't want you anymore."

My jaw falls open. It's by far the nastiest thing she's ever said to me, and yet somehow, against all odds, I don't feel like lashing out. I don't feel the high that normally rushes through my veins. Instead, I pity her because I'm able to really look at her, and I don't think I ever could before. I was too in my head. Too consumed by my own hurt. But I see those wide, darting eyes. She's afraid.

I take a deep breath before speaking. "Mom, I need space from you. I'm leaving."

"You will not take that little girl with you. I promise you, I'll call CPS."

The words don't even hurt this time. They just sound...

absurd. What does she think CPS will do? Take my daughter away from me because I plan to take her out of town for a few weeks?

"Don't worry," I say. "You'll see her again soon. I love her, and although I have my faults, I'm not selfish enough to punish her because I'm mad at you. She loves you and Dad. She'd be sad if we were away too long. But I really do need this time away from you, and I need you to respect that. Cadence is coming with me because she's my daughter, and that's what's best for her."

Her jaw ticks. "I don't know about that."

It doesn't even take effort to keep my eyes from rolling. "You do, though. You know it's not good for her to be away from her mother. She's with me most of the time. I'm her *stability*. You've said that before."

She crosses her arms across her chest. "How can you call yourself her stability when you might have another wild night in Vegas and fall asleep in the bathtub with her?"

I stare at her in silence, stunned that the words don't hurt this time. What's happened? How did that memory lose its hold over me? Maybe I see it now for what it is—her last resort, her final bargaining chip that she pulls out only in moments of absolute desperation.

And she's lost it.

"This is exactly why I need time away from you. You know that day is a big source of guilt for me. You know it haunts me. And the fact that you would say something so cruel to control me shows how immature you are, and I'm not going to play your bullshit games with you anymore. When you've had time to cool down, you'll realize ultimately that's what's best for Cadence."

Her tiny nostrils on her perfect little button nose flare. She looks like she wants to stamp her feet like a child. Later—I hope —she'll reflect on this moment and see how much I've grown. Maybe she'll feel at least a small measure of relief, even if it's only for Cadence's benefit. But even if she doesn't, I don't care.

Not anymore.

TWENTY-SEVEN

Camden

ONE DAY AT A TIME. I can live without trust, as long as I take it one day at a time.

The moment I step inside our house, I inhale deeply. It smells like her, as it has since she first moved in. I love the way she smells. I love coming home to it.

I love coming home to her.

I booked an earlier flight, because an apology like this needs to be in person. I could hardly sit still the whole flight home. There was a nagging fear that she might already be gone by the time I get there, but that's not her style. She'll probably raid my wine collection first. She's probably at this moment in the cellar, her phone in front of her face as she tries to figure out the most expensive bottle I have.

I carry my suitcase through the foyer, smiling to myself like an idiot. Good God, I'm excited to see her. It's been less than twelve hours since we last saw each other and I was an absolute bastard to her, and I'm still excited to see her.

Just as I brush past the living room, my smile vanishes. I know something in my gut that my brain can't quite understand yet.

She isn't here.

I turn around and scan the living room, but everything looks as it should. The succulent she bought a few weeks ago to add color to my blah grays and beiges sits on the coffee table. The decorative blanket Cadence sometimes cuddles up with when she watches her YouTube shows rests over the edge of the couch armrest.

And then it occurs to me. Her tripod. She always keeps it right at the edge of the couch. Why would she have moved it when she has at least three others around the house?

The world around me starts to buzz as I rush from the living room and run up the staircase.

She has to be here. She couldn't have left already.

By the time I make it to her bedroom door, I already know what I'm going to find, but it doesn't stop me from hesitating at the threshold, closing my eyes and willing it not to be true. When I finally work up the courage, I throw open the door, and even though I already knew what I would see, the breath leaves my lungs in an instant.

She's gone.

There's not a trace of her. The room looks almost sterile. The bed's made, the floor and furniture surfaces clear. I ache for the sight of that pile of laundry on the chair by the window, or the tripod at the corner of the room, surrounded by abandoned makeup subscription boxes.

I walk to the bed as if in a dream, my vision blurred at the edges. I lower my hand and run my fingers over the tightly tucked blanket to make sure that it's real. She never used to make the bed. Her blankets stayed in a lumpy mess even when Cadence was gone and she stayed in my bedroom. The only time it looked like this was on Tuesdays and Saturdays after my cleaning service went through her room. I stare down at the bed, my stomach hollowing.

This is different than I thought it would be. This is a pain of my own making. Because I'm a masochist, I force myself to open her closet door, and it feels just like I thought it would. All the color is gone—those bright dresses and high heels and that sparkling jewelry tree. It's fitting, because all the color in my life left with her.

My spirits lift a little when I walk into Cadence's room and find it mostly as it was before, but the feeling is short-lived. The sight of her clothes still folded in her tiny dresser only confirms that this wasn't a childish act on Lauren's part. She didn't disappear without a trace to punish me. This isn't something she'll take back after she cools down. I'll still be a father to Cadence, like Lauren promised.

I just won't have Lauren.

God, I need a drink.

After downing three glasses of whiskey, I pick up my phone and call her, but I already know what to expect. It rings five times in a row before going to voicemail, and I have to hang up the moment her voice comes in. I'm unable to bear the sweet sound of it. I try to check her phone location, because I'm too miserable to listen to my conscience, and I find her name removed from my contact list.

After downing another glass, I decide I need a nap. I make my sluggish way to my bedroom, wishing I could sleep for the next month, that I could shut my brain off from the misery and wake up when it's already over. But it won't be a month. It will be much longer.

I rustle around in bed, spreading my arms and legs out,

trying to relish in the ability to do it. Lauren used to hog every inch of the bed when we slept together. Her long arms and legs would spread far and wide like a starfish. So many times, I'd wake up nearly falling off the bed.

I miss her already. I miss the warmth of her body next to mine, the sweet scent of shampoo lingering on her hair when it brushes my face, and the little sounds she makes when she's sleeping.

I frown when my hand brushes something hard and sharp under the blankets. I grab hold of it and lift it in front of my face. Even with the black-out shades pulled down, I can make out those dangling beads. When I rub the rounded glass with the pad of my thumb, my chest seizes. One of her dangling earrings. She probably left it in my bed the last time we had sex and slept with our limbs entangled.

I must be drunk, because I can't stop myself from pressing it against my lips.

TWENTY-EIGHT

Camden

TWO QUESTIONS COME TO MIND:

Will this rehearsal ever end? And is it possible to die from missing someone?

She's been gone two days, and already this ache in my chest has grown so tight I'm finding it hard to control my breathing while I sing. No matter what chords I play, every song is like a requiem to my ears, both subdued and achingly melancholy.

When I glance down at my fingers on the mandolin strings, I see her face in a flash. Her thick, dark brows drawn together. Her big green eyes fixed on my face.

"I literally wish the banjo could be outlawed."

When my voice cracks, I flinch. How could something so silly make me so profoundly sad? A sadness that's settled in my bones, as if I were born to feel it. As if I were destined to have her and lose her. Hunter's head snaps in my direction, and I look away to get a grip on myself.

Just get through the outro, and then you can walk out of here.

When the song is finally over, I exhale heavily. I glance around the studio to find Hunter's eyes locked on mine. His brows are drawn together. "You doing okay?" he asks.

I sigh. "No."

He nods faintly because he already knows what a wreck I am. Normally, it would be Janie asking me what's wrong, but Hunter's taken on a new role these past few days. After he flew in Sunday night and had a long coffee date with Dave, he's barely left me out of his sight. It feels strange because I used to watch him like it was my job after a relapse. It's a relief to have our roles reversed.

"I think you should call her."

"I've called her at least a hundred times. She finally sent me a text that said we'll talk about custody soon, and that was it." When a thought occurs to me, my head jerks up. "Did she say something to you?"

"No." His tone is hesitant, wary, as if he knows I'm hanging on by a thread and doesn't want me to snap. "But she's very forgiving. I've fucked up a lot over the years, and she's never held a grudge."

I grunt. "I think it's a little easier to forgive an addict. I was dead sober when I accused her of taking my alcoholic brother out for drinks, and then..." I release a humorless chuckle. "Then I kicked her out of my house."

His lips part, but before he gets a chance to speak, my phone rings, and the sound of it vibrates in my bones. The mandolin thuds as I plop it onto the floor, and I sense both Hunter and Janie's surprise without even seeing their faces. I never handle my instruments this roughly. I rush to the corner couch and grab my phone, feeling nearly drunk from relief when I see the name.

Helen Henderson.

It's either Lauren calling from Helen's phone, or Helen calling about Lauren. The latter is less appealing, but I'll take it.

"Hi, Cam," Helen says after I pick up, and my stomach sinks only a little.

"What's up, Helen?" My tone is bright and welcoming, as if it's perfectly natural for her to call me. As if this isn't probably the first time since high school that I've spoken to her on the phone, but the hope in my heart must be sharpening my social skills.

"I know this is sort of awkward getting a call from me." She laughs lightly, and I don't even feel like rolling my eyes. I'd suffer through a lifetime of her flirtation if she tells me Lauren's been as much of a wreck as I have been these past few days.

"And I wouldn't do it," she says, "if I wasn't worried about Lauren."

I hate the smile that rises to my lips. I shouldn't be happy that Lauren's in pain, especially when I'm the one who caused it.

But goddamn, these last few days have been hell, and I ache to know that she feels it like I do, that she loves me as much as I love her.

"We were in a horrible fight on Sunday," Helen says. "And I haven't seen her since."

My whole body grows cold.

"What's wrong?" Hunter mouths to me, his eyes wide.

I wave him off, but his gaze stays fixed on my face. Out of the corner of my eye, I see Janie rest her cello on the stand and start walking in my direction.

"I know she moved out of your house a few days ago," Helen continues, "since she dumped off everything here. In trash bags, too. Her room looks like a junkyard."

I grit my teeth, inwardly begging her to get to the point.

"But you're my last resort. I don't know who else to call. She took Cadence with her, too, so of course both John and I are going crazy."

Now, my pulse is hammering. "Have you talked to Ryder?"

She sighs heavily. "Yes, and he says everything is fine, but I don't think he knows much more than we do. She told him she and Cadence would be out of town for a few weeks and promised to FaceTime him, and that was that." She lowers her voice. "Between you and me, she's run circles around that boy since they were teenagers."

I take a deep breath. This is nothing to worry about. She's probably visiting a friend. She's too responsible a mother to put her daughter at risk.

Our daughter.

"I'm worried because she can be so impulsive when she's angry. She does stupid things without thinking them through. You know her."

My stomach sinks. I *do* know her. I know that even being a wonderful mother, she's still impetuous. She can do wild, reckless things when provoked, especially when she feels trapped and judged. And what could make her feel more trapped and judged than what I did two days ago? Unbearable anxiety claws at my insides, and I'm seized with the need to act. I won't be able to rest until I know they're both safe.

"I'll find her," I say, my tone hard.

"You really don't have to do that. I got the idea you guys broke up when she came home Sunday night, but I was desperate, and that's why I gave you a call, but I don't want to put you out."

I roll my eyes, wondering how in the hell she could care about putting me out if she thought her daughter and granddaughter were missing. "Don't worry about it. I feel sort of responsible for her running off. She and I also got into a pretty terrible fight."

She chuckles humorlessly. "It's hard to *not* fight with her. She's so volatile all the time. Any little thing you say can set her off."

I grit my teeth, wanting to defend Lauren but knowing it won't do any good. "In this case, I said some pretty terrible things I didn't mean. I need to apologize and this will give me the chance. I'll find her."

"Cam, that's just so—"

"Which of her friends have you talked to?" I interrupt, not wanting to even hear a thank you from her, let alone respond to it.

"All of them, I think. At least the ones I know. No one has heard from her. Not even Logan."

Oh God, this is even worse than I thought. Of all the people in Lauren's life, I would expect Logan to know. Hell, I'd expect her to go stay with him, even if it meant flying all the way to Indiana.

"Okay, I need you to do something for me. I need you to send me a list of every friend Lauren's hung out with over the past year."

Helen doesn't seem to mind my high-handedness. We talk for another minute, and she gives me a few suggestions of who to call first. I promise her I'll contact her as soon as I hear something, and then we hang up.

"She skipped town, huh?" Hunter says, not sounding nearly as worried as he ought to be.

"With Cadence, too." I huff, shaking my head. "Goddamn her."

"She's justifiably angry." Hunter's tone is hard. "She probably needed to clear her head."

"I agree," Janie says. "You gave her less than twenty-four hours to vacate your house."

I exhale slowly. "I know. I'm just worried."

Hunter gives me a hard pat on the back. "I hate to be a dick, but you deserve it. You call her impulsive? You forced her to move back in with her parents when you know she has a shit relationship with her mom. That's the whole reason she wanted to move out in the first place. Of course she was going to run off."

The self-loathing that washes over me makes my stomach churn.

"I'm going to find them," I say, and I mean it with every fiber of my being.

TEN HOURS LATER, I'm knocking on a white wooden door, gripped by fear that no one will answer and I'll be left to freeze out here. Logan wouldn't give me a straight answer when I called him, which made me suspect he knows where Lauren and Cadence are and won't tell me.

Or maybe he's hiding them.

Maybe he's not, but once the suspicion took hold, I couldn't rest until I found out for sure. We have a concert in less than twelve hours in Anaheim, and I'm barely going to make it on time. If my flight home from Indiana is delayed by even an hour, I'll be late. But I don't care. I have to find them.

As I wait for the door to open, I reach into my pocket and feel around until my fingers hit the metal clasp. I run the pad of my thumb up and down over the small beads of her earring until my shoulders relax.

When the door opens, a petite, unsmiling girl with large brown eyes and heart-shaped lips stares steadily back at me.

"Lyla," I say, pretty sure—but not certain—that's the name of Logan's girlfriend. "Is Lauren here?"

She stares back at me with unblinking eyes, and I get the distinct impression she knows I'm going out of my mind and wants to extend my misery.

"Leilani," she says.

I exhale heavily. "Sorry. I never remember names because I hate people. In general, I mean. I'm not saying I hate you." I lift a nervous hand and run it through my hair, realizing that exhaustion is dulling my already weak interpersonal skills. The motion catches Leilani's attention. Something flashes in her eyes.

It looks like pity.

God, I must look like a train wreck. I haven't shaved in two days, and my five o'clock shadow is making my face itch so badly I've been scratching it constantly, which has likely turned my skin red and splotchy. I haven't even looked at my hair since I got the call from Helen, but I know it's a mess. I can feel it sticking up in places it shouldn't.

"I kind of hate people, too," Leilani says, a faint smile twinging her lips. "Most people. I have a few I like."

I smile back at her, and the feeling is unfamiliar on my lips after so many days of misery. "I only like five." My smile fades when longing grips me suddenly. "Six now, actually."

"Lauren isn't here." Logan's face appears in the doorway. "I already told you that."

Trying to get my temper under control, I take a deep breath. "I don't believe you."

Logan shrugs, an arrogant smirk tugging at his lips. "Believe it or not, it won't change the fact that she isn't here. Or that you flew across the country for nothing."

I stare at that smug, smiling face, wishing I could hit it.

There's no way in hell I flew here for nothing. I'll see Lauren and Cadence today if it's the last thing I do.

On impulse, I find myself barging through the door. I must have caught them both by surprise, because they immediately move out of my way and let me inside.

"Dude!" Logan shouts.

I ignore him, giving the living room a once over before rushing toward what looks like the entrance to the kitchen. My heart jumps into my throat when I catch sight of a brunette sitting at the table and holding a phone, but my stomach sinks almost immediately.

It's not Lauren.

"Well, hey there. Who are you, a stray mountain man looking for shelter from the cold? I'll keep you warm." As if a thought occurs to her, her eyes widen and her jaw pops open. "Oh shit! You're Camden Hayes, huh?"

"Dude!" It's Logan's voice behind me. "What the fuck do you think you're doing? This is my house. You don't know what kind of stuff Leilani and I are into." He points to the brunette. "Brenna could have been naked."

"And what a missed opportunity." Brenna winks at me. "Maybe next time."

Trying to capitalize on Brenna's good graces, I look at her probingly. "Is Lauren here?"

She looks to Logan and then back to me, wincing. "I don't think I'm allowed to say."

Her admission fills me with hope. I rush out of the kitchen and make my way down the hall. I throw open the next door I find, clearly the master bedroom—tidy and pristine with a tightly made bed. Definitely not my messy Lauren's room, but that doesn't mean she isn't hiding. I make my way to the master bathroom, and when I don't see her right away, I walk to the shower and open the glass door. My lunacy doesn't occur to me until I hear a deep chuckle behind me.

"Lani, come here," Logan says. "You've got to see this. Hurry!"

I turn around slowly. "Where is she?"

"Not in the shower." He holds out his phone, his eyes fixed on the screen. It takes my tired brain a second to realize he's taking a video. Strangely, I don't even care that I'm making a complete ass of myself, and that he now has footage of it. It's worth it to know with certainty that Lauren and Cadence aren't here.

Logan looks up from his phone. "I'm not sure where she is, but I do have a basement." He grins, but then his face becomes mockingly stoic. "You should probably check that, too. You know, to be thorough."

"Logan." Leilani's tone is scolding.

"She isn't here." She turns to Logan, glaring at him. "He's being an asshole."

Logan walks over to her and pulls her against his chest. "Give me this one moment," he says after kissing her hard on the cheek. "For Lauren's sake. I'm going to send all of this to her." He glances at me. "Let's go check out the basement."

When he raises his phone again, an idea occurs to me, but I don't want him to catch on, so I keep my head down as I follow him to the hallway. When we get to what looks like a closet door, he lifts the phone higher, which makes my heart race. He opens the door and gestures down at the concrete staircase. "Go ahead."

Keeping my eyes on the stairs, I walk steadily forward. As I make it to the threshold, I reach out and yank the phone from Logan's hand.

"What the fuck!" he shouts.

Not wasting a moment, I sprint to the front door and burst

outside of the house. While I run, I pull up his contact list and search for Lauren's name. As soon as I find it, I press the call button. Knowing Logan is on my tail, I throw open the door of my rental car and leap inside. After slamming the door, I press the lock button three times in a row to be safe.

Lauren picks up on the third ring. "What's up?" she says, and her high-pitched voice fills my body with an overwhelming warmth. I shut my eyes, relishing the sound of it.

Still, I have to keep my head. I know I can't properly mimic Logan's voice, so I don't even try. Instead, I keep my voice low. "The coast is clear," I say, hoping against all hope that she snuck out the back when she found out I was at the front door.

"What the fuck are you talking about?"

My heart sinks. She isn't here. But I can't let my disappointment get the better of me. I have to find out where she is. I wince when I hear pounding on the roof of my car.

"Lauren!" It's Logan's muffled shout. "Cam stole my phone! Hang up on him!"

"What the fuck is going on?" Lauren's voice is shrill.

Logan keeps pounding and shouting. Accepting that it's a losing battle, I give in. "It's Cam. I was worried about you and Cadence, so I flew to Indiana." I shut my eyes after I say it, worried she's going to hang up.

"Why would you fly to Indiana?"

"I was hoping you went to stay with your brother."

"How did you even get his address?"

"Your mom gave it to me." I wince right after I say it. *Bad move, Cam. Very bad move.*

"You've been talking to *my mom*." She says it with so much disdain, I fear that I might never find her. That I might have sentenced myself to a never-ending chase with her slipping out of my reach whenever I get close.

"We're really worried, Lauren."

"*We.*" Her tone is scathing. "You and my mom are a 'we' now. I don't believe it."

"*She* reached out to *me*. And I needed information from her to help look for you. It's not like we're going out on coffee dates and sending each other pictures of our food. I'm not on *her* side."

She doesn't say anything, but I know she feels betrayed. I'll deal with it later. At least she hasn't hung up. Yet.

I try to keep my voice steady when I ask, "Can you tell me where you guys are?"

"No," she says immediately.

"Can you just..." My throat grows tight. "Come home then?"

"Home," she repeats, and there's something in her voice... something almost melancholy. It gives me the first glimmer of hope I've felt in days.

She misses me, too.

"Yes, home." It's only when my voice quivers that I realize how close I am to tears. "You know it's home. It's home for you, and it's home for Cadence. And for me, it's not home unless both of you are there."

She's quiet for a moment. I hear only the static murmur of ambient noise through the phone, and I find myself holding my breath as I wait for her answer.

"What does that mean?" she eventually asks.

"It means I love you," I say right away. "I love both of you. And I hate myself for everything I said on Saturday night. You'd have every right to hate me, too." I exhale a shaky breath. "But I hope you don't. I hope that you can forgive me."

"Does this mean you trust me?"

I open my mouth, ready to tell her yes. Ready to tell her anything to get her home. But I find that I can't say the word.

I can't lie.

"I'm..." I try to swallow, but my mouth is too dry. "It's really hard for me... You know how I am. But I'm okay not trusting you, and I'm going to try really hard not to be such a jealous control freak—"

"No. That's not good enough."

"Please, Lauren." The words are barely above a whisper. "Just give me some time. Be patient with me." I clench my teeth to fight the sob rising in my throat. "I'm begging you."

"No." Her tone is final. "I've been patient enough. I'm not asking much of you. I'll forgive every control-freak thing you've done these past few months, and you've done a lot of things, honey. You know you have. I'll even forgive you for tracking my location without my knowledge, like a fucking psychopath."

I flinch, hating myself for my lack of conscience. I knew it was wrong the moment I did it, and I didn't care. Knowing where she was made me feel better, and that was enough.

God, I'm a selfish bastard.

"But if you want to be with me," she continues, "you need to say, 'Lauren, I trust you'. And maybe throw in that you promise not to act like a complete psychotic lunatic the next time your brother hugs me. You know, to sweeten the pot a little. But the first one is non-negotiable. I will not come *home* until you tell me you trust me. And if you can't do it, I won't ever come home again. Understand?"

I can only grunt in response, and it feels dangerously close to a sob.

Goddamn it, why can't I say the words? Why is it so hard? She isn't eighteen anymore. She's no longer the wild girl who broke my heart. I've known this for a while now. Maybe I've been holding on to a past version of her, too afraid of what would happen if I let it go. Maybe I've been so terrified of her that I've clung to my mistrust like an amulet, as if it could protect me from getting hurt if I lost her.

But I did lose her.

Mistrust hasn't gotten me anywhere. When self-reflection threatens to choke my throat, I push it away. I can't think about it now. I'm too exhausted, too frantic to find her.

"I have a lot to process," I say. "Can you at least... Can you tell me where you are? So I'll know for sure you're both safe?"

She laughs, and even knowing it's at my expense, the nasally sound of it is so sweet I want to weep.

"Sweetheart, no," she says. "That's your problem right here. You need to *trust me* when I tell you we're both safe.

"We'll be back in San Diego soon, and then you and I can figure out how we're going to ease you into this whole father thing. I'll even let you FaceTime Cadence now if you miss her, but I'm not telling you where we are, and I don't think that's unreasonable."

"Not unreasonable." My voice is so strained I can barely get the words out. "But it still fucking sucks."

"Aww, honey. You sound tired."

"I'm fucking exhausted."

She sighs. "Go home and get some rest."

When the line goes quiet, I fight the urge to slam the phone on the dashboard. Suddenly feeling that I can't breathe, I throw open the car door. I only have one foot planted in the snow when a large hand reaches out and yanks the phone out of my loose grip.

"Dude!" Logan shouts. "Do you realize you broke into my house and stole my phone? We're in Indiana. You pick the wrong house, and you'll get shot for that." He backs away, shaking his head. "I hope it was worth it."

I shut my eyes tightly. "It wasn't."

Logan laughs humorlessly, and my chest is seized with a painful grip of longing as I realize he sounds so much like Lauren.

"Of course it wasn't. You're not going to win her back like this. Trust me. I've been in your position before."

"How will I win her back?" I find myself asking. "How do you win someone back who wants something that you're not ready to give them yet? Would you lie? Would you just tell them what they want to hear?"

His brows draw together. "Do you want a drink? This sounds complicated, and I feel like a glass of whiskey might help."

HOT AIR BLOWS from a kitchen vent, thawing my ice-cold nose. Logan reaches into a high cupboard and grabs a bottle of Macallan. "How do you feel about scotch?"

"Perfect. Can you pour me a pint glass of it?"

He chuckles. "Wow. She really destroyed you on that phone call, huh? I feel your pain. My sister can be fucking mean, especially when you're mean to her first. But it's because she's really sensitive, and she doesn't want people to know."

I shut my eyes, exhaling as I hear the sound of ice hitting glass. A drink is shoved into my hand—not a pint glass, but at least a double of scotch. I take a large gulp, enjoying the burn as the liquid trails down my throat.

"I've been in your position before," he says. "I know exactly how you feel. And it was way worse for me. Trust me when I tell you Leilani is ten times meaner than Lauren."

"Logan." The husky voice floats through from the kitchen. I glance at the entryway where Leilani stands with her hands on her hips. "What are you telling him?"

"I'm giving him advice." He turns back to me. "Okay, here's the thing. If you really can't give her what she wants, you need to tell her that. Don't lie to her. And I'm not only saying that because she's my sister. I know how fucking miserable you are right now, and I would have told Leilani fucking anything to win her back. I would have lied out of my ass."

"Oh my God, Logan." Leilani places a hand on her brow, a faint smile twinging her lips.

He glances in her direction. "I'm just being honest. I was in a really dark place." He turns back to me, his eyes growing hard. "I don't want you to lie to my sister. Lying isn't a good strategy. Not with Lauren. One thing that's awesome about her is she's really accepting of other people's flaws."

"Fuck," I say, shutting my eyes tightly.

"What's wrong?" Logan asks, and he sounds genuinely concerned.

"Nothing." I shake my head. "I just fucking love that about her."

When I open my eyes, Logan looks alarmed. "Dude, you're really a wreck. Do you realize that?"

I sigh. "Yes."

He pats me hard on the back. "It's alright. I think it's a good thing. In fact, I think this should be your strategy. I think you should humble yourself when you finally talk to her face-to-face."

I frown. "How do I do that?"

"Easy. Keep doing exactly what you're doing. Tell her the things you're telling me right now. Give her examples even. What's the most pathetic thing you've done since you haven't been able to find her?"

I groan as I try to sort through the foggy haze of these last few miserable days. I'm not particularly optimistic about Logan's strategy, but I can't think of any alternatives. My head jerks up when a thought occurs to me. "I've been carrying her earring with me." I reach into my pocket and pull out the dangling beads. "I found it in my bed after she moved out."

Logan's jaw drops, his eyes settling on the earring. "Oh my God."

"That's so sweet," Leilani says.

"I'm literally crying right now." It's Brenna's voice, drawing my attention to the kitchen entry, and she doesn't sound like she's crying. That choked quality to her voice sounds a lot more like laughter.

"Oh, Cam... That's so sad, man." He makes a gulping sound, as if holding back laughter. "I don't think I ever did anything that pathetic, which is *really* saying a lot." He places a hand on my shoulder. "Okay, here's what you need to do. You need to show up at her doorstep looking exactly like you do right now, which is like absolute shit."

"False," Brenna cuts in. "He looks great. Like a lumberjack."

"Well, whatever," Logan says. "Show up looking like you haven't showered, and lead with the earring. Make shit up if you have to. Tell her you've been wandering around your house kissing it or something."

"I have been."

Logan sucks in his lips as if to fight a smile. I'd definitely be annoyed with him under any other circumstances, but I'm too exhausted to care.

Too desperate.

Too miserable.

When he starts to laugh in earnest, Leilani punches him in the shoulder. "He's being a jerk," she says after turning to me, "but I don't think it's a terrible idea to show some vulnerability. I can't guarantee she'll respond to it, but I think it's better than the approach you took earlier. When you showed up at Logan's doorstep and..."

"Broke and entered," I fill in for her, running my fingers

through my already disheveled hair. "What the hell am I going to say to her?"

Logan frowns. "That's the easy part. Tell her how you feel. Tell her the truth."

"The truth isn't very romantic."

In an instant, Logan's expression shifts into what I saw earlier when he came to the door. "What is the truth?"

I groan, too tired to even think about it, let alone explain it. "The truth is that I want her so desperately, I don't even care that I can't trust her. That at any moment she might do something like...*this*."

Logan crosses his arms over his chest. "What exactly is *this*?"

"Disappear without a trace because she's mad at me. Take her daughter away from me, who's probably *my* daughter."

Something flashes in Logan's eyes, and I realize he knows. Lauren told him everything. "Even if she is, and the chances are slim, biology doesn't make a father. You barely know Cadence."

I exhale heavily, not wanting to get into this argument again. The truth is that I don't care anymore. I want my new family back so badly that the circumstances don't matter. I don't need proof that I'm Cadence's biological father.

I'm starting to wonder if I only wanted the paternity test as leverage over Lauren, because I always feel like I have something over her or I'll be lost. Her control over my emotions is so complete I've tried to fight it by controlling her behavior. But I should have known all along that I can't do it. This is just like Hunter's addiction.

Control is an illusion.

And I'm starting not to care that she owns me.

"It's worth it," I say with complete confidence this time.

"It's worth being on edge all the time if it means we can be together."

"Why would you be on edge all the time?" Logan asks.

I frown. "Because she's so unpredictable. I could never relax."

Logan shakes his head. "That sounds like a Cam problem. Not a Lauren problem."

A chill runs down my spine. His words take me back to that conversation with Hunter a few days ago. "What do you mean?"

"Lauren's really not that unpredictable. Sure, sometimes she'll get really drunk and dance on top of a bar, or make-out with someone else's boyfriend." He glances at Brenna pointedly. "But that's the extent of it."

"What about running away?" I nearly yell.

"She didn't run away. She's visiting a friend because she needed space. You're the only one who's worried about her."

"Your mom and dad are worried—"

"No," he interrupts. "My mom's manipulating you because she wants Lauren to bring Cadence back to San Diego. Neither of them are worried. You're the only one who's worried, which isn't a Lauren problem. It's a Cam problem."

The denial rises to my lips—it's on the tip of my tongue—but then I'm brought back to that conversation with Janie not that long ago.

"Because for people like you and me—and by that I mean people with anxiety..."

Goddamn it, is that all this is? Am I that lacking in self-awareness that I'd push away the woman I love because I have anxiety? It seems too stupidly simple to be the cause of all my misery, but then it's so in line with all of my problems with Hunter.

I'm scared. I'm scared all the time because this love is so big it's painful. If I lost either of them, my heart would shatter irreparably.

I've blamed them both for my fear, when all along, I should have looked inward.

"I think you're right," I mumble.

"Of course I'm right."

I inhale a shaky breath. "God, this is too much. It's too fucking much. I'm too tired."

"Aww, sweetheart." It's Brenna's voice. "Do you want to go take a nap? Logan will let you use his bed."

"No," I say. "I need to go. I need to apologize to her. As soon as I can."

"Yep," Logan says.

When a thought occurs to me, I pin Logan with a hard stare. "I assume this means you're going to tell me where she is."

He frowns. "Fuck no. I can't betray her like that, and actually, I'd be betraying two people in this case, but don't worry. She'll be back."

"She's with my ex-boyfriend, Armaan."

My eyes dart to Brenna's face.

Logan frowns at her. "Brenna, what the fuck?"

She winces apologetically. "I couldn't help it. Just look at him." She gestures over my body. "He can't take a moment more of this."

I exhale heavily. "Thank you."

She smiles. "You're welcome. I'll give you the address. He's staying at his parents' beach house. They're hella rich—probably even as rich as you—and he manipulates them into giving him whatever he wants. He has plenty of room for Lauren and Cadence."

Jealousy rises, as usual, but I hardly feel it. I'm too exhausted and relieved.

Brenna sets her hand on my shoulder and shoots me a probing look. "But don't do what you did here. Don't break and enter. Think of a way to say you're sorry first. Make sure she knows you're really sorry."

"I don't even have to think about it," I say. "I know exactly what I'm going to tell her."

TWENTY-NINE

Lauren

I LIFT my eyes from the laptop. "All video content has to be of you," I tell Armaan.

We've spent the last several days coming up with a social media plan for the launch of his new company, and it's been surprisingly challenging. Since cannabis is a controlled substance, I had to do a lot of research about how to legally promote it.

I was grateful for the distraction. It kept me from giving in to that agonizingly sweet plea.

"For me, it's not home unless both of you are there."

"I don't think so," he says. "You're so much better at it. You're so much more sincere on camera."

I shake my head sharply. "That's only because I'm talking about the two loves of my life—makeup and skincare—but it wouldn't be the same if I'm talking about cannabis cookies. They aren't my passion, and people can sense insincerity a mile away. They'll know it's advertisement coming from me, and they'll scroll past it. You can talk about the company and really mean it."

He looks away, lifting a hand and scratching the back of his head. "I fucking hate being on camera."

I smile. "You'll get used to it. I'm as vain as it's possible for a human being to be, and it took time even for me." I halt at the sound of a loud knock.

Armaan's eyes widen, his lips parting. "I think that's your boyfriend."

My pulse starts to pound, and it takes tremendous willpower not to rush to the door. The frantic texts and calls had stopped altogether after Cam's trip to Indiana, and even though Logan told me he's planning to apologize, I couldn't help but fear that he had given up. As each day passed—now three and a half in total—I started to wonder if he finally decided I'm too much for him. That he can never trust me.

My stomach flips when Armaan stands up and walks in the direction of the hallway. "Do you want me to tell him to fuck off?"

"Yes... No." I swallow, my breathing growing unsteady. "Maybe see what he wants first, and then I'll decide."

Armaan nods, and I listen intently to his footsteps as he makes his way through the hallway. By the time I hear the front door open, my hands are trembling. The deep rumble of Cam's voice sends a pleasant shiver down my spine, though I can't quite make out what he's saying. I'm about ready to leap from my seat when I'm startled by the sound of the door closing.

That's it? He just came and left?

I don't have time to process the question. Armaan appears again, and my eyes are drawn to a folded piece of paper in his hands. He smiles as he hands it to me.

"Man of few words. He asked me to give this to you, turned

around, and walked away." His smile grows. "Definitely got the feeling he wanted to beat my ass, though. I don't think he likes that you and Cade are staying here."

I hardly hear Armaan's voice as I start to unfold the paper. My eagerness making me clumsy, it slips from my hands on my first try, but before I know it, it's open in front of me. It's the same lined notebook paper he uses when he writes music, and it's tattered and worn, as if he's been fiddling with it. My eyes run over the words, my breathing coming so rapidly, I feel almost faint.

Dear Lauren,

I trust you.

I tried to write a song about it, but in my genre, we tell stories, and no matter what pretty words I choose, recapping our history makes me sound like an unimaginable dick, and I want you to actually take me back. Plus, I've been too depressed to be creative since you and Cadence left.

Lauren, I trust you.

I trust you. I trust you. I trust you.

I'll say it aloud as many times as it takes for you to believe it. I'll say it every day if you want.

I didn't understand until recently that trust needs to come from me. If I want you in my life, and I do more than anything, I need to have faith in you. I'm determined to have faith in you, no matter how much it scares me, because I can't lose you.

I meant it when I said you're my home, and it's terrifying for a control freak like me to find something as wild and bright as you are, and realize that I need you, that without you, I'll forever be adrift.

Oh, and here's my list. Number one has been there for as

*long as I can remember, but I had to demote someone to add
number two.*

   1. Lauren

   2. Cadence

   3. Hunter

   4. Janie

   5. Isaac

Love, Cam

I stare at the letter, barely able to see it anymore though my
blurred vision. Before I turn into a sobbing mess, I jump from
my seat and rush out of the kitchen.

"Go get him, love," Armaan calls out, laughter in his voice.

I make it outside just as Camden starts his car ignition.

"Camden!" I shout.

His head whips in my direction, and even from all the way
over here, I can see the fire in his eyes.

He doesn't waste a moment. He throws open the door and
practically leaps from the car. I shut my eyes as I wipe away a
few more stray tears. When I feel the pressure of his hands on
my shoulders, I glance up at his face, and it's only now he's
close that I see how utterly exhausted he looks. His eyes are
sunken and bloodshot, his coloring pale. Thank God, I hadn't
seen him before now. I would have given in.

"You read it?" he asks, his voice hoarse.

"Yes, and you're full of shit. There's absolutely no way I've
been on your list for as long as you can remember. You're an
absolute fucking liar. You strategically wrote this letter to win
me back, but I don't even care. I love you too much to care." I
take a deep, unsteady breath.

When I release my first sob, he presses me hard against his
chest. "Oh God, Lauren. Does this mean you've forgiven me?"

"Absolutely not." To emphasize my denial, I rub my nose over his peck, wiping my snot on his shirt.

He jerks back. "Gross!" A tender smile tugs at his lips as he lifts his hands and places them both on my cheeks. "Then why did you call me back over here? Why are you crying?"

"I didn't say I wasn't coming back, just that I haven't forgiven you. I'm going to make you grovel for the next six months at least. I'm going to get a whole new wardrobe out of you, darling."

He squeezes my face for a moment before yanking me closer and pressing his mouth against mine. His kiss is hard and desperate. When he pulls away, he gasps, as if breaking to the surface after diving too deep. He rubs the pads of his thumbs against my cheeks. "I love it when you call me darling."

"Yeah?"

He smiles faintly, his eyes heavy-lidded. "I always wanted you to call me darling. You called everyone darling. Even Callum, the psychopath neighbor. But never me."

I smile as I raise my hand and thread my fingers into his hair, and his eyes fall shut. "Yeah, well...only boys who did exactly what I said got special treatment. You never did."

"I wish I did. I wish I had just given in." His eyes snap open. "You were wrong, though. I wasn't lying. You've been number one for as long as I can remember." When his eyes gather moisture, my throat grows tight. "I've loved you for as long as I can remember. You're my home."

He pulls me in closer. "I promise I'm going to be better. You'll be good for me. And I love that you're a firecracker. I love that you'll wear lingerie in public when I tell you to be a good girl." When he pulls away, his eyes settle intently on my face. "And I'm not going to push the issue with Cadence's paternity. Ever again. We'll wait till she's old enough to make the choice for herself. I want to be her father no matter what that DNA test says."

I smile tenderly, my lips quivering. "You don't have to make all of these promises. I'll take you back no matter what. I know I talked a big game about trust, but the truth is I have no principles." My smile grows cheeky. "I'm your ho, honey. Your paid ho."

He smiles tenderly, lifting a hand and tucking a strand of hair behind my ears. "You do have principles, but I love that you would say that. And you'll be my unpaid ho from now on."

He sets his mouth on mine. The kiss is soft and sweet, as chaste as he's ever kissed me, and it makes me that much hungrier for the hours we'll spend in his bed making up for years of stupidity.

EPILOGUE

Camden

HER FACE GLOWS with perspiration as she stares back at me. Those heavy-lidded eyes tell me she's moments from drifting off to sleep.

It's now four in the morning, and every time her eyes have fallen shut, I've pulled her in for another round of fucking. I'm too elated, too overcome with my good fortune to let her sleep. She's back in my bed. Cadence sleeps a few doors down.

And it's permanent now.

Still not willing to let her sleep, I reach over to the bedside table and open the drawer. I've pulled the earring out so many times, my hand knows exactly where to find it. I dangle the strands over her face, letting the sparkling red bead at the end brush the tip of her nose. The tinkling sound makes my chest ache, reminding me of those miserable days without her.

"What's that?" Lauren asks, her voice groggy.

"Your earring. I carried it around with me when I couldn't find you."

Her eyes pop open, and she seems to snap out of her sleepy daze. She stares at me for a moment, as if assessing my seriousness. Seeming to come to some kind of conclusion, she turns into her pillow and buries her face, her chest shaking with laughter.

A sheepish smile tugs at my lips. "In case you couldn't tell by my unhinged voicemails, I was kind of a pathetic mess when you left."

"Apparently." The pillow muffles her voice.

"You really have no idea." I reach out and stroke the dark strands of hair spread over her back. "I wandered around the house aimlessly, holding it in one hand with my phone in the other, calling you for the fiftieth time in a row."

"Where did you find it?"

There's something in her tone... Something that sounds like mischief. "Right here." I point to the edge of my bed.

"And you thought that was a coincidence?"

My brow knits. "You left it there on purpose?"

She sucks in her lips, as if fighting a smile. "I promised myself it was my final childish act. It was just too tempting not to do. I was packing up my jewelry, and after the idea popped into my head, I couldn't let it go. I even wove the prong through one of the threads of your comforter. I was hoping it would stick to it when your cleaning service came and changed the sheets." A slow smile spreads across her face. "I was determined for your next girl to find it."

I stare at her blankly. "I don't believe you."

Her smile grows. "I also chose the ugliest pair of earrings I could find in my collection because I wasn't about to waste something I actually liked. I'm pretty sure I bought that—" she points to the earring, "—at a mall kiosk when I was sixteen."

I stare down at the dangling earring, unable to believe that I've spent the past week pining over this thing, holding it in my hands and rubbing it as if I could conjure her with it.

I reach my hand toward her hips. She clearly anticipates what's going to come, because she squeals and rolls away from me, but I get a good grip on her arm before she makes it off the bed. I hold her tightly, lifting my hand high in the air.

SLAP!

The sound echoes through the room, and the pink print of my hand forms on her skin.

SLAP!

"Oh God!" Her voice is breathy and hoarse. "Do that again!"

"No." I grab her by the shoulders and roughly flip her onto her back, shifting my body over hers. "Not if you want it. This is a punishment, and it's not the only one you're going to get. I can't believe I was pining over that earring when it was a gesture of spite. For that, I'm not going to let you sleep at all tonight."

She hums, wiggling her hips against mine.

"And I'm going to fuck you hard this time."

But I don't. The next thirty minutes are soft and slow and worshipful, because she's given me what I've always wanted and never thought I'd get. Three months ago, this was only a fantasy, and now she's really here.

And she's here for good.

She's home.

AUTHOR'S NOTE

Thank you again for your support and reading Lauren and Camden's story. I'm a new indie author and reviews are really helpful in getting exposure. If you enjoyed *Wild and Bright*, I'd greatly appreciate it if you went to Amazon or Goodreads and told the world what you think.

If you want more Wild and Bright content, go to skylermason.com and sign up for my monthly newsletter. Everyone on my email list will receive a bonus scene with a peek in Lauren and Camden's future.

And follow me on social media here:
instagram.com/authorskymason
facebook.com/authorskymason
twitter.com/authorskymason

ALSO BY SKYLER MASON

Revenge Cake

Revenge Cake *is the first book in the* Toxic Love *series. It's an angsty second chance romance featuring Logan and Leilani from* ***Wild and Bright***, *and it can be read as a standalone.*

Leilani

The moment we locked eyes, I knew he was trouble.

I tried to protect myself, using my natural coldness to resist his compelling warmth.

But he wore me down with his beautiful face and self-deprecating charm.

He made me feel like the center of his universe.

Until one day, I wasn't.

The anxiety and the pills turned me into a different person.

But did I deserve to be abandoned in the darkest moment of my life?

He shattered my heart into a million pieces, and now it's time to make him pay.

Revenge never tasted so sweet.

Logan

I was done with love until the night I saw her.

She opened that sassy, heart-shaped mouth and called me weak.

And just like that, I was a goner.

I knew she was the only woman for me.

And in a moment of weakness, I may have lost her forever.

I was tired of being ignored.

I didn't know what to do with her addiction to anxiety pills.

But did I have to let it cost me my soulmate?

I won't let my mistake ruin us.

And if she thinks I'll just stand by while she moves on, she's got another thing coming.

Warning: This book explores the topics of panic disorder, addiction, and cheating.

ACKNOWLEDGMENTS

My wonderful husband and two sweet little boys, thank you for being patient with me when I spent every waking hour of the last month scrambling to get this book finished. I can't wait to finally get back in to our normal routine!

My amazing editor Heidi Shoham, thank you for teaching me to be a better writer. Without you, this book would be full of unnecessary flashback scenes that could better be summed up in a few sentences.

My excellent proofreader Taylor West, thank you for catching the numerous typos my careless brain overlooked.

To my beautiful critique partners, Gabrielle and Dakota, your support over the last year (has it really only been that long we've been friends??) has meant the world to me. You've helped me grow both as a writer and a marketer. Plus, you're both the best friends a girl who reads could ask for!

To my beta readers, Ellie and Kasey, thank you for spending your time reading *Wild and Bright* before it even went through copy edit. Your support and encouragement has meant so much to me. Writing spicy books has helped me find my community, and I'm so grateful!

9 781087 992280